A MATTER OF MOTIVE

Rudd's mind went back to the cottage that Vaughan had vacated like an actor walking off a stage and for the first time he was aware that the answer to the problem of death might lie not in the actions so much as the character. It was not so much a question of how Vaughan had died, but why. The means and opportunity would, of course, have to be investigated, but suddenly the motive seemed to have much more significance. Someone had wanted Vaughan dead, and the reason, he realised, could be as complex and enigmatic as Vaughan's own personality.

Bantam Books by June Thomson
Ask your bookseller for the books you have missed.

ALIBI IN TIME
CASE CLOSED
DEATH CAP
THE HABIT OF LOVING
A QUESTION OF IDENTITY

ALIBI
IN
TIME

June Thomson

BANTAM BOOKS
TORONTO · NEW YORK · LONDON · SYDNEY

All of the characters in this book
are fictitious, any resemblance
to actual persons, living or dead,
is purely coincidental.

*This low-priced Bantam Book
has been completely reset in a type face
designed for easy reading, and was printed
from new plates. It contains the complete
text of the original hard-cover edition.*
NOT ONE WORD HAS BEEN OMITTED.

ALIBI IN TIME

*A Bantam Book / published by arrangement with
Doubleday & Company Inc.*

PRINTING HISTORY
*Doubleday edition published July 1980
An Alternate Selection of Detective Book Club in August 1980
Bantam edition / October 1981*

*Bantam Books are published by Bantam Books, Inc. Its trademark,
consisting of the words "Bantam Books" and the portrayal of a rooster
is Registered in U.S. Patent and Trademark Office and in other
countries. Marca Registrada. Bantam Books, Inc., 666 Fifth Avenue,
New York, New York 10103.*

PRINTED IN THE UNITED STATES OF AMERICA

0 9 8 7 6 5 4 3 2 1

ALIBI
IN
TIME

1

Kitty hadn't sounded particularly urgent on the telephone, only a little subdued, unlike her usual self. But she had said nothing except, "Are you busy this evening, Lewis? Could you spare an hour?"

So he had walked, taking pleasure in the boisterous late October dusk; the wind northwesterly, he noticed with his careful eye for detail, driving before it great ragged masses of black cloud, that were ripped to pieces and dispersed before they could coalesce. If the wind drops, though, he thought, it will rain.

Once out of the village, he took the path through the wood with the excuse that it was quicker than going all the way round by the road, although he knew he had chosen the short cut mainly to avoid passing the gate cottage where Patrick Vaughan lived. Just seeing the place reminded him unpleasantly of the man and his own irrational dislike of him.

It was quieter down there among the trees, sheltered from the wind, although he could still hear it surge and sough like the sea in the topmost branches. The last of the light was going; only a few faint silvery streaks of brightness were still visible between the rents in the clouds, more like dawn than dusk. The trees were almost bare already where the gale had stripped them and the path ahead of him was littered with torn leaves. Autumn had come roaring in this year; not Keats' season of mellow fruitfulness, replete and golden, but full of wild gusto.

On the far side of the wood, a wicket gate led into the garden of Coppins, Kitty's house, and he paused for a moment to look across at it, standing four-square and safe, anchored in its lawns; immutable, he always felt, a symbol of changelessness in a world that, now he had gone past middle age, seemed to become less and less constant. It was early Victorian, built in the solid, unpretentious style of a country vicarage, its only decorative feature being a long, open verandah of wrought iron with a curving roof that ran along the ground-floor façade, reminding him in its graceful charm of a villa in Brighton or one of those ornate bandstands that adorn some public parks.

It seemed also to epitomize Kitty herself in its simple robustness, as if she, too, like the house, established in her own landscape, would remain untouched by the years.

He was disconcerted, therefore, when on crossing the lawn and approaching the front of the house, he saw Edwin Cotty's car standing in the drive. Kitty had said nothing when she had phoned him about being unwell and, as she lived alone now with only Mrs. Allison coming in daily to help with the housework, she could have called the doctor in only on her own account. He felt suddenly guilty that he hadn't hurried straight over to see her; anxious, too, when Mrs. Allison opened the door to him. Normally she would have left long before.

"Mrs. Fulton's ill?" he asked.

"Came over faint," Mrs. Allison replied with grim satisfaction, letting him into the hall. She was a small woman with hard, tight little features which put Lewis Shand in mind of the medieval carvings on the organ screen in the church; a peasant's face, unsubtle and crudely delineated but possessing a certain rough vigour of its own. "Lucky I was still here when it happened. 'You send for the doctor,' I told her. 'I shan't go till he's been.' Because she wasn't going to bother. He's with her now."

"She didn't say she was ill when she phoned," Lewis Shand said quickly, feeling on the defensive.

"Well, she wouldn't, would she? You know what she's like; doesn't want a fuss. Been doing too much if you ask me. Knocked herself out. Worried about something too just recently. Won't say anything to me but *I* know," Mrs. Allison added, sounding oracular as she took his coat and laid it across the high-backed chair which stood by the door.

She might to you though, her tone also implied, and he was suddenly aware of the fierce protective love that Mrs. Allison had for Kitty and the jealousy she felt towards him in his privileged position as Mrs. Fulton's friend and possible confidant.

He was about to say something pleasantly noncommittal when the drawing-room door opened and Edwin Cotty appeared, bag in hand, walking towards them with that brisk, staccato walk of his, his free arm swinging stiffly. He was a tall, austere man with a chalky look about his skin and hair as if too much exposure to the antiseptics and prescriptions of his profession had withered up the essential juices in his body. It was noticeable too in his hands, always clinically clean, the nails of which were spotted with tiny white marks. Lewis Shand had known him for a long time, ever since his own arrival in the village fifteen years before, and had good reason to be grateful to him for his treatment of his daughter, Hilary, when she had had a nervous breakdown. But he had never felt he had got close to the man. There was something too chilly and brusque in Cotty's manner, a deliberate distancing, as if he preferred not to make too much human contact.

It was a pity, Lewis Shand thought. He would have liked to offer him friendship. Cotty had an invalid wife, Eleanor, a pale, diffident woman, pretty once but faded now like a photograph whose image had lost some of its definition but whom Cotty evidently loved, his stern features relaxing whenever she was present. Lewis Shand, whose own wife was dead, had hoped it might form a bond between them but Cotty had remained aloof.

"Ah, Shand," Cotty was saying as he approached. "I'm glad you're here. Kitty said she'd sent for you."

"How is she?" Lewis Shand broke in anxiously.

"All right. Nothing much to worry about. Just overtired. I've left a couple of sleeping pills for her to take before she goes to bed tonight, although she says she won't need them. Insist she has them, will you?"

"I'll try," he replied. Kitty was not the sort of person one could be insistent with and he felt caught between their two wills, hers and Cotty's, knowing that by satisfying one he would probably displease the other.

"Is she all right to be left then?" Mrs. Allison asked sharply. "Because I ought to be off."

Relief made her sound more belligerent than she intended. Besides, she felt out of it now. The two men seemed to have taken over, the dry-as-an-old-stick doctor and Mr. Shand, Mrs. Fulton's friend, the headmaster, with his mild bespectacled face and thinning hair. Deep down, she would have liked a little more drama, without wishing Mrs. Fulton any real harm, but she had pictured herself at the bedside, offering cups of tea on trays, with Dr. Cotty praising her devotion.

Instead he was saying brusquely, "Do you want a lift down to the village?"

"I've got me bike," she told him, beholden to no one, and,

shrugging on her coat, marched over to the front door and let herself out.

"You won't keep her too long, will you?" Edwin Cotty asked, turning back to Lewis Shand. "She ought to get a good night's rest."

"No, I shan't," he promised. The evening with Kitty that he had been looking forward to with so much pleasure was already tarnished. He felt, in Cotty's eyes, he had no business to be there at all.

"Tell her I'll look in again tomorrow," Cotty was adding at the door.

Then he had gone and, for the first time since he had been coming to Coppins, Lewis Shand was aware how empty, in fact, the house was. The broad polished stairs went up to a dark landing. The grandfather clock ticked sonorously. Yet it had always seemed alive before, even after the children had left home and Richard Fulton had died. Kitty's presence had been enough to fill it. Normally she would have been at the door to meet him, bustling him out of his coat, taking him into the drawing room, where the whisky decanter and glasses would be set out in readiness. He realised how much he had come to rely on her strength, her energy, the simple fact that she was always there.

"Lewis!"

Her voice came through the closed drawing-room door and he hurried across the hall to open it. Entering the room, he was gratified to see how little it had changed. The curtains were drawn, the lamps switched on, a fire burned in the hearth; one of Kitty's huge, extravagant fires, he noticed with a sense of returning pleasure, the light from it glittering on the surfaces of her many possessions, silver and cut-glass, gilt-edged pictures and mirrors, boule and marquetry.

He had been brought up himself in a home where there had been little left over for luxuries, and his own house, apart from his books, reflected the same simple tastes. Until he had come to Coppins, he had never seen such a profusion of beautiful things outside a museum, all of them used, and it had shocked him at first to see Kitty's children actually sitting in the chairs, playing with the ivory chess set, eating from the fragile plates. Afterwards he had come to accept it as part of her attitude to life—that it was to be taken joyfully with both hands, not treated with niggardly caution.

Money, of course, made a difference. A small, tart voice, which he recognised as an echo of his mother's, had reminded him of this on his first visit—an invitation to tea, he remembered, in order that he and Hilary should meet the Fulton family—but as he got to know

Kitty better, he realised that she would have been the same person on a farm labourer's wages.

Would he, he sometimes wondered, have been a different person himself if he had been brought up in the same generous spirit? Less hesitant perhaps? Less timid of soul?

Or Hilary, his own daughter?

But there was no answer to these questions. It was too late to start again. And besides, Kitty was watching him as he crossed the room towards her, sitting upright on the sofa, her sturdy legs crossed at the ankles; looking tired, he could see, a little diminished but still amused, ironic; her strong grey hair pushed back from her forehead; a pillow, that Mrs. Allison had probably provided, thrown down on the floor beside her.

"My dear, don't look so worried," she greeted him. "I'm not dead yet."

"But I am worried," he confessed. "And I blame myself for not coming sooner. I had no idea you were ill."

"Not *ill*." She sounded exasperated; not with him, he realised, but because lying there was a confession of weakness. "Edwin Cotty's done all his tests and I'm perfectly fit—heart, pulse, blood pressure, all normal. I'll be up and about tomorrow. Pour yourself a whisky and one for me, too, please."

"Should you?" he asked, his hand on the decanter. "Cotty said something about you taking some sleeping pills."

"Well, I shan't."

He felt trapped by her stubbornness.

"I did promise I'd try to make you take them."

"Oh, Lewis, how could you!"

She was mocking him, he realised, but he didn't mind and he smiled as he poured a second glass and took it over to her.

"Just a small one then. A compromise."

"To ease your conscience? Very well, but I'm making no promises about helping myself to another larger one after you've gone. Whisky's much better than Edwin's wretched little pills. I sleep like a top most of the time anyway." She broke off suddenly to ask, "How's Hilary?"

"Well," he replied. "Busy."

He was aware of a restraint he always felt at discussing his daughter that he only partly understood. He loved Hilary very much. Aware of her vulnerability, he wanted to protect her. Perhaps it was this quality in her that made him hesitate to speak of her too openly, even to Kitty, although he knew she was fond of the girl. Kitty's own children were so successful: her daughter married to a surgeon; one son a lawyer; the other in politics, like his father, and already spoken of as a possible junior minister; all of them confident of their place in the world.

Compared to them, Hilary had always seemed subdued, a little wan, especially since her breakdown, although her personality had never been strongly defined. It had happened while she had been at college, training to be a teacher. The usual story, he supposed sadly. There was nothing special about her tragedy. She had fallen in love with another student, become engaged, and then, abruptly, the relationship had ended. She had been sent home in a state of collapse after a pathetic, bungled attempt at suicide, a secret he had told no one. She had lived at home ever since. Later, as she improved, she had gone into partnership with a woman friend, Stella Maxton, in running a bookshop in the nearby town of Weldon. She had never married and he supposed now she never would. She was twenty-seven and already he could see that she had settled down into an acceptance of spinsterhood, filling her life with the small, daily routine of the shop, evening classes—it was French this year—and coming home to care for him. He had wanted desperately at times to open doors for her onto those new, marvellous and exciting worlds that Kitty's children seemed to inhabit with such ease. The difficulty was he didn't know how and, as the years went by, he realised with a terrible sense of inevitability that they were both becoming more and more established into the pattern of widowed father and unmarried daughter sharing a quasi life together and that he was too old and selfish now to want it any different.

"I haven't dragged you away from home, have I?" Kitty was asking. "Hilary's not by herself?"

He roused himself to reply.

"No, not at all. As a matter of fact, she stayed on at the shop this evening. Something to do with stock-taking, I believe. She'll get herself a meal in town."

"What about you? Have you eaten?"

It was typical of her that she should pounce on the fact that there was no one to cook for him. As it happened, he had eaten—scrambled eggs on toast; hardly an adequate supper, in Kitty's eyes, for a cold October evening, but it hadn't seemed worth going to much trouble just for himself, even if he didn't like to admit it. Kitty would take it as an excuse to get up and start cooking for him; she had done it before.

"Yes, I've had supper. What did you want to see me about?" he added to change the subject, drawing one of the armchairs close to the sofa.

"Oh, yes, that," she replied, avoiding his eyes, and he realised that whatever it was, she seemed as reluctant to discuss it as he had been to talk about Hilary. It must be something important, however, for her to ask him to come over in the first place and he remembered Mrs. Allison's remark that Kitty had been worried recently. He could see it now for himself in her face. She was looking down into her glass of whisky, a small, deep, V-shaped crease between her eyebrows, her mouth pursed as if she found the subject unpleasant.

"I need your advice, Lewis," she said abruptly. "I don't want to go to a solicitor yet but I do need someone to talk it over with first, as a friend. The fact is, I'm thinking of selling Coppins."

The announcement, so flatly made without any softening preamble, shocked him and he felt a sense of loss as deep as that when Marion had died. And with it came the awareness, a sense of sudden recognition of something that had always been there but had been too close for him to perceive before, that he loved her. Had always loved her. More even than Marion. But as much as Hilary, although in a different way. For Kitty he felt no anxiety, only the desire to commit himself utterly into her hands; to come home at last and be at peace.

But how ironic to realise it only when she was thinking of going away! He had known her for fifteen years; six since her husband had died; plenty of time in which to be aware of his feelings. But perhaps it had been too long since he had been in love for him to recognise the symptoms. Or he had wrongly assumed that passion was only for the young. Certainly, he had always been a little in awe of her, and inhibited also by her marriage to Richard Fulton which had been so happy that, at times, seeing them together, he had felt like a watcher at a feast.

He glanced involuntarily at the photograph of Kitty's dead husband on the mantelpiece above the huge red fire. Beloved husband and father. It said so on his gravestone in the churchyard. And he could have gone on adding to his catalogue of excellencies. Respected member of Parliament for the constituency for over twenty years. Tireless campaigner for many local causes. Popular after-dinner speaker. Wit. Raconteur. A man of taste and letters. What was the point in continuing? Richard Fulton was smiling out of the silver frame and Lewis Shand knew he would never find the courage to tell his widow that he loved her.

"Poor Lewis. You looked terribly shocked," Kitty was saying.

"Of course I am," he said, finding his voice. "I had no

idea . . ."

She shifted restlessly on the sofa.

"It's been at the back of my mind for some time now. A feeling that I'm not getting any younger and perhaps I ought to give in gracefully before the house and the garden get too much for me. I shall miss it all, of course. My roots are here. As you know, Richard bought the place soon after we were married. A family home, he said. And so it was. The children loved it but they're grown up now and I can't afford to be sentimental . . ."

"If it's a question of finances," Lewis Shand interrupted, seizing on the suggestion eagerly, even though he was embarrassed at mentioning money. "Couldn't you sell off some of the land? Or let part of it furnished? The upper floor, for instance?"

But Kitty was shaking her head.

"I didn't mean afford in that sense. Richard left me well provided for—of course, money doesn't go as far as it used to. But I manage. No, that isn't the problem. In fact, that's the reason why I asked you here tonight. If I do decide to sell, what on earth am I going to do about Patrick Vaughan? I can hardly put the place on the market while he's occupying the gatehouse."

The look of displeasure had settled more firmly on her face and Lewis Shand was aware for the first time that she might share his dislike for the man.

"I can't see why you let him have it in the first place," he remarked a little acidly, letting her see his feelings.

"Neither can I now. But that's water under the bridge. It seemed a good idea. The cottage was empty. He was a writer. Nice and quiet, I thought; someone interesting to have about the place."

"But if you were thinking of selling . . ."

"I wasn't *then!*" Her voice rose, sounding oddly sharp. "It's only lately I've been considering it. But before I do I shall have to get him to move out."

"Can't you just tell him to go? I don't know the law on these matters but surely . . ."

"It's on a year's lease."

He spread out his hands.

"Well, then, I don't see you have any problem. Wait for the lease to run out—next January, isn't it?—and then refuse to renew it. A solicitor would be able to advise you."

"Oh yes, I can do that," she said impatiently, as if he had missed the point. "But I don't know his plans, you see, Lewis. That's the difficulty. And I can hardly go to him myself and ask him what he intends doing. Not when I haven't made up my own mind whether or not to sell."

"I see," he said slowly, even though he didn't. The explanation struck him as confused and irrational, not at all like Kitty. Why did her decision depend on Patrick Vaughan? It didn't make sense and he had the distinct feeling that she was being deliberately obtuse, which saddened him. Apart from the one shameful secret of Hilary's attempted suicide, he had always believed they had been open with one another, and it hurt him to think that she might have some secret of her own that she was unwilling to share with him.

"I don't understand what you want me to do," he said helplessly.

She seized quickly on the remark. "Talk to him. Just casually. I don't want you to say anything at all about the possibility I might be selling. In fact, I'd rather you didn't mention it to anyone at this stage, not even Hilary. Try to find out what he plans to do when the lease ends; if he's got somewhere else in mind, for instance."

"I hardly know him," he objected.

"Yes, you do," she interposed. "You've met him here several times and you must have seen him about the village. Oh, please, Lewis, don't be difficult." Her voice rose again. "You could call on him on your way home. You'll have to pass the cottage. It won't seem odd, not if you handle it carefully."

He was about to tell her that he hadn't come in the car but had walked, and then he changed his mind. Kitty was manipulating him into the situation, a thing she had never done before, and he felt suddenly too weary to protest. Let her have her way, he thought. It must be important to her. Her distress was more obvious now that there might be a possibility he would refuse, her mouth trembling and the skin across her forehead stretched high with tension. His love for her rushed in on him again to see her so pitifully exposed.

"Very well, Kitty," he said, rising to his feet. "I'll try sounding him out for you."

"You're going now?"

"I think I'd better. Hilary may be home soon and I don't know how long I shall be talking to Vaughan."

"You'll phone me to let me know what he says?"

"Yes, of course," he assured her. "As soon as I get back."

She took both his hands in hers.

"Dear Lewis. Thank you!"

The endearment touched him with an odd, unexpected compassion. He had never imagined that she would express that kind of gratitude to him and, looking down into her face, he was suddenly

aware that in her own way she might be almost as vulnerable as
Hilary.

He left at once, pausing in the hall only long enough to put on his
coat before stepping out into the gusty twilight. It was darker now, but
enough light remained for him to find his way down the drive. The
trees lining it roared, their branches clashing together, but despite the
cold wind, he walked slowly, hands deep in his pockets, putting off
the moment of meeting Vaughan, which he still viewed with
reluctance, and thinking over, now that he was alone, the implications
behind Kitty's extraordinary request.

Because it *was* extraordinary. Even allowing for the fact that she
was unwell didn't properly explain it. She could have waited a few
days until she was better and then spoken to Vaughan herself, which
would have been much more in character. And yet she had telephoned
him and asked him to come over for the express purpose of getting
him to sound out Vaughan and, in doing so, had offered him an
explanation that was at best lame, at worst downright evasive. Why?

It was obvious she was worried. Mrs. Allison had been right
about that. It was clear, too, that Kitty's concern was connected with
Patrick Vaughan. He had seen Kitty only a fortnight before when she
had called in at the schoolhouse on her way to Weldon with an armful
of dahlias. There had been nothing the matter with her then. She had
been cheerful, full of plans for the garden, looking forward to her two
grandsons, her daughter's boys, spending part of the half-term
holiday with her.

So whatever had happened had taken place since then; something
that perhaps Vaughan had said or done to distress her enough to
consider selling Coppins and moving out but not before she knew
whether or not he would give up the lease of the cottage.

He couldn't imagine what it could be. His own instinctive dislike
of the man clouded his judgement and it was difficult for him to see
beyond it. Besides, as he had pointed out to Kitty, he didn't know him
all that well. He had first met him, he remembered, when Kitty had
invited him to a small party one evening soon after Vaughan's arrival
in order to introduce him to people in the village, and, on entering the
drawing room to find Vaughan already there, he had been struck at
once by something distasteful about the man. It was nothing overt.
Vaughan had been pleasant enough and had gone out of his way to be
sociable. But it was a feeling that long experience as a teacher had
made Lewis Shand unconsciously aware of, almost like a scent: the
faint odour of the troublemaker, the whiff of malice. Over the years
he had learnt to pick out the type; something in the eyes, perhaps, or

the quality of the smile; some jaunty air of knowingness that always put him on his guard.

Kitty had seemed unaware of it. In fact, she had seemed amused at the thought of having a writer as a tenant. The cottage had been occupied by an elderly couple who, when Richard Fulton had been alive, had acted as housekeeper and gardener at Coppins. On their retirement, Kitty had allowed them to stay on and the cottage had become vacant only the previous autumn when, on his wife's death, old Bryant had gone to live with a married daughter. It was then that Kitty had decided to let it. She had discussed it with Lewis Shand, pointing out that it seemed a pity to leave it empty, it would only deteriorate and, now that she was alone, she could perfectly well manage with the Allisons coming in daily to help with the house and the heavy work in the garden. As the cottage was so small, it seemed better to let it furnished to someone single.

The cottage had been redecorated and modernised, the furniture moved in—spare stuff from Coppins, he understood—and Vaughan had arrived the previous January. It had all appeared quite satisfactory.

Now it was evident that something had gone badly wrong, although exactly what he had no idea.

There was no time, anyway, for further speculation. He had reached the end of the drive where the single-storeyed gatehouse stood, overlooking the road. In contrast to the simple style of Coppins, it was deliberately decorative, pillared and pedimented like an ornate doll's house, and set in a small, formal garden, with a brick-built garage at the back facing an opening in the shrubbery lining the drive wide enough to allow a car to pass through, as there was no direct access to the road except for a small gate and garden path leading up to the front door.

Afterwards, Lewis Shand was to ask himself what made him decide to enter through this opening into the back garden. Not knowing Patrick Vaughan all that well, it would have been more natural for him to go round by the path and knock at the front door. Perhaps Kitty's insistence that his visit was to appear casual gave him the idea that it would look less formal if he went to the back. He even had the words ready in his mind. He would say something along the lines that he had been visiting Kitty and, as he was passing on his way home, he thought he'd call in to ask if he could borrow the book on local history that Vaughan had mentioned the last time they met. It wasn't a very good excuse but it would have to do. The subject was a particular interest of his and he had plenty of books of his own.

Vaughan, knowing this, had once remarked that he'd recently bought a book himself in Weldon on Essex churches; from Hilary's shop, as a matter of fact, and the conversation had passed on to a discussion of the business. In fact, Lewis Shand suddenly remembered, he had been annoyed at the time by Vaughan's questions, which had seemed impertinent. Did it do well? he had asked. Surely in a place like Weldon there wasn't much call for a bookshop? The library had always seemed deserted whenever he went in there except for elderly ladies searching the shelves for the latest romance. There had been an amused, inquisitive look on his face, and Lewis Shand had quickly changed the subject.

Now, at least, it gave him a reason for calling. After that he had no idea how he was going to steer the conversation the way Kitty wanted. Vaughan, he suspected, was much too intelligent to be easily fooled, and Lewis Shand, doubting his ability, felt an overwhelming reluctance at the thought of the next half hour, well though he was prepared to face it for Kitty's sake.

A short length of rough grass, rutted by car wheels, led from the opening in the shrubbery to a concreted area extending from the back door to the garage that lay further off from the house, partly obscured by bushes and a trellis, erected to hide its raw, modern brickwork. It was darker there under the trees and Lewis Shand felt his way gingerly. No light was showing at the back of the cottage and he hoped for a moment that Vaughan might be out.

But the hope was short-lived for, as he stepped onto the concrete, he saw a car had been parked in front of the garage doors; not Vaughan's, though. As he got closer, he noticed it was a dark blue Mini, similar to his daughter's. It meant, however, that Vaughan must have a guest so he'd have to postpone his own visit to another evening.

He was in the act of turning back when he glanced at the registration number, a little curious to find out if it was one he knew.

For a moment, he wasn't sure that he had taken it in properly but the combination of letters and figures was too familiar for him to be mistaken. The car was Hilary's.

The shock of it bewildered him at first, and then, just as his love for Kitty had come flashing in on him with that white clarity of recognition, he knew that Vaughan and Hilary were lovers. The fact that she had lied to him about staying on at the shop was enough to convince him. Hilary wouldn't have deceived him for any trivial reason. There had been other occasions, too, over the past few weeks

when she had made some excuse for being late home. Not that he had
suspected anything.

The thought of a relationship between her and Vaughan was
abhorrent, as impossible to accept as the violence of his own reaction.
And with the repugnance came a deep anger and hatred; not against
Hilary, but for Vaughan, the seducer, the violator.

Turning abruptly, Lewis Shand began walking away, aware of
nothing except his need to escape from the place as quickly as
possible. Gradually, as he grew calmer, the nausea died down and
some of the worst of his anger, although it still burned inside him like
a slow, dull fire. There were other considerations to think of now, not
the least of which was what he was going to say to Kitty when he
telephoned her, as he knew he must. She would be waiting for his
call. He could easily make the excuse that Vaughan had been out,
even though he disliked lying to her. He knew he could never bring
himself to tell her the truth. What he found harder to come to terms
with was the thought of facing Hilary when she returned home. In
God's name what was he going to say to her? Nothing, he realised
bleakly. He would have to pretend that he accepted her deceit,
entering into the falsehood with her, a prospect that appalled him. He
felt their relationship would never be the same again. Not that the
realisation of her affair with Vaughan in any way altered his love
towards her. In some curious way that he couldn't properly understand, the knowledge only strengthened it. She seemed more than
ever in need of his protection.

As for Vaughan, he had no idea at all how he was going to deal
with him. He'd have to see him, of course. It was impossible to shirk
his obligation to Kitty. He supposed he'd summon up the courage
when the time came, but the thought of it filled him with dread. But
he had faced worse, he thought, and found the strength to carry him
through. Like the time Marion died and he had come back from the
hospital on that bright summer afternoon, and had seen Hilary's face
at the window, pressed against the glass, and knew, as he opened the
gate and walked towards the house, that he had no idea how he was
going to break the news to her. But the words had come. He had
survived and so, too, had she, although he felt that the loss had left a
flaw in her personality, like a fine, hair crack in a piece of china, to
shatter later.

In the same way, he supposed he would find the words for

Vaughan, hiding his hostility and bitterness, for he suddenly realised that he had as much need as Kitty for wanting Vaughan out of the village.

2

Hilary Shand got out of bed and, turning her back on Patrick Vaughan, began to dress, fumbling in her haste. She was still aware, however, of his scrutiny. It seemed to burn into her bare skin.

"Did anyone tell you that you have a beautiful spine?" he asked suddenly from behind her. His voice sounded relaxed and amused.

"No," she replied and flinched away from his touch as, leaning forward, he ran a finger down the narrow column of bone. She thrust her arms into the sleeves of her blouse, buttoning it awkwardly, and only then was able to turn and face him.

He was lying back on the pillow, still watching her, the sheet pulled up over his legs but the rest of his body naked, showing the dark shield of his chest and its blazon of black hair and the taut, muscular stomach. She still couldn't meet his eyes although she was aware that he was still smiling, his teeth gleaming in his beard.

Yes, I amuse him, she thought bitterly; in all possible senses of the word. Yet, knowing it, I still love him. And hate him, too.

The paradox didn't strike her as strange. The one emotion seemed inextricably part of the other, both as fierce as the desire she felt for him and the shame that accompanied it.

"No one? I really can't believe that, Hilary."

He was openly laughing at her now and she knew exactly how he regarded her—as a woman who was available; no longer young or even very attractive; just someone to invite into his bed and to whom he probably considered he was doing a favour.

"No, no one," she said and stood abruptly to zip up her skirt.

Thank God she had never told him about David. At least she'd not been that much of a fool, because to have done so would have put a weapon in his hand that could really hurt her. She was grateful, too, that Patrick would never have the same power to reduce her to the frenzy of grief and despair when he left her. Because he would leave her. She had seen the inevitability of it as soon as the affair began. It was part of the hatred she felt for him which would finally save her.

That, and the knowledge that she had been there before and this time
would be able to find her own way out of the darkness.

"Won't you stay for a drink?" Patrick was asking.

"No, I mustn't. Thanks all the same."

"Lewis is expecting you home?"

Implying that she was still tied to her father, like a child.

She replied as calmly as she could, accepting the comment.
"Yes, he will be."

"I've told you before, you ought to leave; find a flat of your own
somewhere."

It was the same subject that they had discussed soon after they
had first met and, at that time, she had believed that he was genuinely
concerned about her future. But now that she knew him better, she
wasn't so sure. There was a meddling quality about him; a propensity
for intrigue that made her suspect his motives. She was aware of
another, more obscure reason, as if in pressing her to leave home, he
wanted to punish Lewis in some way. She knew her father didn't like
Patrick, and Lewis was too naïve, or perhaps too honest, to conceal
his antipathy. What surprised her was the fact that Patrick seemed to
mind so much, although he took care to cover it up.

"It's not that easy to walk out," she replied.

"Why not? You're a big girl now, Hilary. You don't need a
daddy to look after you any longer."

It would have been wiser to keep silent but the mocking tone in
his voice stung her into replying.

"I don't like to think of him on his own."

"Hasn't it ever occurred to you that Lewis might welcome the
idea once he's got used to it; perhaps even enjoy it? After all he's a
very self-sufficient person in his own way. Without you around, I can
quite easily imagine him settling down into a comfortable bachelor
existence, busying himself with local affairs and trotting off to look at
churches at the weekends."

This time she said nothing. There was enough unexpected truth
in his remarks to make her reconsider her relationship with her father.
Could Patrick be right? she wondered. Would Lewis in fact be happier
on his own? She had always thought of herself as indispensible but
now she wasn't sure anymore. Patrick had this trick of summing
people up and then dismissing them. She had seen him do it before;
with Kitty Fulton, for example, whom he had described as "much
preferring to sit on the throne than be the power behind it." She had
never been able to meet Kitty since without seeing her through
Patrick's eyes.

Now, faced with his comments about her father, she was uncomfortably aware that he might be right.

"Don't you agree, Hilary?" he asked, insisting on an answer.

"I don't know," she replied, and added more sharply, "I don't think it's any of your business anyway."

"Probably not," he agreed, shrugging. "My dear Hilary, you take life much too seriously. You shouldn't, you know."

"Perhaps I do. But I can't alter myself now."

"Can't you?" His tone of voice was light, as if it didn't really matter. "But people who refuse to change are such bores, don't you agree?"

He was getting out of bed, pulling on his jeans roughly, as if his body didn't mean all that much to him either. And probably it didn't, she thought wryly. Not anymore.

She knew she ought to go but she lingered, waiting for him to ask when he would see her again. But he was intent on buckling his belt before bending down to pick up his shirt from the floor so that in the end she was forced to speak.

"Will you phone me?"

He looked up as if the question had surprised him.

"Oh, yes, of course. Or I'll drop in at the shop sometime."

Sometime.

She knew the signs without being told and she walked to the door, leaving him putting on his shirt. At least, she thought, as she let herself out of the cottage, he hadn't been enough of a Judas to offer to kiss her good-bye. Or perhaps it had simply not occurred to him that some final gesture of affection might be needed.

No, affection was the wrong word, she decided, getting into the car and turning on the headlamps. It implied a tenderness that neither of them felt.

The lights were thrown back from the closed garage doors, leaving the rest of the garden in darkness, but as she backed and turned they swung round, illuminating briefly the wind-tossed evergreens, their leaves glistening thickly, and the tangle of small twigs that had once been lilac bushes.

But that's damned stupid, she told herself angrily. The same trap of self-pity that had closed on her before. They were still lilac bushes. Nothing had altered them because they had lost their leaves. Life went on, even hers. She would go home and exchange conversation with her father. Just before ten o'clock she would make tea and carry it through into the sitting room so that they could drink it together as they watched the news on television. Tomorrow she would drive into

Weldon, be pleasant with customers, discuss the order book with
Stella, make some sense, however trivial, of the day's small events.
She might even be a little happy. It would be no worse, or not much,
than all the other days that had gone before or were to come.

But oh God! she thought suddenly, I shall miss his arms and the
pleasure of human contact; his needing me even though the desire was
totally selfish. Without him I am not nothing, as I was when David
left, but I am all the same reduced, shrunken, as if he had taken part
of me away with him.

As she swung the car through the opening into the drive and drew
up in front of the double gates, set open, that led into the road, she
was aware of another car approaching from her left. She waited,
watching as it came nearer, noticing at the same time that Patrick must
have gone into the sitting room because the light from the uncurtained
window was now streaming out across the narrow strip of front
garden, and she shrank back against the seat, hoping that the driver
was not someone she knew, for the bonnet and front number plate of
her own car must be visible. She saw a face turn briefly towards her
but it was too far away for her to recognise and then the car was gone,
travelling at speed towards the village. Having waited a few moments
to let it get well ahead, she turned into the road behind it.

Police Constable Neave glanced into his rear mirror and grinned
to himself. The headmaster's daughter spending an evening with
Patrick Vaughan. Who would have credited it? She didn't look the
type to appeal to Vaughan. Not that she wasn't attractive, but she was
too tense, too angular for most men to fancy.

Neave was quite sure in his own mind that's where she'd come
from. While he was still some distance up the road, he had noticed the
headlights turn into the drive from behind the cottage so he knew she
hadn't been visiting Mrs. Fulton at Coppins.

I wonder if her father knows? he asked himself. Probably not.
He couldn't imagine Shand approving of her going out with someone
like Vaughan. He had a randy look about him and Neave was willing
to bet he'd known a good few women in his time. A bit of a boozer,
too, by all accounts. She wouldn't get very far mixing herself up with
him, if it was marriage she was after, and he supposed that's what she
would want because she must be pushing thirty. She'd been too
sheltered, that was half the trouble. Shand was a nice enough man,
but he was too anxious about his daughter. You could see it in his face
whenever he looked at her, although you could understand his
concern. Neave had been in the village for only four years but

according to the gossip he'd heard, she'd had some kind of a breakdown. All the same, it never paid to get too involved with your own kids, Neave, whose own children were both under five, added sententiously to himself.

Lewis Shand heard the car draw up outside the house and went quickly into the kitchen to put the kettle on. He wanted to be busy when she came in.

That way, he thought, I can talk to her as if nothing has happened.

He had already decided not to mention his visit to Kitty's. If she knew he had been anywhere near Coppins, she might realise there was a possibility he had seen her car outside the cottage. He had telephoned Kitty earlier to tell her that he had been unable to speak to Vaughan.

Already the situation was beginning to develop into a web of falsehood and deceit; Kitty and Hilary lying to him; himself now part of it, and, in the centre of it all, Patrick Vaughan, as if the thread started there, reaching out to bind them together and to him.

Kitty had accepted his lie, even though he had been aware of her disappointment.

"But you'll go and see him another evening, won't you, Lewis?" she had asked.

He had hesitated fractionally before replying. There was, however, no other way out, and besides, he wanted Vaughan out of the cottage as much as she did.

"Yes, of course," he replied. "I'll try to see him on Thursday."

It gave him two days to summon up the courage and on Thursday there was no chance that Hilary would be visiting Vaughan. It was half-closing day in Weldon and he knew that she and Stella had arranged to drive up to London together to look round a paperback book exhibition and go on from there to the theatre. She couldn't have lied about that. He had seen the tickets.

"I'll phone you after I've seen him," he had added.

"Won't you come up to the house? I'd like to see you again. I wasn't very good company this evening. Do say you'll come and let me make it up to you."

He had agreed reluctantly. The ridiculous thing was that now he realised that he loved her he wanted to avoid being with her. He felt he couldn't trust himself to act in the same way as he had done in the past. There would be some sign, he felt, in his voice or face that would betray him.

"All right, Kitty, I'll come. But only if you promise me you'll take the sleeping pills."

"Must I? I don't want to." Again there was that sharp note in her voice that he had noticed before when he had mentioned the tablets. "I feel a lot better already."

"Please, Kitty," he persisted.

"Oh, very well, although I hate taking anything like that."

"And no more whisky?"

"I know the risks," she had told him briefly.

Hilary came into the kitchen just as he was pouring the boiling water into the teapot so he had an excuse not to look up at her.

"Oh, you're making it," she said. "You needn't have bothered. I could have done it."

Her voice sounded natural enough, perhaps a little too high, and he wondered how practised she was in the art of deception.

"The kettle was already hot," he explained. He still didn't look up at her, intent on fitting the lid onto the pot. As if someone else was speaking, he listened to his own voice add, "Did you finish the stock-taking?"

"Yes, thanks. We had to go through every paperback in the shop to see what we'd need to order on Thursday."

"And you've eaten?"

"I had a sandwich."

"Was that enough? Wouldn't you like something else now?"

In his anxiety, he turned to look at her. She was standing just inside the door, leaning as if tired against the jamb, and, at the sight of her, tenderness overwhelmed him. At the same time, he felt distanced enough from her to see her objectively, as if they had just met. A clear, dispassionate, inner eye took in her features. The dark hair and eyes were attractive. The rest of her face was too bony for beauty but it was the expression rather than any individual detail that marred it. It was too set and rigid, as if the muscles were taut, drawing the skin down with them into small hollows and declivities round the mouth and under the cheeks. She already looks old, he thought, exhausted and joyless, although there were times when she smiled and the whole face came alive again.

"No, thanks. I'm not hungry."

"Won't you have a biscuit with your tea?"

"Oh, Father, don't *fuss!*"

He accepted the rebuke meekly. It was a justifiable criticism. What he couldn't make her understand was that, most of time, it was the only way he knew of expressing his love.

She took the tray from him and preceded him into the sitting room, where a small coal fire was burning in the hearth, his armchair drawn up to it, the book he had been reading, or trying to read since his return from Vaughan's, lying open over the arm. She noticed it as she put down the tray and pulled up her own chair.

"How was your evening? You've been reading?"

"Yes. There wasn't anything on television I wanted to watch."

We have exchanged lies, he thought sadly. Tit for tat. We are now equal.

"Is it interesting?"

He glanced at the cover to remind himself of the title.

"I suppose so. The first chapters are quite good. It tails off a bit after that."

So the evening would continue, he thought, each of them contributing the small change of conversation as if nothing had happened.

Kitty Fulton washed up the whisky glasses and dried them carefully before putting them away. In spite of her assurance to Lewis that she was better, she still felt exhausted, her limbs unaccustomedly heavy as she moved about the kitchen. It exasperated her. She was so rarely ill and had come to count on the vigour and resilience of her body as something that would never fail her.

Switching off the lights, she went back to the drawing room, where the fire still glowed red, and, feeling suddenly cold, she crouched over it, listening to the wind banging in the chimney. Usually she enjoyed a wild evening such as this, the sensation of being warm and sheltered inside the house with the weather shut outside. Tonight she felt only desolation.

The worst part of it had been lying to Lewis. The memory of it still distressed her but there had been no other course that she could take. She could hardly tell him the truth. And the dear man had thought it was money! God, if only it was. She could have coped with that, parting willingly with everything, the pictures, the silver, the furniture, all the things that she and Richard had collected together with so much pleasure over the years, and be content in one room. Because that's all they were in a final court—just things.

Lewis's telephone call had been a great disappointment, although she had tried not to show it. She hoped by tonight it would all be over and she would know exactly where she stood. The uncertainty was hardest to bear. She was, as she acknowledged herself, not very good at waiting.

But that's something I shall have to learn to live with, she told herself grimly.

As for Lewis, well, when everything was over, she'd try to make amends for the part she'd forced him to play in the sordid business. He hadn't liked it; she had seen it in his face. His antipathy towards Vaughan had been obvious. Perhaps, in his quiet way, he was more acute than she was at seeing through someone like Patrick, more sensitive to shades of personality than she was. He watched people, certainly. She had seen him doing it, sitting back, hardly speaking, his eyes going from one person's face to another, absorbing not just the words but the expressions and the gestures of a hand. He was an observer, whereas she had always been a participator, in the centre of the action.

She could only hope to God that he hadn't found out about Vaughan and Hilary. She thought he hadn't—not yet anyway. In her experience, you knew least about those people closest to you, a mistake she'd made herself and had compounded when she'd passed on the comment to Vaughan in one of those thoughtless exchanges that now she bitterly regretted.

But the girl is a fool! she thought angrily, although she found it hard to blame her. Might not she herself have done the same under the circumstances? In an odd way, she felt she understood Hilary better than Hilary's own father did. Even in those early days, when they had moved to the village and Hilary had been about twelve, she had been struck by how much the girl had reminded her of the young Jane Eyre. She had the same lost, orphan look; the grave, solemn expression. But behind it there had been a capacity for passion that Lewis evidently hadn't been aware of because her breakdown had shocked him so deeply.

Yes, she thought, Lewis must be protected. She had too much affection for him to want to see him suffer.

If only he had managed to see Vaughan and found out that he was going to leave! It would all then be at an end. They would be safe once more and she could go on living at Coppins as if none of the nightmare had really happened.

But it was no good brooding, she supposed, and she got stiffly to her feet. She would take Edwin Cotty's sleeping pills because she had promised Lewis she would and because she couldn't face another night of lying awake and going over it all again with the futility of some caged creature, but, as she shook them out of the little square envelope into the palm of her hand, she felt her throat close over at the sight of them.

Lewis Shand closed up the house for the night, going through the ritual of locking the front and back doors, turning off the lights and checking the boiler before mounting the stairs. Hilary had gone to bed early, pleading tiredness, although he could still hear her moving about softly in her bedroom as he passed her closed door.

In his room, he undressed and got into the double bed that he had once shared with Marion. He thought about her, as he often did, but tonight she seemed distanced, as if she no longer had any substantiality in his memory, only a faint image. The reality of Hilary and Kitty overlaid the recollection. Vaughan's face rose up, too, as clearly as if he had actually seen him that evening, dark-bearded and sarcastic, slightly built for a man, and with small neat hands like a woman's. . . .

He jerked his mind away from the thought of those hands and, switching on the bedside lamp again, reached across for the book that lay on the table beside it. If sleep was out of the question, he might as well stay awake and read, although the printed words, as he turned the pages, had no meaning for him.

In the bedroom next door, Hilary Shand also thought of Vaughan and lay, rigid and dry-eyed, staring up at the ceiling.

Kitty had taken the sleeping pills and they were already beginning to have their effect, making her feel slow and clumsy, as if she were wading through deep water. She hated the sensation but at least it numbed reality.

Moving like someone already asleep, she went across to the window to draw the curtains and saw, through the stripped branches of the trees, a light in Vaughan's cottage, blowing to and fro, too, it seemed in the wind and signalling to her in a dreadful parody of friendship.

Patrick Vaughan poured himself another gin and tonic and, glass in hand, moved back to the desk. The reading lamp shone down on the typewriter and the pile of manuscript, and, at the sight of them lying in the pool of light, a line from one of Donne's love poems came into his mind:

"This bed thy centre is, these walls thy sphere."

Substitute the word "desk," he thought sardonically, and it just about sums it all up, the world contracted thus, to further paraphrase that old lecher-poet-priest, to a few square feet of flat surface on which I ply my craft and exercise what talent I possess. But, Christ, it's something! Better than going down in the mire with the other countless millions, happy as pigs in shit, never once lifting their eyes beyond the ruts that they've dug with their own snouts.

I could pick it up, my world, my little universe, and encompass it all in one suitcase; move on as Bruno will do in my book, because it is only in the uncommitted and the unstructured that freedom lies. And that's what none of them—readers, critics, or that huge, amorphous mass, the Great British Public—will ever comprehend. But for God's sake look at them! All those frightened faces, pressing up against the windows of their houses, protected from reality by sheets of glass; little men scurrying to work, hollow men, straw men, their legs moving like scissors as they run for buses and trains; snip! snip! snip! Chopping up life into so many scraps of paper.

Even Moira didn't understand that you have to smash your way out.

But I must be drunk to think about her. She only comes back to haunt me, my ghost of a dead love—no! my genie of the gin bottle, long-lost spirit, 100 per cent proof—at two o'clock in the morning when I'm half-seas over and looking at life darkly through the bottom of a glass.

The aptness of the simile amused him and he laughed out loud.

I could use that in the next chapter, he told himself; Bruno coming back from Hester's and sitting in his room—a room like this one—the curtains drawn and just the one lamp alight, the rented furniture banished to the shadows, drinking and remembering another woman with the same dark hair. . . .

Sitting down at the desk, he opened the notebook that lay beside the typed pages and began to write in his quick, slanting hand.

". . . who seems more real than the woman whose bed he has just left. So it is paradoxically Hester who becomes the ghost and the phantom the reality. He imagines her standing behind his chair and is afraid to turn his head. He realises for the first time that he no longer has the power to control the memory of her. She comes unbidden. This idea might be worth exploring later in the book—how the act of remembering, used first as a conscious art, becomes more and more obsessive until he can recollect even the smallest detail. *Sensual recall very important here.*" He underlined the phrase with a heavy, black stroke. "Texture of skin. Tones of voice. The taste of her hair across his mouth. N.B. recast the opening chapters with this in mind."

Almost as an afterthought, although he was aware of the connection, he added, "Saw H.S. this evening. Strange girl. Very uptight and tense. Possibly a repressed hysteric? Good body, though; lean like a boy's. Surprisingly passionate, too; more than I'd imagined. I thought she'd be frigid—untried virginity—like making love to the Snow Princess. And with her hair loose, she does give the impression of being about sixteen, a schoolgirl in her nicely ironed blouse with its little Peter Pan collar. But I've decided to finish the affair. It's too complicated. If I'm not careful, I could have her round my neck. I think she realised it was over. After all, she's intelligent and sensitive enough. Spoke to her of Lewis and her need to break free, although I doubt if she'll have the courage. If she did, though, it would be a kind of retribution. He dislikes me. I see it in his eyes whenever we meet, although I was prepared to meet him halfway, buying that ridiculous book so that we could chatter about church architecture together. But who bloody cares? He's a prime example of the G.B.P.—a small frog in a small pond, squatting safe and smug on his lily leaf, oblivious to anything outside his piddling world. I wonder if he knows about H. and me? Probably not. His type never does until it's too late, like Hester's middle-aged boy friend."

3

It wasn't possible to walk to Vaughan's on Thursday evening. During the afternoon, the wind dropped, and by seven o'clock, as Lewis Shand was washing up his supper things, it began to rain —huge drops that slashed against the kitchen window; hardly the weather for a social visit but it was too late now to change his mind. He had promised Kitty and there might not be another evening when he could be sure of Hilary's plans. Besides, he had been preparing for the past two days and, although he still dreaded the thought of meeting Vaughan, it seemed better to get it over and done with than go through the same anxiety again.

All the same, he drove slowly, putting off the moment of confrontation. The village was deserted in the rain and mostly in darkness except for a scattering of lighted windows and the lamp over the door of the village hall shining down in a nimbus of water vapour on to the words "The Richard Fulton Memorial Hall" in black lettering picked out with gold, an inscription he had seen often enough over the past six years but which he had never read before with such a keen sense of his own inadequacy.

There was a light on, too, in Vaughan's. He saw it as soon as he turned into the drive of Coppins—a narrow slit of brightness showing between the curtains of the window that faced the road. So Vaughan was at home. Half an hour, an hour at most, and it would all be behind him.

Parking just inside the gate, he walked back to the front door.

Patrick Vaughan came to the door wearing a dressing gown, Lewis Shand noticed distractedly. He was too flustered to take in much more except that he was smiling and there was a lustre about his lips and eyes that contrasted oddly with the matt blackness of his beard and hair.

"Have I come at an awkward time?" he heard himself asking. His voice sounded unnaturally forced.

"Not really," Vaughan replied. He seemed surprised to see him and at the same time amused. "I've just got out of the bath, that's all. But do come in. I'm delighted that you've called."

He sounded genuine enough and yet Lewis Shand had always mistrusted Vaughan's easy social manner. Like his smile, they always appeared a little too facile, he thought, as he followed him down a narrow hall and into a sitting room where Vaughan turned to face him.

"Sit down. Join me in a drink while you're here."

"No thank you," Lewis Shand replied. He sat down on the edge of a sofa, conscious of an inner trembling that he could control only by holding himself very still and rigid.

"But you must. I insist. You've never paid me a visit before so we must celebrate the occasion."

"Very well," Lewis Shand agreed reluctantly. He had no wish to accept Vaughan's hospitality but it might seem churlish to refuse. Besides, there was an assertiveness behind the offer which told him Vaughan intended to have his own way.

"Let me see, you drink whisky, don't you, Lewis?"

Now how on earth did he know that? Lewis Shand thought. He had met Vaughan on only three social occasions, all of them at Kitty's; twice for sherry; once for a buffet supper last spring for about a dozen local people, including the Cottys and the vicar and his wife, at which only wine had been served, and he was unpleasantly reminded of that prying, quizzical side to Vaughan's nature. And it was at that supper party, he also remembered, that Hilary and Vaughan had first met. Had she been attracted to him then? He recalled them briefly, standing together by the window, Vaughan talking to her and smiling, and Hilary, who had her back to him, appearing ill at ease. There had been that awkward look about the set of her shoulders that told him she was on the defensive. She had said little afterwards about Vaughan. But she had said very little about David either, even after the engagement was broken off; nothing that had given him any real understanding of that relationship. He remembered only her ravaged face, and the tears that had poured silently out, and the sense of his own helplessness.

"A small one then," he said primly.

He watched as Vaughan crossed the room to a side table that held bottles and glasses, walking softly in the heel-less mules. He's like a black tomcat, he thought suddenly and was surprised that he hadn't seen the comparison before. He had the same feline, predatory alertness.

He had also, Lewis Shand realised, drunk quite a lot already. It was evident in his voice, which was just a little too loud, and in his manner, every gesture and movement slightly exaggerated and, at the same time, curiously self-regarding, as if Vaughan was forcing Lewis to follow him with his eyes.

As Vaughan came towards him, bringing him his glass of whisky, he was able, too, now that the first embarrassed flurry was over, to take in more details of his appearance. The dark-red dressing gown he was wearing was short, just covering his knees, and revealing bare, dark-skinned legs whose nakedness seemed obscene, and having taken the glass, Lewis Shand looked hurriedly away, as if suddenly interested in his surroundings.

It was a long, low room, running the length of the cottage, with windows at both ends; surprisingly large, considering the dimensions of the building, and furnished with that mixture of elegance and comfort that he recognised as Kitty's. In fact, some of the pieces were familiar; the desk, for example, had stood in the little study at Coppins, while the watercolour over the fireplace had once hung in the hall. But none of it reminded him so much of Kitty as Hilary. God knows how many times she and Vaughan had occupied this room together. Her presence still seemed to fill it.

"Well?" Vaughan was asking. He was standing by the fireplace, one arm thrust up on the mantelshelf. "What do I owe the pleasure to, Lewis, especially on such a ghastly evening?"

"I was on my way to Kitty's," Lewis Shand began. The words, like the furniture, were familiar—after all, he had rehearsed them often enough over the past two days. "I thought I'd call in to ask if I might borrow your book on Essex churches . . ."

"This one you mean?" Vaughan reached negligently for it from the bookshelves that flanked the fireplace. "The one I bought in Hilary's shop. I remember we discussed it but that was quite a long time ago."

There was an inquisitorial note in his voice for which Lewis Shand had no answer.

"Yes, I know. I wanted to check on a detail in an article I was reading the other day," he continued quickly, not yet daring to break away from his prepared explanation. "I'm sure the author had got one or two facts in it wrong."

"Which church was it about?" Vaughan asked. He had put down his glass and was turning over the pages, looking across at Lewis Shand at the same time.

Lewis Shand felt trapped. The conversation was not going at all as he had planned. He had imagined Vaughan would hand him the book, there would be a brief exchange about local history and then, by making some comment about the room or Vaughan's own work, he would be able to pass on to the subject of the lease without too much difficulty.

Instead of which, Vaughan had taken over the questioning. There was, of course, no magazine article and he thought desperately of anything he had read recently that would answer Vaughan's query.

"Mearsden church," he said at last.

Vaughan was turning to the index, running a finger down the list of names before flapping back the pages.

" 'Mearsden church,' " he read out loud, " 'although much restored in the 1870s is a fine building with many interesting features, the nave showing traces of early fourteenth-century work in the arcades. The tower is fifteenth century. In the chancel is a piscina niche with the original credence shelf, while the font with its ball and flower moulding dates to the reign of Edward I.' Is that what you wanted, Lewis?"

"Thank you," Lewis Shand said stiffly.

"Does it answer your question?"

"Yes, perfectly.

"What was the detail you thought was wrong? Was it the arcades or the piscina you had your doubts about?"

He's playing with me, Lewis Shand thought suddenly. He suspects the reason I gave him for coming here is just an excuse and he's deliberately testing me out. The realisation angered him and he felt his hands begin to tremble. But the jauntiness of Vaughan's expression hardened his own resolve.

"It was the font," he replied. The alacrity with which he thought up the lie surprised him. He felt no guilt as he had done with Kitty and Hilary, only a pleasurable sense of success at beating Vaughan at his own game. "The writer of the article ascribed it to the reign of Edward II."

"What a foolish mistake to make," Vaughan said lightly. "But perhaps it was a printer's error." He closed the book, as if acknowledging that the sport was over, and laid it down on top of the desk. "Do borrow it though. You're welcome to take it."

"There's no need now," Lewis Shand replied. He even managed a smile.

He paused and glanced about him to find some way of introducing the subject of the lease. A typewriter stood on the desk close to where Vaughan had placed the book; it might seem natural to ask about his writing. But as he hesitated Vaughan was already speaking.

"By the way, Lewis, how is Hilary these days?"

There was no mistake this time that the question was deliberately chosen. The look on his face, the relaxed, almost drawling voice in which it was asked were intended to be provoking.

But he can't know that I've found out about the affair, Lewis Shand thought helplessly. And then he realised that this wasn't the point. His eyes were on Lewis Shand's face, searching for any change of expression, and there was a quiet, intent quality about his scrutiny in spite of his assumed casualness.

Lewis Shand sensed rather than saw the purpose behind it. It wasn't simply malice; there was an arrogant streak in Vaughan that enjoyed a sense of power over others.

He should have been aware of it before, he realised. Soon after Vaughan's arrival in the village, he had borrowed one of his novels from the library in Weldon out of curiosity but had given up reading it after a few chapters. It was a novel of intrigue with a taut, exciting plot and a background of international banking and finance; not his type of book, although that hadn't been his reason for abandoning it. There had been a quality of ruthlessness and cynicism about the writing that had repelled him. Everyone has his price, Vaughan seemed to be saying. There is no one who can't be bought. It was an angry, sardonic, bitter philosophy that at the time he had thought was a mere literary device, the fashionable cult of the outsider who, like Camus' character, was unable to develop any relationship that really mattered; the observer who stood back and watched even himself. But in Vaughan's case, he saw, there was not that final, compassionate understanding.

We are like characters in one of his books, he thought. Puppets that can be manipulated as he wants, used and then discarded. God knows how he came by such an attitude.

Under any other circumstances he might have felt pity for a man who lacked such basic humanity, but for Vaughan he was conscious only of a sense of alienation and detestation, although, in a dim and half-intelligible way, he could see his attraction for Hilary. Vaughan had a dangerous, glittering quality about him that had a certain fascination. He held out the promise of a kind of love that she, with her own need for the drama of pain and self-humiliation, would find desirable.

How little I understand her, he thought. I offered her a way of life that was suited to my needs, not hers; the quiet, even stream of living when, all along, she had wanted the excitement and hazard of the rapids.

He blamed himself for not having seen it before. Marion, too, had possessed a restlessness that, in her case, had found its outlet in the trivial form of sudden whims and caprices that at times had driven him to the limit of endurance and that in the end had killed her. Driving home one day, she had overtaken a lorry on a hill, lost control of the car and crashed into a tree, receiving injuries from which she had died two days later. So, in a way, her death, too, had been a kind of suicide, a final act of impatience that was partly deliberate, as if she had grown weary of waiting.

He had accused Vaughan of arrogance, but it had been a similar pride which had prevented him from realising before that Hilary might be more like Marion than himself and which, even now, he found difficult to accept.

"Hilary?" he heard himself replying. "She's quite well. She's gone to London."

"Yes, she told me she was going," Vaughan said. "She mentioned it the last time I saw her. I called in at the shop, of course."

"Of course," Lewis Shand repeated foolishly. He could think of nothing else to say.

There was a small silence. Lewis Shand looked down at his hands. They were grasping his glass, the knuckles showing white under the stretched skin. He ought, he realised, to begin soon on the subject that had brought him here before the silence became so protracted that any remark would seem unnaturally forced, but no words seemed to form.

"How's the writing going, Patrick?" he said at last. His lips felt dry and he ran his tongue over them.

"Oh, all right," Vaughan replied easily. He seemed to accept the question as a piece of politeness, awkwardly expressed. For, after all, in Vaughan's eyes, Lewis Shand realised, he must seem socially inept. At times, he was painfully aware of it himself, feeling like an unskilful tennis player, patting the ball of small talk tentatively to and fro. Vaughan was still watching him, head a little on one side, but he had the pleased air of someone encouraged to talk about himself. "I've just begun a new book, as a matter of fact. It's going quite well at the moment."

"So you find the cottage a good place to work in?"

The ease with which he had got onto the subject gave him confidence. After all his anxiety, perhaps it wasn't going to be as difficult as he had imagined.

"Not too bad, I suppose," Vaughan was saying. "Kitty's made it quite comfortable."

There was a grudging tone in his voice.

Something's wrong, Lewis Shand thought. He's bored, he realised suddenly, and the knowledge gave him a feeling of relief and unexpected power. Vaughan, too, was vulnerable and in a way that he hadn't imagined. If only he could handle it properly, he might be able to use it to his advantage.

"Do you think you might settle here?" he asked, and added in his eagerness to keep the conversation going, "you must find you need the quiet."

For a moment he thought the last remark had been a mistake. Vaughan would start talking about his work again and the opportunity would be lost. In fact, Vaughan had put his glass down on the desk, which was neatly organised, Lewis Shand noticed as he followed him with his eyes, the papers on it arranged with a precision that he wouldn't have expected from someone like Vaughan. In addition to the pile of typewritten manuscript, the pages clipped together, and the typewriter, there was a blue mug containing pens and pencils and a flat china dish that held elastic bands, erasers and other small paraphernalia. A notebook with a stiff, red cover lay on top of the typewriter, slightly askew, as if put there hastily.

Vaughan was also looking at the desk, his face in profile. It was difficult to read his expression. The beard masked his mouth but the jauntiness had gone and there was a crouched look about his shoulders.

"Quiet?" he said suddenly, swinging round. "Christ, Lewis, I don't know how I stand it some days. It's all so bucolic and so bloody boring! No one to talk to. Nowhere much to go except the local pub and even there I'm treated like an outsider."

The outburst, with its unexpected bitterness and self-pity, caught Lewis Shand off guard. Coming from anybody else, Lewis Shand might indeed have felt sympathetic, even a little touched, by the confession. In its way, it was oddly flattering, and he could see how Hilary might find it appealing; even Kitty, whose protective, maternal qualities could have been roused by such an admission of loneliness.

In his own case, he felt merely embarrassed.

"Yes, I suppose you must find it very isolated after living in London," he remarked cautiously, feeling his way. As he said it, he realised it was one of the few facts he knew about Vaughan.

Was he married? he wondered. Even if he wasn't, he doubted if the relationship with Hilary was anything more than an affair. He couldn't see Vaughan committing himself further. He lacked any vestige of tenderness or kindness. Probably it had begun in the first place only because Vaughan was looking for amusement. Was she

aware of it? He wasn't sure. But he was certain of one thing
—Vaughan had to go.

"Were you thinking of moving back there when the lease runs
out?" he added.

He had spoken too eagerly. Vaughan was on the alert again,
looking towards him with a sharp, inquisitive expression.

"Why do you ask that? Has Kitty said anything to you about the
cottage?"

"No, no, of course not," Lewis Shand replied. The palms of his
hands were clammy with sweat and he rubbed them surreptitiously
across the knees of his trousers.

Oh, God, he thought despairingly, he's guessed why I'm here.
For a moment he had the wild and ridiculous idea that Vaughan could
read his mind; that it all lay exposed under Vaughan's bright scrutiny.

"She never discusses her business affairs with me. I simply
wondered . . . as you don't seem to like it here . . ."

He trailed off, appalled by his own ineptitude, but Vaughan had
once more taken on the look of brooding displeasure.

"I don't know. I haven't made up my mind yet. The trouble is
London's so bloody expensive. You can't find a decent flat these days
at a reasonable rent and I don't intend paying through the nose for a
couple of crummy rooms."

He paused to drain his glass, and then, walking back to the side
table, added, "Another drink, Lewis?"

"No, thank you," Lewis Shand replied awkwardly.

Vaughan was helping himself to more gin, splashing it carelessly
into his glass. Over his shoulder, he continued in an offhand voice, as
if there had been no break in the previous conversation, "So if Kitty's
curious about my plans, you can tell her that I haven't decided yet
what I'm going to do."

Lewis Shand got slowly to his feet. He felt bruised in the pit of
the stomach, as if Vaughan's remark had struck him like a physical
blow. Yet he felt he ought to say something more in protest. Or would
it only make matters worse? After all, Vaughan only suspected. But
he knew he was clutching at straws.

"Are you going?" Vaughan was asking. "Then I'll see you out."

He was relaxed and affable, as if nothing had happened between
them except an exchange of social pleasantries. "Nice of you to drop
in," he added as he opened the front door. "Call again anytime you're
on your way to Kitty's. Give her my love, by the way."

"Yes," Lewis Shand said automatically.

"And Hilary, too."

There was, thank God, no need to reply. Lewis Shand was already on the doorstep, turning to duck away through the rain, and, when he did look back briefly at the gate, Vaughan had already gone back inside the house.

Kitty must have been listening out for the car for, as soon as he drew up, she appeared on the porch, hugging her arms round her for extra warmth and peering through the curtain of drops that pattered down from the edge of the verandah roof.

What on earth am I going to say to her? Lewis Shand thought as he got slowly out of the car. He knew she was counting on him to bring her good news. He saw, too, with an increasing sense of his own failure, that she had dressed up for the occasion in a long skirt of green wool with a silk blouse, as if for a celebration. But before he could speak, she had clasped him by the arm and was drawing him inside the house, exclaiming about the weather.

"Heavens, Lewis, what a night! I'd never have asked you to come if I thought it was going to be like this. Are you soaked, my dear? Give me your coat; there's a fire in the drawing room."

He submitted to her hands, watching as she shook out his mackintosh and hung it over the back of the chair to dry, giving it a little approving pat as she did so, as if transferring to the coat some of the affection she felt towards him.

The drawing room had also been prepared for his coming. The chair he usually occupied was already drawn up to the fire and a bowl of late roses stood on the low table beside the decanter and the glasses.

"I picked them this morning," Kitty explained. "Thank goodness I did. The rain would have ruined them. Now, Lewis, help yourself to a drink and sit down by the fire."

He poured two glasses, taking one across to her. Her smile as she thanked him was open, quite without guile, and he thought how easy it would be to confess everything to her, not just the disastrous interview with Vaughan but all the other things that pressed so heavily on him—Hilary's affair and his own feelings towards her.

But the same cool, objective eye that had regarded Hilary with such dispassion on the evening she came home from Vaughan's was turned this time on himself.

After all, what was he? A headmaster of a country school, nothing more, and lacking both the drive and the ambition to rise any further. It was too late now anyway and, besides, the boundaries of his life had been imposed long before, he realised, in his cautious upbringing that had taught him not to take too many risks.

"Are you sure you're doing the right thing?" How often had his parents asked him that? With loving concern, of course. He recognised that. But he had learnt to question every decision he ever made with the same anxiety, always looking over his shoulder in case he made a mistake, never quite ready to commit himself.

The same question faced him now, and the answer, he realised, was probably no. He wasn't at all sure that he would be doing the right thing. Better, perhaps, to leave the situation as it was. At the moment, he was at least assured of Kitty's friendship. To admit to more might destroy what he had.

For much the same reason, he would say nothing to her about Vaughan and Hilary.

"Did you see Patrick?" Kitty was asking. She made no attempt to hide her eagerness.

"Yes, I saw him." Lewis Shand sat down, holding the glass of whisky between both hands. "I called at the cottage on my way here."

"And what did he say?"

"Nothing positive, I'm afraid, Kitty. He hadn't made up his mind what he's going to do. My fault, I must admit. I didn't handle it at all well . . ."

"He didn't suspect I'd asked you to talk to him?" she broke in. Her face had taken on again the same drawn look he had seen the other evening, the eyes dark and full, brimming with a desperate appeal.

She's afraid of him, he thought suddenly. But in God's name why? Seeing her expression, he knew it was going to be impossible to tell her the truth.

"No, of course not. I made the excuse of calling on him to borrow a book. He seemed to accept it."

He was talking too quickly in his anxiety to reassure her. But she was only half listening. She had got up from the sofa as if she could no longer bear to be still and was walking up and down in front of the fire, each time she turned her long skirt brushing the tops of his shoes while he watched her helplessly.

"What shall I do now?" she asked at last.

"My dear, I don't know." He made a futile gesture with one hand. "If only I understood what was the matter . . ."

"I've already told you. I can't do anything about selling Coppins until I've got him out of the gatehouse. And he's not a very good tenant."

"No," agreed Lewis Shand. That, at least, made sense.

"I don't think he's trustworthy, either," Kitty added quickly. She wanted to go on and warn him about Hilary and Vaughan but how could she when he sat there looking up at her with such obvious concern at her own distress? She couldn't burden him any further. Besides, she remembered too clearly his unhappiness when Hilary had had her breakdown. He had suffered every agony with her. It would be too cruel to thrust him back again into the pit.

"I don't trust him either," Lewis Shand replied with a touch of asperity. "And I've never liked him. But I could try talking to him again if you like."

If only he'd had the sense to bring the book with him! It would have given him the excuse to go back another day in order to return it. He blamed himself for not having seen the opportunity.

"I don't think it would do any good," Kitty said.

She was probably right, he thought. Vaughan was already suspicious. To try reintroducing the question of the lease would only make it worse.

"Of course, he may decide to move out anyway," he continued with a deliberate attempt at cheerfulness. "I know for a fact he's bored. He mentioned it while I was talking to him. It's too quiet for him here; not enough to do. He may find as the weather gets worse he can't stand it any longer."

"Oh, I knew that," Kitty said. There was an odd note of weary bitterness in her voice that made him look at her in surprise. Why hadn't she told him that before? he wondered. It might have helped him prepare for the interview. As it was, Vaughan's dislike of the countryside had taken him aback and he felt now he could have made better use of it. "He gets depressed at times," she added. Her mouth had twisted into a grimace of distaste that he couldn't understand either.

"Did he tell you that?" he asked, aware suddenly of conversations that Kitty must have had with Vaughan of which he knew nothing. He was touched by an unexpected feeling of jealousy at the thought.

"He mentioned it once," she said dismissively, as if she didn't want him to pursue the subject any further. "Well, Lewis, my dear, you've obviously done all you can and I'm very grateful. Now let's talk about something more agreeable."

The conversation passed on to other matters—village affairs, mostly: his plans for the Christmas fete and the school party, the vagaries of the local bus service about which Kitty was campaigning, but neither of them had their heart in it and the subject of Patrick Vaughan seemed to lie like a shadow across the evening.

For Lewis Shand it took the form of a question that he dared not ask. What was going to happen to Coppins now? he wanted to say to Kitty.

As he sat talking, he took small, covert glances about the room that over the years had become as familiar to him as his own. Would it all go? he wondered. The collection of watercolours? The walnut bureau? The cabinet of Chinese porcelain?

He had a vivid mental picture, almost visionary in its detail, of the room stripped of everything, of cold, angular sunlight pouring in through the sash windows and lying in oblongs across the bare floors. It was based to a large extent, he realised, on his own experience of selling the house in Kent after Marion died, before moving to Chellfield. It had been intended as a fresh start, an escape from the past. Even Marion's death, distanced by time, seemed bearable compared to the prospect of losing Kitty.

The matter wasn't referred to again until he was on the point of leaving and she came with him into the hall.

"Don't come out," he told her. "It's too cold."

She helped him on with his coat, and then, as he stood with his back to her, he felt her lean her weight briefly against him, both hands resting on his shoulders, as if she were suddenly exhausted.

"Oh, Lewis," he heard her say, "how am I going to get rid of him?"

He could have spoken then, he realised. It would have been the most natural thing in the world to turn and take her in his arms. But he hesitated a moment too long. He felt the pressure of her hands slacken and when he looked into her face he saw it was too late.

"I don't know, Kitty. But don't worry. I'll think of something," he assured her.

God knows what, he thought as he went down the steps and got into the car. Passing Vaughan's cottage and seeing the streak of light still shining out onto the front garden, he remembered her words and repeated them to himself:

How am I going to get rid of him?

He was to recall them the next day with a sense of terrible apprehension when he heard that Patrick Vaughan was dead.

4

About four hours after Lewis Shand had left Coppins, the telephone extension on Edwin Cotty's bedside table rang. Stretching out an arm above the bedclothes, he fumbled for the lamp switch before picking up the receiver.

As he replaced it and got out of bed, Eleanor Cotty turned in her sleep and awoke.

"Edwin?" she asked.

He was standing at the foot of the bed, hurriedly pulling on his clothes over his pyjamas.

"I'm sorry, my dear," he replied. "Did the phone wake you up? I've got to go out on a call, I'm afraid."

"What's the time?" She glanced at the alarm clock and saw it was just gone half-past one.

"There's been an accident. Someone's just phoned through to report it. I must go."

He came to the bedside and bent down to kiss her, then, drawing back, looked into her face. Her head lay lightly on the pillow, the fine, grey hair scattered, the features blurred and dominated by her eyes, a huge, drenched blue.

"Are you in any discomfort?" he asked anxiously.

Strange that, he thought. I never call it pain, as if the word were dirty.

"A little," she whispered.

"I'll give you one of your tablets."

"Should I take one so soon?" she asked, dragging herself into a sitting position as he leaned across the bed to reach the bottle of pills and the glass of water that stood on her side of the bed. It was her usual protest.

"It won't do any harm."

He spoke in the coaxing voice that he always used when she woke in the night and needed another tablet, as he might to a child, and she took the pill he held out in the palm of his hand, putting it into her mouth and swallowing it down with a sip of water. He saw the tendons in her throat, too obvious now since she had lost weight, tighten painfully and then relax. He patted her hand.

"Now you're to go back to sleep again and not lie awake worrying. I'll be home as soon as I can."

He kissed her again before snapping off the light and closing the bedroom door. She heard him go down the stairs and enter the surgery to collect his bag. The front door clicked quietly shut and then came the subdued rumble as he opened the garage: familiar night noises that she had heard so many times over the years as he went out on emergency calls. She had never really got accustomed to the emptiness he left behind. In the old days, she used to get up with him to make sure he had everything he needed, seeing him off at the front door before going back to the kitchen to prepare a tray, with the biscuit barrel and a flask of tea, for his return. Now she was grateful for the tablet and the opportunity to slip back again into blessed oblivion.

The sound of his car died away up the road and there was silence except for the faint prickling of rain against the window behind the closed curtains.

At one thirty-two a telephone call also woke up Bob Neave but not his wife, who was capable of sleeping, as he often told her, through the last trump. Like Edwin Cotty, he dressed hastily before going downstairs to start the car.

It was a lousy night to be called out; thick darkness and rain, although not as heavy, thank Christ, as it had been earlier in the evening.

He checked his watch before driving off. One thirty-five precisely. Not bad going. Three minutes from receiving the call to leaving the house. Another four, say, to reach the accident. In all, less than ten minutes.

In fact, it took him nearly six, for the road surface was too dangerous for him to drive above fifty even on the straight, and some damned fool had left a car parked right on the S bend in the centre of the village in spite of the double yellow lines, forcing him to slow down in order to pass it. He'd bloody have the number on the way back.

Once clear of the houses, he was able to put his foot down; past the gates of Coppins, his lights picking out the toy façade of the cottage, and somewhere along here, according to the man who'd phoned in to report, he should be at the scene. A few moments later, he saw headlamps ahead of him, full on, shining in a double shaft onto the grass verge on his left. Then he saw the car itself, parked slightly askew with its off-side wheels up on the verge and a figure squatting down over what looked like a bundle of old clothes lying huddled a few feet in from the edge.

Drawing in just behind the other car, Neave got out as the figure rose to its feet and turned to face him. He saw it was Dr. Cotty, his stethoscope hanging loose round his neck.

"Is that you, Neave?" he asked.

He was looking straight into the headlamps and could see only a dark shape that seemed familiar.

"Yes, Doctor. What's happened?"

"I don't know," Dr. Cotty replied impatiently. "I've only just got here myself. It looks like a hit-and-run accident. Fatal, I'm afraid."

"Who is it?"

As he asked the question, Neave bent down over the body and saw for himself. Patrick Vaughan was lying on his back, his face turned towards the headlamps, which lit up with cruel clarity every detail of his features. The eyes were open, staring upwards, Neave noticed, and the beard and hair were wet with rain and spattered with mud, while the clothing, open to the waist, was also drenched.

"Is that how you found him?" he asked, looking up at Dr. Cotty, who had remained standing.

"No. He was lying facedown. I turned him over to see if he was still alive but I couldn't find a heartbeat," Dr. Cotty replied in his clipped voice.

That would account for the clothes being pulled open, Neave thought.

"And the injuries?"

"I haven't had time to examine them properly. As I told you, I've only just arrived myself. From a cursory examination, I'd say certainly broken legs and possibly spine, as well as internal injuries."

"Hit from behind," Neave commented, half to himself.

"It would seem so," Dr. Cotty replied, as if the remark had been addressed to him. "From the way he was lying when I found him, it looked as if he'd been struck in the lower back and the impact had thrown him onto the side of the road. By the way, I assume you also had a telephone call about the accident?"

It was a question that Neave had intended asking the doctor and it exasperated him a little that the initiative had been taken out of his hands. Cotty might be damned good as a doctor but there was a remote, unapproachable air about him that Neave found difficult to take. He had worked with him before and Cotty had never shown the slightest emotional reaction. While Neave admired his control, he would have preferred some sign that the doctor shared his own feelings of revulsion and pity.

The other characteristic that annoyed him was Cotty's tendency to treat him as a subordinate.

"Yes, I got a phone call," he replied. "What time was yours, sir?"

"Almost exactly half-past one."

"Mine was a couple of minutes later. So he must have phoned you first and then me."

"He?"

He's bloody doing it again, Neave thought angrily. But the doctor was quite right. It sounded as if he was assuming the caller was a man, which, in fact, was exactly what he was doing.

"He or she," he corrected himself. "The voice could have been either. Rather husky, wouldn't you say, Dr. Cotty?"

"No more than a whisper. I had difficulty hearing all the words."

"Can you remember them? I'll have to put in a report."

"Let me see. It was quite brief. I was asked first if I was Dr. Cotty and when I said yes, I was, the caller went on to say, 'There's been an accident just past Coppins. You'd better come at once.' "

"And that was all?" Neave asked. He was squatting down in the light of the headlamps, his notebook balanced on one knee.

"Yes. The caller rang off immediately afterwards."

"Did you recognise the voice?"

"No."

Neave closed his notebook and stood up. The words were exactly the same as the ones he had heard and he hadn't been able to recognise the voice either, although he suspected that it had been disguised.

"I assume it was the driver of the car involved," Dr. Cotty added.

Neave had assumed the same, but as he didn't want to appear to agree too readily with the doctor, he replied cagily, "It's possible."

He had reached other conclusions as well. It seemed likely, from the position in which the body was lying, that Patrick Vaughan had been struck down as he walked away from his cottage towards the Cross, a small hamlet of about half a dozen houses a quarter of a mile up the road, although what he was doing out at half-past one on a wet Friday morning was anybody's guess. Knowing Vaughan, or rather seeing him about the village, Neave had mentally categorised him as the arty type and consequently a bit odd, so there was no way of telling what someone like him would take it into his head to do. He was fond of the booze, too, so it was possible he'd been walking off the effects of having a bit too much to drink, a fact that would come out at the postmortem and might also account for the accident. If Vaughan was tight, he could have staggered out into the path of a passing car.

As for the car itself, it must have been travelling in the same direction, that is away from the village towards the Cross, and moving fairly fast for the impact not only to kill Vaughan but to throw his body onto the side of the road. And this linked in with the phone calls. There was a public kiosk at the Cross where the driver could have stopped to ring up first the doctor and then himself before driving on.

There was another point about this, too, that was worth bearing in mind. The man—and Neave was still convinced in his own mind that the caller had been a man, even though he wouldn't be prepared to swear to it—might be local or at least know the village fairly well for, although he could find Neave's own number by looking up "Police" in the directory, he must have known Dr. Cotty by name to find his. Anyway, a stranger wanting help in an accident would be more likely to dial 999 and ask for the emergency services.

Given a bit more evidence, Neave thought, flakes of paint off the car, for instance, on Vaughan's clothes, and it might be possible to trace the driver.

Meanwhile there was one fact he could establish immediately —the speed the car was travelling by measuring the length of the skid marks on the road, a piece of investigation that was routine in a traffic accident.

Turning to Dr. Cotty, he said, "If we could shift the cars forward, sir . . ."

"You'd like to do your measuring, I suppose." Dr. Cotty completed the sentence for him with a testy air, as if he found police duties trivial and time-consuming. But he complied, driving a little distance up the road, with Neave following.

"Is that far enough?" he called out through the open window as he halted.

"I think that'll do," Neave replied, getting out of his own car with his torch and tape ready in his hand.

"Do you want me to hold the other end of the tape?" Cotty asked.

Cotty's face, looking up at him, was grey with fatigue, and Neave was suddenly aware that, compared to himself, the doctor was an elderly man, well on into his fifties, with a sick wife, too, who ought to be home in his bed, not turning out in the rain to examine a dead body in the early hours of the morning.

"Thanks, sir, but I'll manage," Neave replied, with more warmth than usual in his voice.

Switching on the torch, he walked back along the road to near where Vaughan's body lay on the verge. It wasn't easy to find the tyre marks of the car that had knocked him down. The treads of his own and the doctor's had overlaid them and, besides, a wet surface wasn't nearly as good as a dry one for holding them. But they were there all right, faintly traced out on the tarmac; too blurred, though, for him to tell the make of the tyres.

He put down the metal tab of the tape on the spot where the tyre marks ended, some yards past Vaughan's body, holding it in place with a heavy spanner he'd brought with him from the car, and, walking carefully backwards, reeled out the tape, holding the torch tucked under his left arm. It was slow and laborious and made it difficult for him to estimate the distance, so that, when he reached the point where the tyre marks began, he had no idea how many feet he had covered.

Bending down to check the tape, he was surprised to see that it was only a little over forty. But that couldn't be right. The car had to be travelling at more than twenty miles an hour. He must have dragged the tape with him, so he'd have the whole bloody job to do again.

"Oh, Christ! And in all this sodding rain, too," he said out loud.

This time he'd forget about doing the doctor a good turn and he'd root him out of the car to hold the other end while he remeasured it.

But the spanner was still in place when he reached it.

He stood for a moment shining the torch down on it, oblivious of the rain, and then, his mind made up, he walked back to the doctor's car and tapped on the window.

"I'm sorry," he said as Cotty wound it open, "but I'm afraid I've got to ask you to move the body back to where you found it."

"Very well," the doctor replied. He got stiffly out of the car.

"I'm not too happy about the skid marks," Neave added gratuitously, feeling the need to give some reason.

Cotty didn't answer. He had turned up the collar of his overcoat and was trudging ahead, bowed against the rain. Neave hurried to catch up with him.

"I'll give you a hand," he offered as, reaching the place where Vaughan's body lay, they both bent down over it.

"Thanks," Cotty said briefly. They turned it over together, Neave noticing as he did so that it was already beginning to cool under the wet clothing. He stood back, leaving the doctor to move the head and limbs. Vaughan now lay on his face with his right leg drawn up, while his hands were arranged palms downward on the wet grass, almost parallel with the head, which was turned a little towards the left, a position that was consistent with it having been thrown from the bonnet, say, of a car, but one moving a damned sight faster, Neave suspected, than twenty miles an hour.

"That's as near as I can get it," Dr. Cotty was saying. "I can't vouch for it being absolutely exact."

Neave hardly heard him. He had squatted down again and was moving the light of the torch over the body. When it reached the head, he stopped and, bending lower, looked more carefully at the dark hair, black now with rain. And something else. Neave stretched out a tentative hand and touched it. Blood. It clung to his fingers, sticky and viscous.

"Could you have a look here?" he asked, addressing Dr. Cotty over his shoulder. "I think he's got head injuries as well."

"Hold the torch," Cotty replied snappily.

He knelt down in the soaking grass while Neave stood beside him.

"What sort of injury?" Neave asked quickly.

Cotty moved his shoulders in a gesture of impatience at the constable's eagerness and took his time before replying.

"It's difficulty to say exactly but it's approximately three inches long and an inch wide. It's not the cause of death, if that's what you're thinking. The skin's barely broken."

Too wide to have been caused by the rim along a car's roof, Neave decided. That would have left a narrow cut in the scalp. But he might have got it by striking his head on a kerbstone as he was thrown sideways. The only trouble with that theory was the road wasn't kerbed. There was just grass.

"Hang on a minute," he told Cotty and, stepping back, flashed his torch across the area immediately round the body. Nothing there either. Not a stone or even a tree branch left lying about.

"I must admit I didn't notice the head injury when I first examined him."

Dr. Cotty's voice came out of the darkness sounding stiffly defensive, as if his medical expertise had been called into question.

Understandable, Neave thought. He'd arrived only a few minutes before me. Time for only a quick examination in the car's headlamps before he'd turned Vaughan over to find out if he was still alive. And with the hair wringing wet, the blood wouldn't be obvious. But he was more concerned about his own problems. He knew he'd have to explain his suspicions when he rang in to report. There was enough evidence in the length of the skid marks, let alone the head injury, to make him uneasy about it being just a hit-and-run accident. He shied away, however, from thinking what it could be, if not that. Let the sergeant at Turnleigh decide whether or not the CID ought to be called in, although he knew, once he'd spoken to Morrow, that he might be setting in motion a process of law that, once started, could lead God knows where.

"I'm going back to the village to phone," he said abruptly.

Better not use the kiosk at the Cross although it was nearer, he decided. There might be prints on the receiver that could be useful as evidence.

"I'd like you to stay on here, Doctor, just in case someone else drives past and decides to stop," he continued. And messes up the skid marks, not to mention touching the body, he added to himself.

"Yes, of course," Dr. Cotty replied.

"I'd sit in the car if I were you."

He wasn't sure himself why he said it. After all, he'd never felt much sympathy for Cotty and yet he was suddenly moved by a protective instinct towards the older man.

Leaving him to make his own way back to his car, Neave strode ahead to his and, getting in, did a brisk U-turn in the road before heading back to Chellfield. But he changed his mind about phoning from the other public kiosk outside the post office and drove home instead. The call could be lengthy, and he didn't fancy standing there feeding small change into the coin box.

In the event, however, it didn't take all that long. Morrow heard him out but didn't say much except, "All right. Leave it with me, lad. I'll be out there myself anyway as soon as I can."

Feeling deflated, Neave collected a tarpaulin from the garage that was used in winter to cover up the kids' sandpit in the back garden and a couple of yellow warning cones that were knocking about under the workbench and set off once more for the scene of the accident.

Perhaps he was wrong after all, he thought, and it was only an accident. Morrow hadn't sounded all that impressed but then Morrow wasn't keen on shifting himself unless he had to. He'd never get further than sergeant. Neave had set his own sights a good bit higher than that.

All the same, he couldn't get it out of his head that there was something not right about it. Stick to the evidence. That had been drummed into him often enough. Well, the evidence was iffy. You couldn't deny that. And added to this was a feeling that there were other things wrong about it, too; not just the fact that Vaughan was out walking in the rain at that God-awful hour in the morning. A gut reaction, if you like. Like being convinced that the caller had been a man.

But it was only now, on the return journey, that he began to consider some of the implications behind Vaughan's death if it wasn't an accident, although he still couldn't bring himself to frame the word "murder" in his mind.

And then his foot jabbed automatically on the brake and he found himself skidding to a halt at the side of the road.

Oh Christ! In his excitement, he'd forgotten the incident the other evening when he'd seen Hilary Shand drive away from Vaughan's cottage. At the time, it had merely amused him. Now he wasn't so sure. Supposing they were having an affair and they'd quarrelled? As he'd thought then, Vaughan wasn't likely to settle down with the headmaster's daughter. But it might give her a motive, especially as she was one of those emotional, highly strung women.

Putting the car into gear, he started to drive on. Let the CID follow that one up themselves if they weren't satisfied with Vaughan's death. Besides, there wasn't time to think it out. He was approaching the scene now, with Vaughan's body lying where he had left it and the doctor's car still parked a little further up the road.

Drawing in just behind it, he got out and looked in at the driver's window. Cotty's face, more grey than ever and twisted with pain, peered up at him, putting Hilary Shand out of his mind.

"Something the matter, Doctor?" he asked quickly. It was obvious the man was ill.

"My damned ulcer," Cotty replied.

It was the first time Neave had ever seen him show any kind of emotion, let alone swear, and he was impressed.

"You look really rotten," he sympathised. "Can I do anything?"

"No, there's nothing. How long am I likely to be kept hanging about here?"

"It shouldn't be too long," Neave said. Morrow ought to be arriving soon and possibly, if the sergeant had thought it necessary to phone through to headquarters at Chelmsford, the CID as well, although he didn't like to tell Cotty that. It might take another half hour before they turned up.

"From my experience of the police, I doubt that very much," Cotty snapped, and Neave felt his sympathy drain away.

Without replying, he walked off up the road, although once he was out of Cotty's hearing he swore out loud to relieve his feelings.

He couldn't seek refuge in his car until he'd covered up the body with the tarpaulin and set the markers out on the road; all of which was damned futile anyway. The body must be wet through already and the markers, one at each end of the skid marks, were almost as useless. But at least he'd be doing what he could and he only hoped Morrow would notice, not that Neave believed for a moment he would.

5

Rudd, too, cursed the rain. Within a short time of arriving, the bottoms of his trouser legs were soaked and water had found its way inside the collar of his coat.

He swore for other reasons, too. The case couldn't have come at a worse time. Both he and the men were already tired, having just finished a complicated investigation into a series of robberies, and none of them had had more than a few hours sleep before they had been called out again.

On his own part, he was under added pressure. He had put in for promotion to the rank of detective chief inspector and much would depend on how he handled this case. In the event, he would have preferred a straightforward, honest-to-God murder rather than a road accident that had happened under suspicious circumstances which didn't look as if it would be cleared up quickly or satisfactorily.

But quite a lot had already been achieved. Two constables were measuring the skid marks in the road. More were erecting a plastic tent over the body, and the uniformed men, under Stapleton's charge, were searching the area with torches while Kyle had been despatched to the public kiosk up the road to fingerprint it and bring back anything lying about on the floor inside.

So far, though, he had only a sketchy idea of what had happened and most of that he had learned secondhand through Morrow. Neave, the local bobby, his face haggard with worry as the convoy of official cars drew up, had been more anxious to justify himself for having had the CID called out at that hour in the morning. It was time, Rudd thought, that he found out a few facts—from the doctor, for instance, who having verified the position of the body, had retired to wait in his car.

Dr. Cotty watched the inspector approach, a stocky figure, hunched up against the rain, hands plunged deep in his raincoat pockets, and, guessing his purpose, leaned across to open the passenger door for him. Rudd got in, bringing with him a gust of cold, wet air.

"Dr. Cotty?" The voice was pleasant enough, with a faint intonation of the local dialect. "I'm Detective Inspector Rudd. Rotten weather for an investigation."

Dr. Cotty murmured an agreement. He sat huddled up in the driver's seat.

"Mind if we have the light on?" Rudd added, and, as Cotty reached back to switch on the interior light, they were each revealed to one another. The doctor saw a bland, fresh-complexioned face wearing the contented and imperturbable expression of a farmer well pleased with his lot. Rudd, in his turn, saw an austere, high-nosed profile, with thinning grey hair that lay close to the scalp, and skin that had the same drawn appearance as if both had shrunk to fit more tightly to the bony structure beneath. The man looked ill, Rudd thought.

"Now, Dr. Cotty, I believe you were first on the scene?"

"Yes. I left the house soon after receiving the phone call."

"At what time was that?" Rudd asked.

"I can tell you precisely," Dr. Cotty replied. He sounded impatient at being interrupted and Rudd settled back to let him make his statement in his own way. As a witness, Cotty seemed to know what he was about. "It came at almost exactly half-past one. Perhaps a couple of seconds later. My wife can verify it if necessary. The call woke her up. The voice was little more than a muffled whisper and I can't say whether it was a man or a woman. But it was made from a pay box, of that I am sure. I heard the tone before the money was put in. He or she spoke quickly. The words as far as I can remember them and I believe I'm correct were, 'There's been an accident just past Coppins. You'd better come at once.' Then the receiver was put down. I got dressed, drove out of the village in the direction I'd been told and found the body without any difficulty. It was lying, as you've seen it, on the side of the road and my headlamps picked it out quite easily. I could see at once that the legs were probably broken but at that stage I was more concerned whether or not the man was still alive. I felt for a pulse but couldn't find one so I turned the body over, opened the clothing and had just finished listening for a heartbeat when Neave arrived. As I couldn't find one, I assumed the man was dead."

He stopped and, feeling in his pocket, produced a handkerchief and wiped his lips. The account seemed to be over.

"I might add," he continued unexpectedly, putting the handkerchief away, "that the body temperature was consistent with death having occurred only shortly before."

"Still warm, was he?" Rudd asked. He had assumed the interested expression of a bright schoolboy eager to learn more. Dr. Cotty folded his lips as if offended by the manner in which the question was put.

"Yes, but the body was cooling rapidly. The clothing was already wet and . . ."

"It's a cold night," Rudd added.

"Quite so."

"You recognised him?"

"Of course, once I'd turned him over."

Cotty again sounded impatient, as if the identity of the dead man was a mere incidental matter, and Rudd decided to leave it there. He had known doctors like him before who were more interested in the corpse than the living man it had once been, although in his experience they were usually pathologists or specialists of some kind. It was less common to find a GP who showed such lack of curiosity.

Better to ask Neave, he decided. He had already spoken to the young constable, who had struck him as much less of a cold fish. Neave, he was willing to bet, would know far more about the dead man and be more ready to talk about him.

But first there were one or two facts he had to verify.

"A patient of yours?" he suggested.

"No, he had never consulted me professionally. I had met him once socially and seen him about the village. That was all."

"And the head wound?"

There was a small, stiff silence in which Rudd was aware he was treading on dangerous ground. Dr. Cotty was a man who was easily affronted and Rudd knew, from his brief talk with Neave, that it was the constable who had discovered the injury.

"I must admit I overlooked that in my preliminary examination," Dr. Cotty said at last, although, to be fair to him, he made no attempt to justify his omission. "When Neave pointed it out to me, I examined the wound and found an area of broken skin about three inches long and an inch wide, not serious enough to cause death."

"Consistent with a car accident?"

"I would have thought so, although it was impossible to examine it thoroughly under the conditions."

"My police surgeon will have a look at it," Rudd assured him. "And I expect the path lab will have another go. Well," he added with deliberate cheerfulness as Cotty made no comment, "I don't think we need keep you any longer. I'll have to ask you later to make an official statement but that can wait for the moment. You can go home, Dr. Cotty."

"Thank you."

The reply was abrupt and bleakly formal. Rudd got out of the car and stood for a moment watching as it turned and headed back towards the village. A difficult man, he thought. Not much warmth there. Odd, that, in a doctor. But it takes all sorts.

He began walking back to the scene of the accident, if accident it was, which was now brightly lit up in the slanting rain, a small area of brilliance and activity in the surrounding darkness. A row of warning lights ran along one perimeter of it, blinking on and off, and in their intermittent orange glow, two uniformed men, their capes glistening, were bending down. Beyond them torches flashed onto patches of wet grass and the lower branches of trees as Stapleton's men made their search. And in the middle of it all, looking oddly cosy and domestic, stood the small plastic tent over the body, illuminated from inside like a miniature greenhouse as McCullum took his photographs. As soon as he had finished, Pardoe would move in to make his examination, and then Rudd would be able to take a closer look at the body. He had seen it briefly and it remained vividly in his mind—a man in his late thirties, of medium height, lying sprawled out, his bearded face turned away so that only the back of his head was visible; thick dark hair matted with mud and rain; blood, too, he supposed.

What the hell he had been doing out at half-past one on a country road in the rain he had yet to find out.

Neave was one of the men taking part in the search and, having beckoned him over and sent another constable to take his place, Rudd led him to where his own car was parked.

"Might as well sit in the dry," he remarked as they got inside. Neave removed his helmet and mopped the rain off his face with his sleeve. He was a thin-featured, bright-eyed young man with a moustache, grown, Rudd suspected, to make him look older, although there was no disguising the eager, boyish air. Keen for promotion, the inspector decided, and felt a fellow sympathy for the young constable's aspirations. And he'd probably make it eventually, though he'd have to slow down a bit first. Everything about him—his voice, his gestures, his eyes—expressed excitability. No good if he was to be in charge of other men. It led to too much indiscipline, subordinates rushing about half-cocked, witnesses hustled into making statements. He'd have to learn if he wanted to do CID work that most of it was a matter of getting your head down and plodding through a lot of dull and seemingly trivial routine, of checking and rechecking the facts, and for that you needed a still, quiet centre that he felt Neave hadn't acquired yet, although, to give the man his due, he'd been sharp enough to notice the significance of the skid marks and the head injury that Cotty had overlooked. Whether or not they added up to something more than a hit-and-run accident had yet to be established.

"Now," Rudd said comfortably, folding his arms over the steering wheel, "I've got a rough outline of what happened, but let's go over it again in more detail. And take it steady. There's plenty of time." He hoped Neave would take the hint. "I believe you got a phone call, like Dr. Cotty. What time was this?"

"At one thirty-two this morning, sir."

"And made from a call box?"

"That's right. As I said, it could have been made from the box down the road . . ."

"Never mind the theory; it's the facts I want to establish," Rudd said. He had no intention of letting Neave take charge of the interview. Unlike Dr. Cotty, the constable seemed more interested in his own suppositions. "Let's get back to the call. What was the voice like?"

"A whisper, that's all. He could have been speaking through a handkerchief or a cupped hand . . ."

"*He?*" Rudd repeated in a quick, pouncing manner that disconcerted Neave. Dr. Cotty had pulled him up in exactly the same way and he had resented it. Coming from the inspector, it was more alarming. Rudd, for all his disarmingly relaxed manner, was sharp enough, a point he'd have to watch out for.

"I wouldn't swear to it, sir," he replied, choosing his words more carefully, "but that's the impression I got. A man rather than a woman."

"All right," Rudd said more gently. He was aware of an increased tension in Neave, which wasn't a bad thing. "Go on. Can you tell me anything more about the voice?"

"It was hurried," Neave added after a moment's pause.

"Anything else?"

"Again I'm not sure, but I got the impression it was disguised." Neave gestured with one hand, indicating his inability to find the right words. "I can't say why. It just didn't sound natural, not even for someone speaking in a whisper as if he . . ." He broke off and looked sideways at Rudd, half expecting to be corrected again, but as Rudd remained silent, he continued, ". . . as if he was deliberately making it sound different."

The explanation sounded lame even to his own ears. Different from what? Rudd asked himself but he didn't express the question out loud. Was Neave trying to say that he might have recognised the voice if it hadn't been disguised? But perhaps that was impossible to answer. It was, after all, only an impression, too subtle, Rudd understood, to convey. He compromised by asking, "Was the voice at all familiar?"

Neave was quite sure on this point.

"No, sir. Definitely not."

"Right. What did the caller say?"

"Only a few words. 'There's been an accident just past Coppins. You'd better come at once.' "

Exactly word for word what Dr. Cotty had heard. Wasn't that a little strange? Rudd thought. Wouldn't someone phoning for help in a serious accident be panicked into saying more, or at least altering the statement? It sounded too controlled, almost rehearsed.

"Go on," Rudd said encouragingly. "Tell me what you did after that but leave out the assumptions."

"Very good, sir."

Neave sat up straight, assuming his courtroom manner.

"I left the house at one thirty-five, got in the car and arrived at the scene just after one-forty, where I found Dr. Cotty already examining the body. It was then lying on its back, with the clothing undone, as the doctor had been trying to find a heartbeat. I recognised the dead man as Patrick Vaughan. I say dead," he added hastily, in case the inspector should pick him up on this as well, "because the doctor told me he was. I then measured the skid marks on the road and not being satisfied because"—he checked himself in time—"I went back to Dr. Cotty, who was waiting in his car, and asked him to place the body back as near as he could to the position he'd found it in. I helped him turn it over. It was then I noticed the blood on the back of the head. I searched the area round the body to see if there was anything that could have caused it. I then asked Dr. Cotty to remain on the scene while I went back to the village to phone Sergeant Morrow. By the way, how is the doctor?" Neave added unexpectedly. "Has he gone home?"

"Yes, he's left," Rudd replied, surprised at the concern in the constable's voice. "Why do you ask?"

"He wasn't at all well; said it was his ulcer playing him up," Neave explained. "I felt a bit guilty about it, keeping him waiting in the cold."

"Oh, I see," Rudd said. The ulcer probably accounted for the doctor's drawn expression and abrupt manner. It wasn't an easy complaint to live with. "Well, now," he continued, "I'd like to find out a bit more about the dead man, Patrick Vaughan. Do you know him?"

"Not all that well, sir, although I've seen him about the village. He's a writer; from London, I believe; been here less than a year. He's renting a cottage just a short way down the road, about ten minutes' walk, in fact. It's the gatehouse to Coppins. I understand Mrs. Fulton, who owns the place, had let it to him furnished. You may have seen it as you drove past."

Rudd hadn't noticed it but he looked interested.

Encouraged, Neave added, "He's a bit, well, odd. An outsider. Doesn't have a lot to do with the local people, though I understand he's quite friendly with Mrs. Fulton."

"Odd in what way?" Rudd asked.

Neave looked embarrassed. "Different things. The way he looks for a start. Jeans and a beard. Arty, if you get my drift."

Neave sounded disapproving and Rudd wondered why. Surely not just the dead man's beard and clothes could have aroused the constable's disapprobation?

"What else?" he asked.

Neave hesitated, wondering whether to mention Hilary Shand and deciding to leave it for the time being. Rudd had said nothing yet to suggest he was treating Vaughan's death as anything other than an accident and, besides, the Shands were part of the village. It was Vaughan who was the stranger.

"He drank rather a lot, sir," he went on, compromising. "I've seen him myself knocking it back in the Red Lion. Mind you, he could carry it. I've never noticed him the worse for drink."

Rudd nodded but didn't speak. Head turned sideways, he watched the young constable's profile. There was something more and Neave would finally spill it.

Neave shifted his buttocks uneasily. Aware of Rudd's scrutiny, he felt the silence gather.

"I think he may have been having an affair with the headmaster's daughter," he heard himself saying, and, having started, it all came out.

Rudd listened without comment, making a mental note only of the name, Hilary Shand. Better for Neave's sake that he left it casual. The man seemed ashamed enough of his admission, although that was something else he'd have to guard against. To do his job properly, a policeman couldn't afford to have divided loyalties. But he watched him climb out of the car into the rain with a small stir of sympathy. After all, it was his patch and he had to live with these people.

Boyce, who had been hanging about waiting for the opportunity, eased his big bulk into the empty seat, glad to be in the dry.

"McCullum's finished," he announced, "and Pardoe's taken over. After that, I suppose you'll want another look at him yourself?"

By "him" they both knew he meant the dead man.

"Christ," he added in gloomy parenthesis, "what a bloody awful night."

For a few seconds, they both stared in silence through the rain-spattered windscreen, beyond which they could see, like figures in another, silent world, oddly distorted by the small lenses of the water drops, the men moving to and fro among the lights. Inside the car, protected and insulated, they could have been watching an old movie.

"How's the search going?" Rudd asked, rousing himself.

"Nearly finished. Not that they're likely to turn up anything that's useful. Find out anything yourself?"

"Quite a lot, though I'm not sure yet what it adds up to."

He gave Boyce a brief summary of what he had learned from Dr. Cotty and Neave, including Neave's account of seeing Hilary Shand leaving Vaughan's cottage.

"Could give her a motive," Boyce pointed out. "If Neave's right and they were having an affair . . ."

"Until the path report comes through we can't be sure what it is, accidental death or murder," Rudd interrupted, voicing the word that Neave had hesitated to express even to himself. "We may not even know then for certain. So it's no good talking about motives at this stage. Anyway, she may have a perfectly good alibi for the time he was killed. All we can do is make discreet inquiries. And I mean discreet. I don't want to stir up any local hornets' nests."

"Neave seemed suspicious," Boyce pointed out.

"Neave's an eager beaver," Rudd replied. "Too keen, perhaps. He's full of theories which may or may not be correct. Like the body being flung off the car onto the side of the road. It's possible Vaughan went under the wheels and the driver moved him onto the verge afterwards. It's feasible and, if that's what happened, the car needn't have been travelling all that fast. Dr. Cotty seemed satisfied it was a hit-and-run. But Neave was right to report his suspicions. There's Pardoe now," he added, catching sight of the police surgeon as he came ducking out of the plastic tent, bag in hand.

Boyce sighed under his breath and heaved himself reluctantly out of the car.

"It's no good asking me to give you a detailed report," Pardoe said briskly as Rudd and Boyce approached. "I'll have to have him on the slab for that. In fact, at this stage, I can't add much more to what Dr. Cotty's already told you. He's got broken legs and pelvis, internal injuries, which is probably what he died of, and a crack on the back of the skull, all of them consistent with a road accident. And according to the body and rectal temperature, he's not been dead all that long; say an hour, which would fit in with Cotty's evidence that he was called out at half-past one. I'll be in touch again after the P.M. Meanwhile, he's all yours. I've turned him over on his back again to examine him, as you'll see. One of your men had already marked out the position of the body. I'll be off then." He lifted his face briefly to the rain. "God, what a night! I'll be glad to be out of it."

As he walked off towards his car, Rudd and Boyce, lowering their heads, entered the confined space of the shelter where Vaughan, stretched out now on his back, lay gazing up at the plastic sheeting above him that sucked and rustled in the wet gusts of wind. In death, he looked oddly debauched, as if he had fallen down in a drunken stupor, his mouth slightly ajar in his beard and smeared with dried blood, his hair tousled. Someone, presumably Pardoe or Cotty, had unfastened his trousers and the fly still gaped, the zip only half done up.

He was wearing the sort of clothes that Rudd had expected from Neave's description of him: a checked cotton shirt worn under a loose cardigan-type knitted jacket; jeans and a military-looking raincoat with buttoned pockets and shoulder tabs. Sticking out of the bottom of the trouser legs, looking absurd and slightly incongruous, were a pair of scuffed but expensive leather boots with elevated heels; out of keeping with the rest of the clothes, which were conventionally casual but hardly stylish.

They gave him, however, the first clue to the dead man's personality. Vaughan had been a little below average height, and the raised heels would have given him another couple of inches; a minor point, perhaps, but revealing that it had mattered to Vaughan.

"Do you want me to go through his pockets?" Boyce was asking.

"Yes. See if you can find a door key," Rudd replied. "I'd like to have a look over his place before the village wakes up and gets interested in what's going on. We might come up with something."

He stood back watching while Boyce quickly frisked the dead man's clothing with the expertise of a professional pickpocket. The

jeans yielded nothing but he found an envelope in the left-hand
raincoat pocket which he handed over to Rudd, remarking, "It looks
as if he was going out to post this."

Rudd took it gingerly by the edges. It was crumpled and damp
from contact with Vaughan's coat but still decipherable, addressed in
a slanting, impatient handwriting to the manager of the National
Westminster Bank in Weldon, the stamp still unfranked. For the first
time, Rudd felt an unaccountable stirring of suspicion, a vague sense
of some other personality present besides Vaughan's, like a dark
shadow flickering just beyond his circle of consciousness that was
gone in an instant.

Striding over to the entrance, he stuck his head between the flaps
and shouted for Neave, who detached himself from the group of men
now waiting at the side of the road, the search having been finished.

"Yes, sir?"

"Is there a post box up the road as well as a kiosk?"

"Yes. Right next to it."

"And what time is the next collection?"

Neave looked bewildered.

"I'm not exactly sure, sir. It's sometime tomorrow morning,
about ten o'clock, I think. It's the last box to be cleared on the round,
anyway."

Rudd merely nodded. His next question seemed just as inconse-
quential to Neave.

"Did Vaughan own a car?"

"Yes, sir. An old Vauxhall."

"Right. You men finished the search? Then ask Inspector
Stapleton to step over, will you?"

Ducking back inside the tent, he said to Boyce, "You heard that?
There's no collection until ten o'clock tomorrow morning. Then why
was Vaughan so anxious to get that letter in the post at half-past one?
And why not take the car anyway?"

Boyce had time only to shrug before Stapleton joined them.

"Found anything?" Rudd asked, turning towards him.

"Nothing that you're likely to be interested in," Stapleton
replied. He was a slow-moving, patient man, too tall for the shelter,
and he stood with his head bent just inside the entrance. "It's all
packed up if you want to have a look at it. Nothing that could have
caused the head wound either. Neave was right there." He glanced
down at the dead body without curiosity. "What about him? Accident,
you reckon?"

"Too early to say," Rudd said noncommittally. "Well, if you've finished, we'll pack up. I'd like someone left on duty. Better make it a couple of men in a patrol car. We'll pick up the search again tomorrow. And we'll get him moved, too." He nodded down towards Vaughan's body. "The sooner the postmortem's done and the path boys have a look at him, the sooner we'll know where we are." As Stapleton withdrew, he added to Boyce, "No key on him? Then we'll take a chance he's left his place unlocked."

"What about the letter?" Boyce asked.

"Kyle can give it the once-over for prints and make it clear to him that I want it done tonight, no hanging about. Then I can deliver it to the bank manager myself in the morning. Maybe he'll tell me what's in it that's so important it had to be posted in the middle of the night."

If that's what happened, he added to himself.

Boyce nodded and, taking the envelope, slipped it into a plastic bag before going outside to find Kyle.

Left alone, Rudd took a last look at the body. It could tell him nothing more for the moment. The experts would now have to take over, scrutinising the clothing, examining the hair, the skin, the fingernails, laying him out on a mortuary slab to open him up. It would all be in the reports. Vaughan was a silent witness to his own death, slowly stiffening into rigor mortis, the face blank, the eyes staring up at the flapping plastic above him. Soon the white tapes that marked the outline of his body would be all that remained.

The ambulance men arrived and Rudd retreated, leaving them to it. Outside, the scene was already breaking up like a fairground on the last night. Men were moving towards the police vans, doors slammed, engines were started. Headlamps momentarily raked the road as the cars turned and headed back towards the village, lighting up wet tarmac, wet grass, wet leaves.

Boyce loomed beside him, looking bulkier than ever, like a hen ruffling out its feathers against the rain.

"All set?" he asked unenthusiastically. He was aching for hot tea and a chance to take his shoes off.

"We'll take the car," Rudd replied.

6

It took only a few minutes to reach Vaughan's cottage, and, as Rudd parked the car and got out, torch in hand, he flashed it briefly over the façade. Ornate. Pretty. With those fancy, pointed windows, all little diamond panes.

The front door was locked and he tramped round to the rear, with Boyce behind him, following a paved path, aware of low bushes brushing against his trouser legs and giving off the smell of lavender, released into the wet air.

It was easier to see the back of the cottage in the light that came streaming out from an uncurtained window, illuminating a concreted area with unkempt grass beyond it. Further back stood a brick-built garage behind a trellis, facing an opening in a thick mass of shrubbery that gave onto a drive leading, presumably, to Coppins, invisible among the trees and the darkness.

Boyce, who had gone to shine his torch through the garage window, came back to report.

"Padlocked but there's a car inside. Vaughan's, I reckon. It's a Vauxhall, anyway."

"He didn't bother to lock this," Rudd commented, mounting the step to try the back door and finding it open.

They walked into a small kitchen. Water dripped from the cold tap onto dirty dishes piled up in the sink.

"Didn't bother to wash up, either," Boyce added.

Another door led directly into a long, narrow hall, carpeted, with the front door at the far end. Two more doors, facing each other, were placed halfway down the hall. Rudd opened the one on the right, switching on the light as he entered.

Beyond was a bedroom, small like the kitchen and, like it, equipped with the minimum of furniture because of the limited space, just a single divan bed with a table beside it, a built-in wardrobe and a chest of drawers that did double duty as a dressing table. A man's hairbrush stood on top of it. Apart from this and a full ashtray on the

bedside table there was nothing else in the way of personal possessions left about.

"Do you want me to start searching?" Boyce asked. He had
followed Rudd into the room and was standing by the chest of
drawers.

"No, not yet," Rudd replied. "We'll just take a look around to
begin with."

All the same, he slid open the wardrobe and took a cursory
glance inside. It contained very little in the way of clothes: a corduroy
jacket with leather patches on the elbows, shabby and well-worn; an
overcoat; a pair of jeans thrust anyhow over the bar of a hanger,
another pair lying crumpled on the floor of the wardrobe where a
couple of pairs of shoes were lined up.

In the corner, partitioned off from the bedroom of which the
wardrobe formed one wall, was a tiny bathroom, its door ajar. Rudd
glanced briefly into that, too, pulling on the light cord as he stuck his
head inside. A towel had been flung down over the rim of the bath,
still damp, as he discovered when he ran his hand over it. A cake of
soap lay in a moist slime between the taps.

"Right," he said, coming back into the bedroom. "Let's try the
other door."

It led into a sitting room, surprisingly large. Standing just inside
the doorway, Rudd took it in with a few rapid glances. A woman's
room, he decided, with everything in it chosen to fit in with the scale
and period of the cottage, some of it good quality stuff, too; and he
remembered that Neave had said Mrs. Fulton had let it furnished to
Vaughan. Not that he seemed to have taken care of it. There was dust
on the surfaces and what looked like a coffee stain on the carpet near
the desk.

He was aware also of another impression that for a moment he
couldn't exactly define. And then he realised what it reminded him of.
It was like a stage set just after the actor playing the leading role has
made his exit and walked off into the wings, the moment before the
curtain comes down.

Stage centre was the fireplace, an electric fire still burning in the
hearth, with a sofa, its back to him, drawn up in front of it. Stage
right, a mahogany kneehole desk, facing the front window and
standing sideways onto the white-painted bookshelves that filled the
chimney alcove. A gooseneck lamp, which had also been left
switched on, stood on the desk top. Stage left, a small table
containing bottles and glasses occupied the other alcove, and farther
left still, under the back window, was a gate-leg table, one leaf of

which was opened out and scattered with crumbs from a meal recently eaten.

Only a moment ago, it seemed, Vaughan had moved about this set, eaten from that table, sat at that desk before walking out into the rain and the darkness to play out the last part of the drama on the verge of a country road.

Stepping into the room, he crossed to the desk and stood looking down on its contents, his hands behind his back, touching nothing. On the front stood a typewriter, a half-completed page still in the roller; a couple of paragraphs from a novel, he imagined, leaning forward to read through it quickly. It seemed to be part of a conversation between a man called Bruno and an unnamed girl, referred to simply as "she." Beside it, lying facedown as if completed and set aside, were three or four more loose sheets of paper, while at the back of the desk was another small pile of typed manuscript, clipped together this time and face-upwards, the top sheet headed "Journey Into Yesterday," with the words "Chapter One" beneath it on the next line. The page had been corrected in the same slanting handwriting as on the envelope found in Vaughan's pocket. Next to it were a mug of pencils and a tray containing small odds and ends, while a book had been placed across the far corner, cover uppermost, showing the title *An Illustrated Guide to Essex Churches*.

An odd choice to find there, Rudd thought, unless Vaughan was using it for reference. The desk seemed to contain only the materials for his writing, organised in a workmanlike manner, although he noticed several recent-looking rings on the mahogany top behind the loose sheets of typescript, as if a damp glass had been placed there. He was bending forward to examine them more closely when Boyce called to him across the room.

"Come and have a look at this!"

He was standing in front of the small table that contained the tray of drinks and was pointing, with a pleased air, to two glasses.

"Both used," he continued as Rudd joined him, "and this evening, too, I reckon. They've got dregs left in the bottom and they're still liquid. I've already sniffed them," he added as Rudd lowered his head. "One's had gin in it, the other whisky. Interesting, eh? It looks as if Vaughan had a visitor, so . . ."

He broke off in surprise as Rudd, his attention caught by something else, turned away as if he had lost interest in the glasses. Boyce couldn't understand it. They were evidence and damned good evidence at that. Someone had called on Vaughan; Vaughan had been found dead, possibly murdered. The two facts seemed to link up and yet Rudd had strolled off to look at a dressing gown thrown down over the seat of the sofa and a pair of leather mules lying discarded on the carpet nearby.

"Don't you want them parcelled up for forensic?" he asked, sounding aggrieved.

"Yes, yes, of course," Rudd replied abstractedly. He was fingering the red woollen fabric of the dressing gown as if testing its quality before squatting down to peer at the mules. It was the first time he had noticed them.

A room like a stage set, he repeated to himself. A half-completed page in the typewriter, two dirty glasses, a discarded dressing gown; theatrical props left lying about after the action and the dialogue are over. But something was wrong and he couldn't quite put his finger on it.

To Boyce's increased surprise, he stood up abruptly and walked over to the table, stared down for a moment at the crumbs littering its surface and then swung round.

"It doesn't add up," he announced.

"What doesn't?" Boyce asked.

"This." He gestured briefly at the desk, the glasses, the dressing gown. "Look at it, Tom. We've got enough evidence here to make a fairly detailed list of what Vaughan did this evening before he was killed; not necessarily in the right order, though, and that's where the problem lies. Let's run through it together. He has a meal. He does some work on his novel; at least, I'm assuming he does. There's a page still in the typewriter and several damp-looking rings where a glass has been standing on top of the desk so it seems he sat there long enough to have more than one drink. I'm also assuming he wrote that letter to his bank we found in his pocket. All right so far?"

"Yes, I'm with you," Boyce agreed. He couldn't understand what the fuss was about. It all seemed perfectly straightforward to him.

"Now we come to the tricky bit," Rudd continued. "Sometime during the evening he has a bath and puts on his dressing gown and slippers. He also has a visitor who stayed long enough to have a drink, so it must have been someone he knew fairly well, not just a casual caller at the door. Now which came first? Did Vaughan have a bath and then entertain his guest? Or was it the other way round? And at what point did he get dressed and why?"

"Perhaps because he had a visitor," Boyce suggested in an offhand manner.

"You mean Vaughan lets his guest in, says something like, 'Excuse me while I put some clothes on'?"

"Yes, if you like." Boyce looked faintly uncomfortable at the way in which the inspector had picked up the imaginary conversation.

"But that won't stand up. Even supposing Vaughan bothered to get changed—and from what Neave's told us about him, I can't imagine he'd mind very much—all the evidence points to the fact that he got dressed *in here*. Why not in the bedroom? I know that's what I'd do. If I felt embarrassed at being seen in my dressing gown in front of a guest, I'm damned sure I wouldn't strip off in front of them."

"I get your drift," Boyce said. "All right then. What's the alternative? That he got dressed in order to go out and post the letter?"

"No," Rudd replied with emphasis. "I don't accept that either, though I think that's what we're meant to believe. Look at the room. Everything about it suggests Vaughan had settled down for an evening at home. I don't know at what point he wrote that letter, but I'm assuming he wrote it after he had a bath. I can't imagine anybody, not even Vaughan, saying to himself, 'I'll have a bath first and then go out to the post box.' It doesn't make sense. It's a cold night, pouring with rain. But if he wrote it after he had a bath, doesn't that suggest it wasn't all that urgent? Suddenly, at half-past one in the morning, we're asked to believe that he got dressed and walked up the road to the letter box. If that's what happened, why didn't he take the car, as I said before?"

"If he'd had a few drinks, he might have been too tight to risk driving," Boyce suggested.

"It's possible," Rudd agreed, although he didn't sound very convinced. "I still can't get over the feeling that something or somebody else persuaded Vaughan to walk out of this room."

"Couldn't his visitor have done that?" Boyce asked tentatively.

"How?" Rudd demanded, looking across at him quickly.

"Well, I haven't worked out the details," Boyce replied. He sounded defensive. "But supposing his visitor calls fairly late. Vaughan's already had his bath and he's wearing his dressing gown and slippers. Like you said, he's settled down for an evening at home. The letter's written, although Vaughan doesn't intend posting it until the morning. The guest notices it and he or she offers to give Vaughan a lift down to the post box at the Cross. Vaughan agrees because the letter's quite important, gets changed hurriedly in here . . ."

"Which would suggest he knew the person very well," Rudd broke in.

"Agreed. Vaughan goes out to the car. A little way down the road, the killer persuades him to get out . . ."

"On what pretext?"

"Oh, I don't know," Boyce replied, shrugging. "What about a pretended flat tyre?"

"It'll do," Rudd said, looking interested. "Go on."

"Vaughan bends down in front of the car to take a look, the driver slams his foot down on the accelerator and runs him over."

"I've got two objections to that," Rudd said. "In the first place, Vaughan was knocked down from behind. And, secondly, I doubt if a driver would be able to get enough speed to kill someone standing immediately in front of a car. But let's accept it as a theory for the time being. Vaughan could have walked a little way up the road." He didn't sound too happy with the idea, though he looked encouragingly at Boyce. "What happens next?"

"The driver gets out, moves Vaughan's body to the grass verge and fakes the skid marks to make it look like a hit-and-run accident before driving to the Cross to put through those two phone calls."

"And forgets to go back to the cottage to remove the glass with his fingerprints on it?"

"Well, yes." That hadn't occurred to Boyce and he looked crest-fallen.

"Not a very clever murderer," Rudd remarked, and then added, to the sergeant's surprise, "it makes some kind of sense though; more than the other theory—that Vaughan walked out of the cottage in the rain to post a letter. Assuming that's what happened, we can start making a few guesses about the murderer. For instance, it must be someone local."

"I don't see why," Boyce objected.

"Don't you? The facts point that way. If your theory's right, the murder can't have been premeditated because the killer couldn't have known beforehand that Vaughan would have a letter ready for the post. But the opportunity was there and the murderer made use of it. And yet he knew Cotty's name and that suggests someone living in the area. If it was an outsider, one of Vaughan's London friends, for instance, he must have looked it up *before* the murder was committed."

"I see your point," Boyce conceded.

"And, assuming you're correct, it's someone fairly quick-witted but not intelligent enough to see the significance of the glass and remove it; also basically cautious and not very knowledgeable about cars."

"Why do you say that?"

"The evidence of the tyre marks," Rudd replied. "Whoever it was either didn't know about the braking distance or didn't dare go much above twenty miles an hour on a wet road before skidding to a halt."

"Could be a woman," Boyce suggested.

"Possibly. But it's too early yet to start jumping to that sort of conclusion. It could just as easily be a man whose instinct would be to drive carefully in the rain. It could, of course, still be an accident."

"But you're not convinced of that," Boyce told him.

"No, I'm not," Rudd said. He walked back to the desk and stood for a few moments in silence, looking down at the sheet of paper in the typewriter. "Who do we have that's keen on reading?"

"Kyle?" Boyce replied. "Whenever I've seen him in the canteen, he's always had his head stuck in a book."

"Then we'll get him in. I'll need someone to read through Vaughan's manuscript. And while you're at it, tell him to bring the envelope that was found in Vaughan's pocket with him. I'll need it later this morning. Give McCullum a call, too. This lot on the desk had better be photographed; also the dressing gown and slippers and the table with the glasses and bottles on it before they're packed up for forensic. We'll need them for evidence. Then I'll want the whole place gone over for fingerprints. We'll get Marsh in on it as well. What are you waiting for?" he added, seeing the sergeant hesitate. "I want them rounded up."

"You mean *now?*" Boyce asked. He looked significantly at his watch. "Do you know what the time is? Three o'clock."

"Well?"

"They'll have just about arrived home and got back into bed."

"Then they'll have to get out of it again," Rudd told him. "And quick. Time's running out and I want a search done, and a thorough one, too, before the village realises something's wrong and starts turning up here to rubberneck. So tell them to park round the back, out of sight of the road."

"They're not going to like it," Boyce muttered, making for the door.

They didn't. They came tramping in, looking tired and disgruntled. Rudd felt his own exasperation return at the sight of their exhausted faces. What in God's name did they expect he could do about it? Working long hours was part of the job and they'd bloody well have to put up with it or get out. McCullum, not very loquacious at the best of times, was more taciturn than ever, merely nodding when the inspector pointed out the shots he wanted taken, and, having completed them, departed, a look of relief on his face as he lugged his equipment out of the back door.

"Right," Rudd said when he'd gone. "We'll start fingerprinting and then turn the place over."

"What are we looking for?" Boyce asked.

"How the hell should I know?" Rudd snapped, unable to control his irritability. "Papers. Bills. Letters. Anything that can tell us something about Vaughan," he went on. "You'd better start in the bedroom."

He left them to it, wandering moodily round the sitting room, surveying its contents in an apparently desultory manner.

Usually he enjoyed the start of an investigation, the official bustle as the men got down to the routine tasks, the feeling that he was beginning to gather the threads of evidence into his hands. Now, suddenly, he wasn't so sure. Vaughan had been murdered. He was still certain of that, though not with the same strength of conviction that he had expressed to Boyce. He had a theory, too, of how it might have happened. But was it good enough? Take those glasses, for example. It was possible that someone quite unconnected with Vaughan's death had drunk from one of them. It was even possible that Vaughan had left the cottage to post that letter after all, in spite of the niggling doubt at the back of his mind that it was a plant. It smelt like one. It was just a little too pat. In fact, perversely, he would have been happier with the situation if Vaughan had had no apparent motive for taking a walk at half-past one in the morning. People did strange things for no obvious reason except out of the complexity of human behaviour and it could be a mistake to try to impose any kind of relevance on their actions. That was too neat and simplistic.

Had the murderer seen it that way? He had already described him to Boyce as someone who was probably cautious and unlikely to take risks. Did that letter suggest another quality? A man, or a woman, with the kind of tidy mind that liked everything to have a reason?

He broke off abruptly. He was making exactly the same mistake that he assumed Vaughan's killer had done by trying to supply motives where there might be none at all. A sign of his own dwindling confidence perhaps. Because when it came down to hard facts he had very little to go on. A dead body, that was all—the rest of it was mere supposition.

It was too damned early in the case for that. A lot more questions would have to be asked before he came to that sort of conclusion. And there lay his problem. Without proof that Vaughan had in fact been murdered, he would have to watch every step he took. People would have to be interviewed, of course. He had already drawn up a preliminary list in his mind—the Shands, Mrs. Fulton, who owned the cottage, Vaughan's manager—but in questioning them he would have to appear to go along with the theory that Vaughan had been killed accidentally.

It wasn't going to be easy. It would mean a hell of a lot of pussyfooting about, and, at the end of it, he might be left exactly where he had started, with nothing more than a hunch that it was murder, not a very satisfactory state of affairs when he was in the running for promotion. All the same, he'd have to begin somewhere and Neave seemed the obvious person to question first. He'd know something about the local people connected with Vaughan and that would give him an opening.

Walking across to the window, he pulled aside the curtains. It was still raining, a steady, persistent drizzle now, but at last it was beginning to get light, if you could call the all-pervading greyness anything as positive as dawn. The trees surrounding the garden were just discernible and he could pick out the oblong shape of the garage, each runnel in the corrugated asbestos roof hung with water drops that slowly gathered and then fell in a slow, melancholy rhythm.

An English autumn, drab and uninspiring, the only colour a clump of Michaelmas daisies, a washed-out mauve, bent down to the ground with the weight of the rain, their petals dragging in the mud. The sight of them did nothing to cheer him.

The village was quiet in the wan, early morning light as he drove through it on his way to Neave's. Having only glimpsed it in the light of his headlamps on the journey from headquarters, he kept his speed down and looked about him rapidly. It was obviously a prosperous, well-to-do village, its nucleus more like a small country town with tiled and plastered houses packed tightly together on a sharp S bend, presenting a pleasant period façade of pargetting, sash windows and brightly polished door knockers. There was the look of money about them and preservation orders. The small collection of shops had the same affluent air.

The council estate where Neave lived was on the far side of the village, tucked away behind a row of trees, too young yet though to form an adequate screen, each sapling encased in a corset of wire netting.

Opposite it stood the school, a Victorian building with two steep gables, set in an asphalt playground. It reminded him of the village school he had gone to as a child. It had the same look of heavy, earnest endeavour, as if trying to convey in its very structure that education was a serious business, not to be taken lightly, although an attempt had been made at decoration in the zig-zag pattern of black bricks that outlined the gables and the windows.

The schoolhouse was placed next to it, as Rudd guessed it might be, built in the same period, and he glanced at it curiously as he drove past. One detail, at least, of Hilary Shand's background was filled in. He was counting on Neave to give him a good deal more.

Neave's house was the first on the estate, distinguishable from the others by the police notice board in the front garden and a single-storeyed addition on the side that was presumably his office. As Rudd drew up outside the gate, he noticed the curtains were still drawn; Neave was evidently not up yet, although, when he rang the bell, the young constable was quick enough to let him in. He had dressed hastily and was still stuffing his shirt into the waistband of his trousers.

The fact was Neave had slept hardly at all since his return in the early hours of the morning. Instead he had lain awake fretting about the case and his own involvement in it. He regretted passing on to Rudd the information about Hilary Shand. There was probably nothing at all in her visit to Vaughan. She could have been calling on him to deliver something—a book, for instance—though he knew it wasn't very likely. All the same, he'd have to go on facing these people long after Rudd and the others had packed up and left, and he felt obscurely resentful that the inspector should have come trampling in over his patch, upsetting the relationships that he had worked so hard over the past four years to establish. His eldest child was due to start at the school next September. How was Shand going to feel about that? Not that he'd take it out on the child, of course. Shand was too fair-minded a man for that. But nevertheless it was bound to lead to all kinds of embarrassments, Neave realised, and, as the hours passed, his disquiet grew until, just before Rudd rang the bell, he had worked the situation up to its final, dramatic climax—Hilary Shand arrested, himself giving evidence at her trial and everyone in the village turning their backs on him. He had even got round to drafting a letter in his mind requesting a transfer.

The inspector's arrival on his doorstep at that early hour of the morning only deepened his gloom. It was obvious that the investigation had started and that Rudd was going to ask a lot of questions, and, as Neave showed him into his office, he tried to postpone the coming interview with the offer of tea.

"Yes, please," Rudd said promptly.

Neave had switched on the electric fire and the inspector seated himself in front of it, feeling the heat draw the damp out of his trouser legs, and by the time the constable returned with the tray of tea things, he already looked at home.

"Nice here," Rudd remarked conversationally, looking round him at the official notices about stolen cars and antirabies regulations. He was aware of Neave's anxiety and wanted to put him at his ease, remembering his own feelings of intimidation the first time he had been interviewed on a case by an inspector from headquarters and regarding Neave with some sympathy as he awkwardly poured the tea and handed him the sugar bowl.

"About Hilary Shand," Neave began with an air of desperation. "I've been thinking . . ."

"Then don't," Rudd warned him quickly, guessing what was coming. "Your part in it's over except for some routine work I want you to do for me and a few questions I'd like you to answer. And don't jump to too many conclusions, Neave. It may still be an accident. At least, that's the way I'm going to handle it until I've got proof it was murder." He heard Neave give a little sharp intake of breath and his cup rattled in his saucer. "Yes, murder," he repeated. "It's possible and I can't rule it out. But as far as anyone outside the investigation is concerned we're inquiring into a hit-and-run accident. Is that quite clear?"

"Yes, sir," Neave replied, sounding even more subdued.

"Right. Now for the routine stuff first. I want you to interview the people living at the Cross, where it looks as if Vaughan was making for when he was killed. How many houses are there?"

"Only about half a dozen."

"Good. I'll leave it to you then. I expect you can guess the sort of questions I'd like asked. Did anyone hear a car draw up outside the phone box? If so, at what time? If we're lucky someone may have seen it. I don't hold out too much hope of that, but if they did, I want a description."

"Very good, sir," Neave replied. He had been jotting down notes on a small pad with a more positive air, as if having a job to do had consoled him.

"Now for the second part," Rudd continued. "Before I start my inquiries, I must know a bit more about the people involved and for that I'm relying on you. You know them; I don't. It's as simple as that. So to start with, what can you tell me about the dead man, Patrick Vaughan?"

"Not a lot," Neave admitted. "I think I've told you all I know."

"Yes, the facts," Rudd said in a dismissive voice. "What I'm interested in is impressions. What sort of a man was he? Was he popular in the village, for example?"

"Not really. A good few people thought him a bit, well, stuck-up."

"Why was that?" Rudd asked, looking interested.

"He had a cocky look about him," Neave replied. "I can't explain it exactly. Sort of amused, as if he wasn't taking anybody seriously. Nosey, too."

"Nosey? In what way?"

"Asked a lot of questions; none of them very important but some people resented it. I've seen him doing it some evenings down at the Red Lion. He'd go up to someone and start a conversation. He had a go at me once. 'Did I like being a policeman? What sort of cases had I been on?' That sort of thing."

"It could have been a writer's curiosity," Rudd suggested. "He'd be interested in other people."

"It wasn't like that," Neave said. There was a flushed look about his face, as if the memory still rankled. "You felt he was poking fun at you. He wasn't a very tall man; you saw that for yourself; but all the time he was talking to you, you got the impression he was looking down on you."

"Yes, I know the feeling," Rudd agreed. "Did anybody have a positive dislike for him?"

"Enough to kill him, you mean?" Neave asked with a new, bold air. "I don't think so. People mainly avoided him if they could."

"You said he moved down here from London," Rudd continued. "Do you know of any visitors from outside calling on him?"

"I haven't noticed any cars parked outside his place, but it's on the edge of the village and I don't go past it all that often. Besides, if a car was left round the back, I wouldn't be able to see it from the road."

"That's true," agreed Rudd. It was only by chance that Neave had noticed Hilary Shand's car turning into the drive from behind the cottage. But he didn't want to get onto that subject quite yet. It was obvious Neave was having second thoughts about mentioning her and he preferred to leave it to the end of the interview when the young constable would be more relaxed.

"But I believe you said he was fairly friendly with Mrs. Fulton, who leased him the cottage?"

"Yes?" Neave said more warily.

"I'll have to go and see her later today," Rudd continued, "to break the news of Vaughan's death. What sort of a person is she?"

"Oh, very pleasant," he assured the inspector. "Very well liked in the village. Does a lot for the people round here. She's on the Parish Council, for instance, and is one of the school governors. She's Richard Fulton's widow, by the way, sir; you know, the MP."

"Is she?" Rudd asked. That was indeed an interesting piece of information. He had met Richard Fulton once several years before at an official police function; a tall, good-looking man with an easy, assured air; a very witty after-dinner speaker, too. His death had caused quite a lot of excitement, not only in the local press but in the nationals as well. He had been the second Member of Parliament to die of a heart attack in the same year and the media had taken it up like a crusade. Questions were asked about the amount of stress that MPs were subjected to and how much longer the custom of all-night sittings in the House of Commons should be allowed to continue. In Richard Fulton's case, the argument had been particularly fierce. He had evidently had a heart attack two years earlier and had been advised by his doctor to take things easier; advice that he obviously hadn't followed because he had been found dead in bed. But not here in Chellfield, Rudd thought, although the details of it escaped him for the moment.

"Would Mrs. Fulton be likely to call on Patrick Vaughan in the evenings?"

"I'm afraid I couldn't say, sir," Neave replied.

"Hilary Shand must have known him though," Rudd pointed out. "And quite well, too, by the sound of it." Enough time had been spent circling round the subject. "You know the rules of the game as well as I do. Someone's been killed and, even if it turns out to be an accident after all, questions have still got to be asked. Vaughan had a visitor sometime yesterday evening. It may not have been Hilary Shand. That's something I'll have to check with her. But we know she called on him Tuesday evening, two days before he died, and for that reason alone I'll have to talk to her. Before I do, I want some information about her and you're the only person who can give it to me. So what do you know about her?"

"Not a lot," Neave replied. He seemed relieved now that the decision to talk had been taken out of his hands. "And most of what I do know I've picked up since I moved here. She's not married; in her late twenties, I think; runs a bookshop in Weldon with a woman partner. As I told you, her father's the headmaster of the local school. They've been here about fifteen years. Mr. Shand's very highly thought of. Respected." He shot a look at the inspector that was oddly appealing. "You may not know what it's like, sir . . ."

"Yes, I do," Rudd assured him. He had been brought up himself in the country and knew from his own experience that in most villages there is a group of people, usually consisting of the vicar, the doctor, the headmaster and perhaps one or two of the more prosperous farmers as well, who form a select circle of individuals who, while not above being discussed in the village, are not gossiped about with outsiders like himself. "Go on. There's been talk about her." He had gathered that from Neave's own comment. "What's been said?"

"Well, I understand she had some kind of a breakdown while she was away at college. It was hushed up at the time and Mr. Shand was anxious to put it about that she'd been overworking. But she'd stopped wearing her engagement ring and it didn't take long for people to put two and two together."

"Who treated her? Dr. Cotty?"

"I suppose so," Neave replied after a moment's hesitation. "I hadn't really thought about it before."

"And now she runs a bookshop in Weldon?"

"Yes. From what I've heard, she didn't go back to college. She was at home for several months, and then Mr. Shand put up the money for a half share in the business."

"What sort of a car does she own?"

"A Mini."

Not a very powerful car, Rudd thought, to run someone down with, and the width between the tyre marks on the road suggested a vehicle with a bigger wheelbase, but it would have to be checked. It was too early in the case to start dismissing anyone from the investigation.

"When did she meet Patrick Vaughan?"

"I'm not sure. He's been living in the gatehouse since last January so I suppose she could have known him for some time. She might have met him at Mrs. Fulton's. The Shands are very friendly with her and I know Mr. Shand calls at Coppins quite often."

"Do her parents know about the relationship?"

"There's only Mr. Shand, sir. He's a widower. His wife died before they moved here; I believe in a car accident."

He stopped suddenly, aware of what he had said, and added quickly, "There's no connection. It happened fifteen years ago at Broadstairs, where they were living then."

"A coincidence, I expect," Rudd murmured blandly. All the

same, it was an interesting one and worth following up. "Do you know how it happened?"

"I'm sorry, sir, I'm afraid I don't," Neave said. His face had taken on an apologetically blank look. "And I'm not sure if Mr. Shand knows," he added. "I mean about his daughter and Vaughan."

Something in his tone of voice made Rudd ask, "Would he approve if he did?"

"I can't see him liking the idea very much. Vaughan was a bit . . ." Neave paused, hesitating to use the word "randy" in front of the inspector. "Not the marrying kind," he concluded lamely. The phrase sounded strangely prim.

"And you think that marriage was what Hilary Shand was after?"

"I don't know." Neave sounded harassed. The inspector had the disconcerting habit of dragging his suppositions out into the open and submitting them to the kind of scrutiny that he knew they wouldn't stand up to.

To Neave's relief, Rudd had finished his tea and was getting to his feet and buttoning his coat.

"Is that all, sir?" he asked hopefully.

"For the time being," Rudd replied. "I'd like a report on the inquiry at the Cross by this evening. If you need me during the day, I'll either be in the village interviewing Mrs. Fulton and Mr. Shand or in Weldon having a chat with his daughter. Oh, don't worry," he added. "I shan't let on to her father about the affair."

"Thank you, sir," Neave said. He didn't appear to be much conforted by this reassurance and, as he watched from the doorstep as Rudd drove away in the rain, he looked a deeply troubled man.

7

By the time Rudd returned to the cottage, Boyce and the others had finished searching the bedroom and had moved into the sitting room, where the sergeant was going systematically through the drawers in the desk while the two constables, Kyle and Marsh, were taking every book from the shelves and shaking open the pages before returning them to their places. A cardboard box already contained the contents of the desk and the side table, wrapped inside plastic bags.

"Found anything?" Rudd asked.

Boyce raised his shoulders doubtfully.

"Not much. I've left everything that seems at all interesting over there on the desk for you to look at. There are a couple of files of papers, one of receipts, the other of correspondence; nothing personal in it, though; mostly business letters to do with his writing. You'll find an accounts book with them, too, up to date to last Tuesday." He pointed to a narrow, black-bound ledger lying on top of the desk, cleared now of its other contents. "His current cheque book's with it. I came across that in the top drawer. And his keys. I found those hanging on a hook in the kitchen. Oh, and one photograph," he added, suddenly remembering. "It was in his wallet in that corduroy jacket. There was nothing much else in it except for a cheque card and a bill from a wine merchant's in Weldon that he evidently hadn't got round to paying yet."

The photograph lay beside the cheque book and Rudd picked it up to look at it. It was a snapshot of a young, attractive, dark-haired woman, taken out of doors in a garden or a park. She was standing under a tree, laughing, one hand holding back her hair from blowing in her face. Judging by the clothes, it had been taken about ten years before, and had been carried about and handled a good deal since then. The edges of the paper were furred with use and the glazed finish had cracked in several places. On the back of it, written in Vaughan's distinctive handwriting, was the one word "Moira."

"Girl friend?" Boyce suggested, coming up to look at it over the inspector's shoulder.

"Or his wife," Rudd replied. "Obviously someone he cared a lot about if he carried it round with him. Mrs. Fulton may know. If not we can check the records to find out whether he was married." He laid the photograph down again. "Nothing else that's personal?"

"No."

"Odd, that," mused Rudd.

"Perhaps he believed in travelling light," Boyce said offhand-edly. "All his papers suggest he was well organised where his business affairs were concerned. He may have cleared all the other stuff out when he moved here."

"Maybe," Rudd agreed. He had the feeling, however, that the absence of other mementoes told him something significant about Vaughan, in the same way that the boots had done. "How much longer will you be before you've finished the search?" he asked.

"About an hour," Boyce replied. "We're nearly through in here. That'll leave just the kitchen and the garage. Stapleton's arrived, by the way. He and the others have gone back to finish searching the area where Vaughan's body was found. After that, they'll take a look round the garden."

"And Neave's going to handle the house-to-house at the Cross," Rudd put in, "so that's got the routine part of it organised."

"Did you find out anything much from Neave?" Boyce asked, lowering his voice and glancing across at the two constables.

"I'll tell you later," Rudd replied. "One or two bits were interesting, including the fact that Mrs. Fulton, who owns the cottage, is the widow of Richard Fulton the MP. But look, Tom, I can't hang about here too long. It's nearly nine so I'll walk up to the house and have a chat with her now. Give me half an hour and then join me. I want you to examine her car, assuming she's got one. . . ."

"You don't think she had anything to do with Vaughan's death, do you?" Boyce broke in, looking faintly scandalised. "I mean, if she's Fulton's widow. . . ."

"I don't think anything at the moment," Rudd replied. Except I'm bloody tired, he wanted to add. "But I've got to talk to her anyway. She must have known Vaughan and she may be able to fill in a bit of his background for us. As far as checking her car's concerned, it's merely routine at this stage. At least that's the line I'm proposing to take and I want you to do the same. After I've seen her, I'm going to have a talk with Shand, the local headmaster, and then drive into Weldon to interview his daughter. That ought to take us up to lunchtime. What about meeting in the Red Lion for a snack round about one o'clock?"

"Right," Boyce agreed, and Rudd crossed the room to speak to Kyle, who got to his feet as the inspector approached.

He looked exhausted, Rudd thought, and remembered suddenly that Kyle's wife had recently had a baby so the constable probably wasn't getting much sleep even on the nights when he was off duty.

"I suppose you haven't had a chance to read through Vaughan's manuscript yet?" Rudd asked.

"Not yet, sir."

"I'd like a report on it as soon as possible. What about the envelope that was found in Vaughan's pocket?"

"I've checked it for prints but I haven't had time to write up my notes yet," Kyle explained, looking defensive. "I could give you a verbal report."

"You know my rules," Rudd snapped. "I want it down on paper. See that it's done straightaway. I shall need it when I see the bank manager later this morning. You can give it to Sergeant Boyce to hand to me."

"Very good, sir."

"And when you've finished here, you can go home," Rudd added, in a kindlier tone. "You, too, Marsh."

"Thank you, sir," they said together, the relief obvious in their voices.

God alone knew when he'd be able to go home himself, Rudd thought, as he trudged up the drive towards Coppins in the fine rain that was still falling. Every leaf and twig was coated with moisture and the gravel oozed softly underneath his feet.

The drive swung round in a wide semicircle in front of the house and, as he rang the bell and waited, he looked about him. The garden, although depleted of colour, was carefully tended. Rose beds, their bushes trimly pruned, flanked the drive, and a wide herbaceous border, backed by evergreens, ran along the far side of the lawn. It all looked established and well ordered.

The woman who answered the door to him was obviously Mrs. Fulton, the owner of the place. Although dressed casually in a skirt and sweater, there was an air of authority about her. It was a handsome face, he noticed, with strong features; dark eyes that contrasted with the short, grey hair; the sort of woman who was used to serving on committees; capable, with a brisk, no-nonsense approach to life; a bit of a manager of other people, he suspected, although the impression was softened by a humourous look about her mouth.

"Mrs. Fulton?" he asked pleasantly. "I'm Detective Inspector

Rudd. I'm afraid I have bad news about Patrick Vaughan. May I come inside?"

He was watching her carefully as he spoke and saw her face close over at the mention of Vaughan's name.

Without speaking, she stood aside to let him enter and then led the way across a large hall into a drawing room that faced the back garden.

He took it in quickly as he entered. It was a beautiful room, its pale-green walls hung with watercolours, the polished floor scattered with rugs that even to his untutored eye looked valuable, and yet, in spite of its elegance, there was a lived-in quality about it. Books and magazines lay about and the bureau that stood in front of one of the windows was littered with papers. A small table in front of the fire had been set informally for breakfast and Rudd took heart at the sight of the used cup and the smears of marmalade left behind on the plate. All the same, he was aware that he wasn't looking his best, his chin rough with a night's growth of stubble and his eyes small and puffy through lack of sleep. Usually such things didn't bother him too much. But this morning he felt at a distinct disadvantage.

"Bad news?" Mrs. Fulton repeated. She had sat down by the fire and indicated an armchair opposite. Rudd lowered himself carefully onto its petit-point cover. She still hadn't mentioned Vaughan's name and he had the impression that she was deliberately avoiding it.

"There's been an accident," he explained. "I'm sorry to have to tell you that Mr. Vaughan was knocked down and killed sometime late last night or early this morning."

He saw her mouth open in a little gasp of horrified surprise, a conventional enough reaction. What was less expected was the complex expression that followed it. It was difficult to analyse because it had gone in a moment, but, in that fleeting instance, he thought he recognised relief in her face.

"How did it happen?" she asked.

"We're not too sure about that," Rudd replied blandly. "That's one of the reasons why I shall have to ask a few questions. We've had a look round the cottage, trying to find out his next of kin." He said it casually, as if the search had been a matter of merely examining Vaughan's papers. "But I'm afraid we haven't come up with any personal addresses. I wondered if you could help us there. I understand Mr. Vaughan was your tenant."

"Yes, that's right. He leased the cottage from me last January. But I'm afraid I can't tell you much about him. He came from London. I believe I have his original address somewhere in my desk. . . ."

She half got to her feet as if to go and look for it but Rudd interrupted her. There was an eagerness about her that suggested to him that she would have welcomed the diversion and he didn't want to give her the opportunity of fully recovering her poise.

"It'll do later, Mrs. Fulton," he said. "What else can you tell me about him? Was he married, for instance?"

"He was divorced. He did mention it to me. But if you're hoping to contact his ex-wife, I can't help you there. I understood from Patrick that she had remarried and gone abroad."

She had spoken his name at last, but with a curious reluctance.

"Was her name Moira?" Rudd asked, thinking of the photograph that Boyce had found in Vaughan's wallet.

"Yes, it was."

"Did he say anything more about her?"

He had assumed his listening pose, although he doubted if it would have much effect on Mrs. Fulton. She didn't look the type who would settle down to a gossip about her dead tenant. To his surprise, however, she picked up the subject with the same eagerness with which she had offered to look for Vaughan's London address and he wondered why. Was it to divert his attention from some other topic?

"Yes, he mentioned her several times. He came here to the house on quite a few occasions, usually in the evenings. I think sometimes he needed company. I had said to him call in any time, though I hadn't expected him to take the invitation quite so literally." Her voice had sharpened as if she still found Vaughan's habit of dropping in unexpectedly a source of irritation. "Of course, I'd offer him a drink when he came and he'd stay to talk, sometimes about his work, sometimes about his private life, although not so often. But I understood from what he told me that the divorce had left him feeling very bitter."

"What were the grounds,"

"Desertion, I believe."

"His?"

"Oh, no, hers," she said, as if there was no question about the matter. "He told me that she walked out on him about a year after they were married."

"Do you know of any women friends he might have had since he moved here?" Rudd asked, thinking of Hilary Shand.

"No, I don't," she replied, but it came too quickly and positively. Did she in fact know about the relationship? Rudd wondered. The possibility wasn't all that farfetched. Vaughan could have mentioned it himself, although he didn't think it likely. According to Neave, Mrs. Fulton was friendly with the Shands, and, knowing this, Vaughan might not have confided in Mrs. Fulton that he was having an affair with her friend's daughter. On the other hand, she could have seen Hilary Shand's car parked outside Vaughan's cottage, as Neave had done, and come to the same conclusion. One thing was clear, however; he had touched on a subject that Mrs. Fulton was unwilling to discuss and he decided to move back to less controversial ground.

"You said he sometimes discussed his writing with you. He was evidently typing out a chapter of his novel yesterday evening before he was killed. Can you tell me anything about his working habits? We'd like to establish a little more precisely the time of death."

A lie, of course. He knew that fairly precisely. "Did he usually work late in the evenings?"

"Yes, he did. He told me once that he preferred working at night. Besides, I've noticed myself that the lights have still been on in the cottage when I've gone to bed. From what he said, I gathered he'd rough out an outline for a book, using notes for the plot and the basic characters, and then get the first draft down straight onto the typewriter, correcting by hand and then retyping from that version. I believe he was fairly successful as a writer, even though he didn't make a lot of money from his books. He once said rather bitterly that he'd be better off as an unskilled labourer."

She was speaking more freely again, as if Vaughan's work had genuinely interested her, and Rudd was aware that, despite her obvious exasperation at Vaughan calling on her uninvited, there had been times when the conversation must have flowed easily between them. Yet underneath it was still the same reluctance to use his name. She seemed, in talking of him, to differentiate between the writer for whom she evidently had some fellow feelings—the public man, if you like, whose life and working habits had roused her curiosity—and the private individual for whom she had felt much less sympathy. This realisation prompted Rudd to ask the next question.

"What was he like as a person?"

He already had Neave's opinion. It would be interesting to learn hers.

The query disconcerted her and for a moment she seemed at a loss to know what to reply.

"Oh, quite interesting to talk to," she replied at last. "He was very widely read and could be very amusing, too, at times."

Rudd noticed the qualifications in the remarks and waited, cocking his head in an invitation for her to continue.

"A lonely man too, I felt," she added. It was said less guardedly, as if, trapped into saying more, she had chosen this last comment as a more sincere summary of Vaughan's personality.

"Did he have many friends?"

"Very few, I should imagine. He mentioned one or two acquaintances in London but I got the impression that there was no one in his life who meant much to him." She hesitated again and then added in a sudden burst of words almost like a confession, "I think I ought to explain to you, Inspector, that he was quite a heavy drinker and once or twice when he turned up here he was obviously not sober. Not that he ever got unpleasantly drunk, at least in my presence, you understand, but on those occasions he tended to be more talkative and he would tell me things about himself that, quite frankly, I would have preferred not to hear. I tried to keep the relationship on a more formal basis but it's very difficult when someone is clearly anxious to talk not to listen to what he has to say. He once told me that his work meant everything to him. He had nothing else that really mattered and he was reluctant, after the breakup of his marriage, to get deeply involved with another woman. It had left him very disillusioned and bitter about love."

She stopped as abruptly as she had begun. It was a strange, emotional outburst, quite out of character, Rudd felt, and, behind it, he was aware that she was trying to say something else, not just about Vaughan but about herself, too, as if she wanted to explain and justify for her own benefit more than his some quality of her relationship with Vaughan that she still did not properly understand. Was she also trying in the same oblique manner to express her feelings about Vaughan and Hilary Shand? he wondered. The reference to Vaughan's attitude to women seemed gratuitous and, while she had no reason to suspect that Rudd knew anything about a possible affair between them, he had the distinct impression that Mrs. Fulton, in fact, was aware of it and was trying to come to terms with that, too.

She was not a very subtle or complex woman, he imagined. It was in her nature to be direct and she would find it difficult to deal with someone more devious than herself. Vaughan's personality had evidently puzzled and disturbed her, rousing in her a more confused reaction than Neave's simple and uncomplicated dislike. He was, on the one hand, someone who could be amusing and interesting to talk to, whose life as a writer had evidently held a certain fascination for her, perhaps because of some latent creative talent in herself that had never found a satisfactory outlet. On the other hand, she had spoken of him as someone lonely, bitter and disillusioned, a far cry from Neave's picture of a cocky, self-assured man.

His mind went back to the cottage that Vaughan had vacated like an actor walking off a stage and for the first time he was aware that the answer to the problem of his death might lie not in the actions so much as the character. It was not so much a question of how Vaughan had died, but why. The means and opportunity would, of course, have to be investigated, but suddenly the motive seemed to have much more significance. Someone had wanted Vaughan dead, and the reason, he realised, could be as complex and enigmatic as Vaughan's own personality.

"Did Vaughan have any visitors that you know of?" he asked. "Anyone who might have called in yesterday evening to see him?"

The question obviously shocked her. There was a silence so sudden and abrupt that it was almost palpable. He saw her face stiffen until only her eyes, dark and unexpectedly frightened, appeared to have any life in the rigid features. But she recovered quickly, tilting her head to one side as if considering his query, a deliberate movement, Rudd felt, in order to break her own state of dazed immobility.

"Oh yes, I believe Lewis Shand called on him yesterday to borrow a book." It was meant to be casual but she spoke a little too hastily. "He was on his way to see me and stopped at the cottage. I remember now he mentioned it."

"Lewis Shand?" Rudd asked, as if the name meant nothing to him.

"The headmaster of the village school," Mrs. Fulton explained.

"Did he know Mr. Vaughan well?"

"He'd met Patrick here a few times."

Her voice had a clipped, crisp edge to it, as if, having recovered her self-possession, she was determined to keep control of the interview and reply to any further questions with only the minimum of words.

He had lost her, Rudd decided. The woman who faced him now was much less vulnerable. Years of experience in public life, first as Richard Fulton's wife and then his widow, had trained her to present this polite, noncommittal face to the world that gave nothing away. All the same, he'd have to plod on with the interview even if he got nothing much else out of it.

"What time did he call on Mr. Vaughan?"

"I have no idea. Mr. Shand arrived here at about quarter to eight. That's all I can tell you."

"Was he in the habit of visiting him?"

"I think you had better ask Mr. Shand that, Inspector."

She was putting him in his place, Rudd thought wryly. But he couldn't complain. He'd not had too bad a run for his money and he'd managed to find out several interesting facts about Vaughan, including the possible identity of his visitor, although that would have to be checked with Shand himself.

He saw she was glancing pointedly at her watch and he decided to take the hint and close the interview. It was unlikely anyway that she'd give much more away. "There's only a couple more questions I'd like to ask," he said blandly. "I believe you said that you could see the windows of the cottage from your bedroom. Did you notice any lights on late last night?"

"At what time?"

"After midnight," Rudd replied. He had no intention of revealing the exact time of Vaughan's death.

"No I didn't. I went to bed about eleven o'clock. There was a light on then when I drew the curtains. I noticed nothing after that."

"Did you hear anything? A car, for instance, drawing up outside the cottage?"

"I've already told you, Inspector, I noticed nothing after I went to bed." She seemed aware herself that the reply was unnecessarily curt because she added in a less abrupt manner, "It was a very windy night, Inspector, and the rain was on the front of the house, where I sleep. Besides, the cottage is some distance away."

"Of course," Rudd murmured. "Could you tell me then if Mr. Vaughan was in the habit of taking walks late at night?"

"I'm afraid I don't know."

"One last question, Mrs. Fulton. Had you met Mr. Vaughan before he moved here?"

"No. The lease was handled by Wilcox and Bailey, the estate agents in Weldon. I believe they advertised the cottage locally and in one or two national newspapers where Mr. Vaughan saw the notice. I gather the lease on his own flat had run out and he wanted a chance to get out of London. My solicitor dealt with Mr. Vaughan's application and references. His bank manager was one and his publisher or agent the other, I forget which."

She rose to her feet and, crossing the room, opened the bureau and came back with a letter in her hand.

"You wanted Mr. Vaughan's London address. Here it is. He

wrote to me once before he moved here. As you'll see, it was a formal letter, introducing himself as my tenant."

Rudd scanned it quickly before copying down the heading into his notebook, a West Kensington address, he noticed.

"Is that all?" Mrs. Fulton asked as he returned the sheet of paper to her.

"For the moment. I may have to bother you again later, I'm afraid. Oh, there is one more thing," he continued, as if the thought had suddenly occurred to him. "Would you object if my sergeant examined your car? It's merely a routine matter. We shall be checking on all the vehicles in the area."

"Of course," she replied. "The garage is at the side of the house. It's unlocked."

There was no flicker of reaction this time. Either Mrs. Fulton had herself under strict control or the request had no significance for her.

"Before you leave, there's one question I'd like to ask you, Inspector," she added unexpectedly. "You're not from the Weldon force, I believe?"

"No," he replied, a little surprised by the query.

"So you don't know Inspector Hallam?"

"I have met him a couple of times," Rudd replied cautiously. He wasn't sure what was behind the question and didn't much care for her tone of voice.

"Who is your superior officer?"

"Detective Superintendent Davies."

"I see."

The remark was said coldly, with the note of implied threat that over the years in the force he had heard on more than one occasion; the voice of the middle-class taxpayer who is determined that no policeman, however exalted his rank, is going to be allowed to forget the fact that he is a public servant.

There was no time to reply even if he could have thought up an adequate answer. Mrs. Fulton was opening the door and was showing him politely but firmly out of the house.

"Oh, hell and blast!" he said out loud, retreating down the steps just as Boyce came trudging up the drive.

"The garage is round the side of the house. Check her car, will you? I've got her permission. I'm on my way to see Shand. Evidently he called on Vaughan yesterday evening but quite early, according to Mrs. Fulton."

"Won't that knock on the head our theory of how Vaughan might have been killed?"

"I don't know," Rudd said irritably. He didn't intend standing in full view of the house discussing the case with Boyce. Besides, the closing stages of the interview with Mrs. Fulton had left a sour taste in his mouth. The barriers were up and there would be no chance now that she'd speak frankly to him again. He felt he had been relegated to the role of the outsider, as Vaughan, too, undoubtedly had been. He hoped to God that Shand wouldn't make the same kind of difficulties. It was bad enough having to pretend that Vaughan's death was an accident.

"Look, Tom. We'll talk about it later. All right?"

Boyce shrugged and, taking an envelope out of his pocket, handed it to Rudd, saying, "I don't want to keep you but I think you wanted this. It's Vaughan's letter to the bank manager. Kyle's put a report in with it."

Then he turned abruptly and walked off, leaving Rudd with the uncomfortable feeling that he had treated Boyce in the same dismissive manner that Mrs. Fulton had used to him and that the sergeant was as thin-skinned about it as he had been.

Had he witnessed it, he would have been consoled by Kitty Fulton's obvious alarm as soon as he left the house. Not daring to risk being seen at the window, she had watched Rudd's departure through the opaque, greenish glass in the front-door panels that gave her only an obscure view of his figure, curiously dwarfed and blunted, as it descended the steps. Another figure joined his and the two outlines merged for a few moments as they met and talked. Then they parted and she heard heavy footsteps crossing the gravel and receding round the side of the house. It was obviously the sergeant who had come to check her car. So much, she thought, for Rudd's pretence that the idea had occurred to him only at the last minute. He had had it planned out well in advance and it worried her. Rudd had presented himself as an amiable enough man, not very intelligent or particularly perceptive. But, as the interview continued, she had been aware of a quiet, listening quality about him that she had realised, too late, was part of his technique. It had fooled her into speaking too freely of Patrick Vaughan, which she now regretted, though she didn't think she had said anything that really mattered. The news of his death had shocked her and caught her momentarily offguard. It was only after she had recovered that she was able to think more calmly about Rudd's exact role and it was this that really frightened her.

She would have to warn Lewis, not just about Patrick's death but about the part the police were taking in the inquiry, and, as soon as the sergeant's footsteps died away, she returned immediately to the drawing room, where, picking up the phone, she dialled the number of the school.

It rang and rang for several exasperating minutes before a woman's voice, Mrs. Dyson's, the school secretary, answered it.

"Chellfield Primary School."

"This is Mrs. Fulton," Kitty said hurriedly. "I want to speak to Mr. Shand."

"He's taking morning assembly," Mrs. Dyson replied. "Could you ring back later?"

Oh God! Kitty thought. In her anxiety, she had forgotten that Lewis would be busy with school prayers until half-past nine. And meanwhile Rudd might arrive there within the next few minutes.

"It's most important I speak to him immediately," she said, aware that her voice was too peremptory.

There was a small, surprised silence and then Mrs. Dyson said reluctantly, "Very well, Mrs. Fulton. I'll fetch him."

Kitty heard the rattle as the receiver was put down and then there was another long, maddening pause during which she could hear faintly in the background children's voices singing before Lewis came on the line.

"Kitty?"

"Lewis, are you alone?"

"Yes." He sounded bewildered. "What's the matter? Mrs. Dyson said you wanted to speak to me urgently."

"Yes, I do. It's about Patrick. He's dead."

There was no time to break the news more circumspectly. Rudd might be drawing up outside the school at that very moment. She heard Lewis catch his breath, but before he could say anything she hurried on.

"He was knocked down by a car sometime last night and killed. I don't know any more details than that. But listen, Lewis, the police have been here, a Detective Inspector Rudd, asking about any visitors Patrick might have had yesterday evening. I had to tell him that you'd called at the cottage to borrow a book. There didn't seem any other way out of it. If I'd lied, it could have made it worse. He's on his way now to question you. I phoned to warn you not to say anything about the real reason you went to see him. You know what I mean?"

"Yes, I understand, Kitty. I shan't mention it at all. It's quite dreadful, about Vaughan, I mean . . ."

She broke in again.

"There's something else that you ought to know. Before Rudd left, I asked him if he was from Weldon and he said no. I thought he wasn't. As you know, Richard was very involved with trying to get better pay and conditions for the police and I've kept up the interest. Last summer I was asked by the Weldon force to their Open Day. Rudd wasn't there and his name wasn't mentioned . . ."

"I don't understand . . ." Lewis Shand began.

"For God's sake!" she cried, suddenly exasperated by his obtuseness. "Can't you see the implications? If it was just a straightforward accident, one of the local inspectors like Hallam would be dealing with it. I don't know much about police procedure but I'm quite sure that's what would normally happen. So, if he isn't from Weldon, I've got the awful feeling he might be from headquarters . . ."

"I'm sorry, Kitty," Lewis Shand broke in. "I can't hear you very well. Assembly's just finished and there's quite a lot of noise outside. What did you say? From headquarters? Does that matter?"

Her patience finally broke, not just because of Lewis, although his ingenuousness was aggravatingly mistimed, but at the whole ridiculous and frightening situation. She could hear the regular thump-thump of the piano playing as the children left the hall and the confused murmur of voices as they passed along the corridor outside Lewis's office. It was absurd that he had so little privacy and that she was forced into raising her voice to make herself heard.

"Yes it does! It could mean that the police don't think his death was an accident."

"Not an accident? Then what . . . ?"

He stopped as if appalled at what he had been about to say.

"I must see you," Kitty said hurriedly. "I think we ought to discuss it but not over the phone. Can you come up to the house this evening?"

"I can't tonight. There's a meeting of the Antiquarian Society in Weldon that I must attend. I'm presenting a paper . . ."

"Tomorrow then?"

It was Saturday and the school would be closed. He was about to suggest that he come in the morning, but Kitty was saying, "Make it the afternoon. Mrs. Allison will be here until twelve."

"Yes, of course, I'll come immediately after lunch."

"And, Lewis," she added just before she rang off, "do please be very careful what you say to Rudd."

Lewis Shand replaced the receiver and stood for a moment, his hand still resting on it. During the conversation with Kitty, he had experienced a complexity of emotions and reactions, none of which he had been able properly to assimilate or rationalise. Vaughan was dead. That much, at least, he had grasped, and, after the initial shock had passed, he had been aware only of relief. With Vaughan gone, Kitty and Hilary would be safe. He felt no guilt. It was as if a great burden had dropped from his back, leaving him light and young again. The fact that the police were inquiring into his death hadn't struck him at first as particularly significant. Of course there would have to be some kind of investigation; there had been when Marion died; Kitty's concern at the inspector's exact identity had seemed unnecessary. It was only when she had said that it might not be an accident that the full implications had at last occurred to him.

His first concern was for Hilary. Would the police inquiry uncover her relationship with Vaughan? He knew that he would say nothing about it himself. There was no question of that. But would she? On the first shock of hearing of it, she might feel some perverse desire to confess everything. He couldn't begin even to guess at what her reactions to it might be, but he was suddenly and frighteningly aware of her emotional instability. He had never dared to admit it before, but he knew now that the fear had always been there and that his need to protect her was, in reality, an awareness of some deeply destructive quality in herself. He was conscious, too, that, in this situation, he could no longer protect her. She would be alone.

His apprehension poured over to include Kitty. She, too, was vulnerable, but to what he was less clear. Her anxiety to get Vaughan out of the cottage seemed to take on new and dangerous connotations.

That was only yesterday, he realised. Vaughan had been alive then; vividly alive, it appeared to Lewis Shand, as he recalled in a series of clear, unconnected images the sheen about his lips and hair; the dark, bare legs; the strange, compelling glitter that he had seemed to radiate.

He felt no fear on his own account about any possible inquiry, only a sensation of inadequacy and doubt as to how well he would be able to handle the situation for Hilary's sake and Kitty's. The excuse he had given Vaughan for calling at the cottage, which he realised he would have to repeat to the police, seemed woefully inadequate. Vaughan had seen through it. Would the police tear it open like paper pasted over a crack?

As the word came into his mind with its sharp, metallic crackle of consonants, he was aware that the sound had been repeated somewhere outside himself, like an echo, and, glancing up, he saw through the window that a car had drawn up outside the school gates and that a stocky figure in a mackintosh was in the act of slamming shut the driver's door with a quick, decisive movement.

It was only then, as the man began to walk across the playground, surveying the building with an interested cock of his head, that Lewis Shand realised it must be the inspector from headquarters, come to inquire into the accident. No, not accident, he remembered, and his mind was suddenly emptied of all other thoughts and ideas except for the one word—murder.

8

As Rudd pushed open the door, he paused for a moment to absorb the smell of the place, which reminded him in one of those jolts of sensory recall more keenly vivid than the familiarity of mere remembered objects of his own early school days spent in a similar building. It was a complex odour, hard to analyse, composed of floor polish, chalk dust and the sweetish scent of disinfectant mingled with the indefinable exhalation of small children en masse, or damp coats and wellington boots, warm skin and hair.

In his day, school had been a grim place of brown glazed bricks and cream distempered walls darkened by dirt and hung with shiny maps suspended from wooden poles, the only picture one of Christ, surrounded by boys and girls of different nationalities, illustrating the text "Suffer Little Children," which had bewildered him at the time. Why should they have to suffer? And why was there no sign of pain on their faces?

There had been changes since then, he thought, and for the better, looking round at the bright colours, the display of children's paintings, the shelves filled with books.

The school hall opened off the entrance foyer and he lingered for a few more moments watching a class of eight-year-olds, stripped to their pants and undershirts, moving rhythmically to the music of Saint-Saëns' "Carnival of Animals," a far cry from the misery of his own physical-training lessons held in the school-yard under the choleric eye of the fierce little Welshman who had been responsible for boys' games and who, judging by his barking cries and the incessant piercing blasts on his whistle, had hated every moment of it.

"May I help you?"

The voice startled Rudd and, turning from his contemplation of the children, he saw a man coming towards him; Shand, he guessed, watching him as he approached. He was a tall man but slightly built, making him seem smaller than he actually was; with grey hair of a fine, loose texture; and steel-rimmed glasses that gave a scholarly air to the lean face that had an acetic, fastidious look about it. Anxious, too. Rudd was aware of tension even though it was disguised under the formal, guarded politeness of his voice.

"Mr. Shand? I'm Detective Inspector Rudd. I wondered if I might speak to you alone for a few moments?"

Lewis Shand hesitated and glanced back at his office, which Mrs. Dyson, carrying the class registers, had just entered. Through lack of space they had to share the one small room, an inconvenience that for once he was grateful for. He had no wish to be interviewed on the school premises. The reason for Rudd's visit concerned his private affairs and he had always been careful to keep them separate from his professional life. Even in the weeks following Marion's death, and later, during Hilary's breakdown, he had managed to go on teaching and carrying out his duties as if he had left his other concerns behind him once he closed his front door.

"It might be better if we went to the house to talk," he said. "There isn't much privacy here . . ."

He left the sentence unfinished as he led the way back into the playground where a small iron gate in the railings opened into the front garden of the house and, as he unlocked the door and showed Rudd into the sitting room, he was glad of the few moments' respite, which gave him time to collect his thoughts.

Rudd's appearance also helped to restore his confidence. He wasn't sure quite what he had expected from Kitty's telephone call warning him about the inspector in charge of the case; certainly not this rather shabby figure in a crumpled raincoat with the tired eyes who seemed thankful for a chance to sit down. There appeared to be nothing threatening about him and Lewis Shand wondered if Kitty hadn't dramatised the situation, though it wasn't like her to over-react.

"Yes?" he asked and waited, his arms deliberately folded, holding himself expectant for what he knew was about to come.

"I'm afraid I have bad news," Rudd began. "Mr. Vaughan, whom I believe you knew, was knocked down and killed last night in a road accident."

He was watching for Shand's reaction and it came just a little too quickly, as if he had been prepared. There wasn't that fractional pause he might have expected while the shock of it was assimilated, although Rudd was prepared to accept the conventional phrase that Shand used. After all, there aren't all that number of ways in which one can express surprise and consternation and most people fall back on a few well-worn examples, however genuine their feelings might be.

"How perfectly dreadful! What exactly happened?"

"We're not sure," Rudd replied. "It looks as if he was out walking not far from his cottage when he was hit by a car. I understand from Mrs. Fulton that you had called to see him yesterday evening . . ."

"Yes, to borrow a book," Lewis Shand put in. Again, the response was too quick and eager.

"Ah," Rudd said blandly, as if that explained a great deal. "What time was this, Mr. Shand?"

"About quarter past seven, though I'm not precisely sure. It could have been nearer twenty past. I was on my way to visit Kitty —Mrs. Fulton—and I stopped at the cottage for about half an hour."

"I wonder if you'd mind going into a little more detail about what happened yesterday evening when you saw Mr. Vaughan. We're trying to find out what he was doing before he was killed so that we can establish the time of death more accurately."

It was the same lie he had used for Mrs. Fulton and Shand seemed to accept it, as she had done.

"I see. What do you want to know, Inspector?"

"Well, for example, we believe Mr. Vaughan had a bath sometime during the evening and put on his dressing gown and slippers . . ."

"That was before I arrived," Lewis Shand said. "He was wearing them when I got there. As a matter of fact, he mentioned that he had just got out of the bath."

"Did he get changed while you were there?"

"No."

"So he was still wearing them when you left?"

"Yes, that's correct."

"And what time was that? About a quarter to eight?"

"Roughly. As I said, I stayed about half an hour."

"Could you tell me if Mr. Vaughan had already had supper by the time you arrived?"

This time Lewis Shand took his time before replying. It was obvious that he hadn't noticed this piece of evidence and Rudd prompted him gently.

"The gate-legged table under the far window, Mr. Shand. Was it opened out as if Mr. Vaughan had been sitting at it to eat a meal?"

Lewis Shand tried to recall the room as he had seen it the previous evening, and after a few moments' thought he replied, "No, it was closed. I was sitting on the sofa facing the desk, and the table was behind me. But I'm quite sure it wasn't opened out."

"Yes, the desk. I wanted to ask you about that," Rudd continued. "Can you describe how it looked? Was there a piece of paper in the typewriter, for example?"

For the first time Shand's face relaxed and he smiled.

"It's a bit like Kim's game, isn't it, Inspector? I remember playing it as a child at parties. It's a very good test of memory and concentration. Let me see." He paused again and then went on. "No, I'm quite sure there was nothing in the typewriter. But I remember seeing a small pile of typed manuscript towards the back of the desk, part of the book he was working on, I imagine. He mentioned that he'd started a new novel. There was a mug, too, containing pencils, and a tray of odds and ends; I think that was all. No, there was something else," he added suddenly, "a notebook on top of the typewriter."

"A notebook?" Rudd repeated sharply. "Can you describe it?"

"It was fairly large and had a stiff, red cover."

"Long and thin, like a ledger?" Rudd asked, remembering the accounts book that Boyce had found in the desk drawer.

"Oh, no, Inspector." Shand sounded quite positive. "This was more square, like a thick exercise book or one of those desk diaries you can buy in Boots."

That was a piece of information worth having, Rudd thought, and something he'd have to check with Boyce when he saw him later. As far as he knew, no notebook of that description had been found, although Kyle and Marsh hadn't finished the search of the sitting room when he'd left to interview Mrs. Fulton. It would have to be found, of course. If it was on the desk when Shand visited Vaughan at quarter past seven it seemed likely that he had been using it in connection with his writing and it might be crucial in helping to determine how Vaughan had spent those last few hours before his death.

"Did you notice anything else on the desk?" he asked. "There was a book on church architecture lying at the back of it this morning when we examined the room."

As he spoke, he was aware of a change in Shand's expression. The muscles in his face had tightened so that the flesh seemed to drop away, leaving the features exposed and bony, like the knuckles of a hand, while two patches of dull red burned on the cheekbones, hectic and unnatural.

"That would be the book I called in to borrow," Lewis Shand replied. He sounded flustered, his voice pitched a little too high, although he managed a nervous laugh that was not entirely convincing. "I knew Vaughan had a copy and I wanted to check on one or two details about a church I was interested in. He looked up the reference while I was there so there was no need, after all, for me to take the book home. I remember he put it down on the desk."

It might have held up as an explanation, Rudd thought, if it wasn't for Shand's distress, and if, facing him across the room, there hadn't been a large oak bookcase, taking up almost the entire wall, several shelves of which were filled with books on local history. Whatever the reason for Shand's visit to Vaughan, he doubted very much if it was to borrow his copy of the *Illustrated Guide to Essex Churches*.

Could it have been to confront Vaughan with his relationship with his daughter? It was possible Shand knew about it and, as Neave had suggested, hadn't approved. But was it enough motive for murder? Hilary Shand was nearly thirty, no mere adolescent whose virginity might need protecting. On the other hand, Shand was a widower and his daughter was an only child. It was the kind of setup in which normal family affection might have become unnatural and obsessive. Shand looked too mild-mannered to be the type but that was nothing to go on. So had Crippen, and even Christie had been one of those nondescript little men you don't give a second glance at in the street.

The room gave nothing away either. Apart from the books, it was furnished with one of those comfortable but quite ordinary suites of armchairs and matching sofa that can be seen in any furniture shop, bought to last and covered with a rust-coloured fabric whose innocuous pattern was designed to tone in with almost anything. The carpet showed the same inconspicuous taste. There was not even a photograph that might have given him a clue as to his relationship with his daughter.

What did Shand and Hilary talk about as they sat together in this room in the evenings? Rudd wondered. Had they ever discussed Vaughan? Come to that, did either of them have an alibi for the time he was killed?

The trouble was he couldn't ask any of those questions directly. Until he had evidence that Vaughan's death was murder, his hands were tied. The normal technique of investigation was closed to him and he hesitated even to pose the direct question: Did you know your daughter might have been having an affair with Vaughan?

It was mere nicety on his part, he realised. Not all his colleagues would have shown the same consideration. But, sitting opposite Shand, watching his harassed face, with its deeply lined forehead and small, rather prim mouth, he was reluctant to blunder in. Not yet, anyway. Until he was more sure of his ground, he preferred to wait, feeling his way cautiously.

He compromised by asking, "How did Mr. Vaughan seem yesterday evening?"

The question appeared to take Shand unawares.

"Seem? I don't understand, Inspector."

"Well, was he depressed, for instance?" He chose the word almost at random. It was one that Mrs. Fulton had used to describe Vaughan.

Lewis Shand hesitated. It was obvious he would have to make some reply. After all, he could hardly expect Rudd to believe that he had spent half an hour in Vaughan's company without being aware of his mood, but he knew he must avoid at all costs mentioning Vaughan's outburst. That might lead to the even more dangerous subject of why he had called at the cottage in the first place.

"He seemed all right," he said at last, and then, conscious that it sounded hopelessly inadequate, he added, "Quite pleasant and affable. We had a drink together and talked about his writing for a time . . ."

"A drink?" Rudd put in quickly. "Could you tell me what you both had?"

"I had a whisky," Shand said, "and Vaughan had a gin and tonic."

So that explained the two glasses, Rudd thought with disgust, and neatly disposed of the one bit of evidence that had looked at all useful. He was back to square one and the whole damned theory would have to be worked out again, which ought to teach him a lesson —not to put too much faith in speculation.

"As a matter of fact," Shand was saying, "I had the impression that Vaughan had already had quite a lot to drink."

He wasn't sure himself why he made the remark. Some residue of hostility and dislike towards Vaughan still lingered, but that wasn't the real motive behind it. In some perverse and only dimly perceived way, he wanted to make this one gesture of honesty. Vaughan was dead and his death should have removed the necessity for all the lies and deceit, leaving the record wiped clean so that the three of them, Hilary, Kitty and himself, could start again. But it wasn't going to be like that, he realised. The falsehoods were self-perpetuating, springing up again like weeds.

Rudd, too, was surprised by the comment, and he had the feeling that Shand was trying to express something more, in much the same way as Mrs. Fulton had done. It was an odd circumstance to bind them together, almost like a shared secret, and he was suddenly aware that he might have part of the answer to the real reason why Shand had called on Vaughan. He had been on his way to Mrs. Fulton's. Could Shand have visited Vaughan on her behalf and gone on to Coppins to report on what had been said? It seemed farfetched and yet both of them, Shand and Mrs. Fulton, had been too eager to explain that Shand had called simply to borrow a book, as if the excuse had been agreed between them.

"Did you know Mr. Vaughan well?" he asked. It seemed an innocuous enough question to start with.

"Not very. I had met him . . ."

"At Mrs. Fulton's, I believe."

Rudd dropped the remark casually but behind it was the unspoken suggestion that he had already been making inquiries into their relationship, a hint that wasn't lost on Shand, who looked uncomfortable.

"Yes, I'd met him at Coppins a few times."

"Had you called on him before?"

The patches of dull colour reappeared on Shand's cheeks.

"No, it was the first time. As I said, I was anxious to borrow the book . . ."

"Of course," Rudd said agreeable. "Who else might have met Mr. Vaughan at Mrs. Fulton's?"

"On two occasions, there were only the three of us, that is Kitty, Vaughan and myself, but Mrs. Fulton gave a party soon after Vaughan arrived to which quite a few people from the village were invited. Let me see—there was the vicar and his wife, the Cottys —he's the local doctor; a retired army man, Major Barry; the Newsons—they have a farm in the area; and one or two people from Weldon, friends of Mrs. Fulton whose names I can't remember. I think that was all."

"And your daughter?" Rudd prompted gently.

There was no mistaking Shand's reaction as being anything but genuine this time. The flush that had stained his cheeks drained away, leaving it white and drawn.

"Yes, Hilary was at the party," he said abruptly.

The reply sounded too curt but he was afraid to say any more. It didn't seem possible that Rudd had found out about Hilary's relationship with Vaughan; no one knew of it, not even Kitty. Then why had he asked about her? Or was it merely a routine question that had no real significance? Rudd was getting to his feet as if the interview was over and his face gave nothing away.

"Just a couple more questions, Mr. Shand," he added. "Did Mr. Vaughan happen to mention if he was expecting any other visitors later that evening?"

"No, he didn't."

"And while you were in the cottage, did you notice a letter anywhere, on the desk, say, or the mantelpiece, ready for posting?"

"No."

"That's all then," Rudd said, smiling and holding out his hand. "Thank you for letting me take up so much of your time, Mr. Shand. I'm very grateful."

It was all over, Lewis Shand thought, as he showed Rudd out of the front door. He should have followed him out but, all at once, he felt incapable of going straight back to school. He needed time alone —five minutes, no more—in which to think over what had been said during the interview and to grasp the pattern of the questions that had come too quickly and almost too inconsequentially at times for him to see beyond them to what Rudd had really had in his mind.

Was it murder? On reflection, there had been nothing in Rudd's manner to suggest he was treating Vaughan's death as anything but an accident, and apart from the two questions about Hilary's first meeting with Vaughan and the reason for his own visit to the cottage the previous evening, the rest of the interview had seemed harmless enough. And, anyway, wouldn't the police have to carry out some kind of inquiry in the case of sudden death? He supposed they would have to be thorough so that they could bring a charge of dangerous driving, perhaps even manslaughter, against the driver, and certain aspects, such as proving the exact time of death, which, according to Rudd, had been late last night, would be important. It was only then that the phrase that he had heard but had not yet properly assimilated struck him with the full force of its significance.

Late last night! Hilary had been out until gone one o'clock, although he wasn't sure of the exact time she had returned. He had slept fitfully, as he always did when she was away from home, and had heard the clock in the dining room strike the hour. After that he had dozed again until he had been wakened by the sound of her car outside. By then he had been properly awake and had lain listening as she came upstairs and went into her own bedroom. Soon afterwards, the house had become quiet again and he had gone back to sleep.

In the morning—this morning, he realised, although it seemed another age away—they had spoken briefly about her trip to London.

There hadn't been time for her to say much. They always shared the preparation of breakfast and the conversation had been snatched between making coffee and toast. The book exhibition had been very interesting, she had told him. A bit crowded but she was glad she had gone. She and Stella had been able to order most of what they needed.

—And the theatre? he had asked her. They had gone to see *Twelfth Night* at the National.

—Oh, marvellous. One of the best productions I've ever seen, she had said, and added, I'll tell you about it tonight.

She had moved into the hall as she spoke and was putting on her coat as he watched her from the open door of the kitchen and, as he sat now in the armchair by the fireplace, he seemed to be watching her and listening to her voice as if the conversation were still going on.

—I hope I didn't wake you up when I came home?

—No, he had lied. A small falsehood this time but surely justifiable? There seemed no point in telling her that he had, in fact, heard her come in.

—I went back to Stella's flat afterwards for coffee and we got talking.

The collar of her coat had become caught up at the back and she put up one hand to release it with a quick gesture of impatience. Like Marion. He had seen her, too, react in just the same way when she was in a hurry.

—I must rush or I'll be late.

She came forward to kiss him quickly on the cheek. But how had she looked? he thought. He could remember almost word for word what she had said and the way she had moved. He could even recall her beige coat with its dark-brown fur collar and the way she had done her hair, tucked under at the back in a small plait that was fastened with a tortoise-shell clip in the shape of a buckle. But her expression eluded him.

Wasn't that a good sign? he asked himself. If there had been anything strange about her, he would have noticed it. Looking back, it seemed a morning much like any other, with nothing special to mark it out, and she had behaved as if, for her, too, it was the same, and yet Vaughan must already have been dead.

And last night? What had happened then? This time he could follow her only in his imagination. She had gone back to Stella's flat —that much he did know—presumably to pick up her car because he had gathered they intended driving to London in Stella's.

Where had Vaughan been killed? Rudd hadn't specified the place. He had merely said that Vaughan had been walking not far from the cottage when he had been knocked down by a car.

But it was unthinkable! he told himself. Hilary wasn't capable of running someone down deliberately. And even if it had happened accidentally, she would have had the sense to report it, which obviously hadn't happened, otherwise Rudd wouldn't have come asking questions, trying to establish the time of death.

Besides, I would have known! he cried out passionately. Something in her face or manner would have told me. And yet the very passion of his conviction made him doubt. It had the flavour of fear about it. He couldn't rationalise it properly. It took the form of images that defied analysis, mere scraps of memory that came too quickly, like photographs glimpsed in an album as the pages are flicked over, which had gone before he could centre his attention on them: Vaughan's face, smiling, his teeth gleaming in his beard; Hilary's at the time of her breakdown, unrecognisable, swollen and shiny with grief, turning away from him; and then the more recent memory of her hand going up to the collar of her coat. Like Marion! Oh God, how like Marion!

He found himself on his feet, making for the hall, and his hand was on the telephone receiver, in the act of lifting it before he was aware of what he was doing. He replaced it slowly. He couldn't warn her, as Kitty had warned him, that Rudd might question her about Vaughan's death. To do so would presuppose his own knowledge of the relationship. Otherwise, why should it occur to him that it would matter to her?

He would have to remain silent, keeping up the pretence that he knew nothing, still trapped in the mesh of lies that Vaughan had spun for them and over which, in dying, he hadn't yet relinquished his control.

9

Rudd took the road to Weldon, passing Vaughan's cottage as he drove out of the village. There was no sign of life about it. Either the search was finished and the men had gone home or the cars were parked out of sight at the back. Nor was there anyone lingering in the road outside, so it seemed likely that the news of Vaughan's death wasn't yet generally enough known for any of the local people to walk past to have a look. Not that there was much to see if they did. Even the site of the accident had been cleared. Stapleton and his men must have completed their search of the area and left. Seen in the daylight, it was just another anonymous stretch of roadside verge, the grass along it flattened by the feet that had trampled over it, and that was all. It seemed that already Vaughan was distanced in space as well as time, as if his death was of little consequence.

But it had meaning for someone. Rudd was still convinced of that even though Shand's statement had disposed of the significance of the two glasses. Indeed, looking back, the whole interview had been unsatisfactory. His own hands had been doubly tied; not only by the fact that he'd had to pretend that he was inquiring into an accidental death, but he had also to hide from Shand his own knowledge of the affair between Shand's daughter and Vaughan.

Did Shand know about it? Rudd was fairly sure he did. Shand's reaction when asked about her presence at Mrs. Fulton's party had seemed to suggest it, and, if he were right, it could give Shand a motive. Opportunity was trickier. According to Shand, he had called at the cottage earlier in the evening, too early for his visit to have anything to do with Vaughan's death, and the timing had been corroborated by Mrs. Fulton. There was no real reason to doubt either of their statements on this point except for an overwhelming feeling that none of it quite added up and the whole business of Shand's visit raised more questions than it answered. It was obvious that Shand wasn't in the habit of dropping in on Vaughan socially so why had he taken the trouble to do so yesterday evening? The reason he had given was so palpably weak as to be hardly worth considering.

Besides, there was also his own hunch that Mrs. Fulton was somehow linked in with the visit, but Rudd had no real evidence for that either.

He switched his thoughts to her. She certainly had more opportunity than Shand appeared to have. She lived alone and the cottage was only a short distance from the house. It would be easy enough for her to call in on some pretext or other. She might even have found a better excuse than someone like Shand for persuading Vaughan to go with her in the car.

Physically, she'd be capable of it, too. Vaughan wasn't a very big man, and if the theory that his body had been carried onto the grass verge after he had been killed was correct, then Mrs. Fulton could quite easily have managed. She gave the impression of strength. There was a psychological toughness about her also, but whether she was ruthless enough to murder was another matter. She would appear to have no motive, although he had gathered from her guarded remarks during the interview that her relationship with Vaughan was far from straightforward.

On the other hand, Hilary Shand could have an obvious reason for wanting Vaughan dead, as Boyce had pointed out. If Neave was right and she'd already had one disastrous love affair, she could have been desperate enough to kill if Vaughan, too, had rejected her.

And it was motive that mattered. He had felt that during his interview with Mrs. Fulton and he had no reason to go back on that particular hunch. But motive implied relationships and here he was on tricky ground. You couldn't submit them to forensic tests. The path lab wouldn't supply the kind of scientific evidence that would hold up under cross-examination in a court of law.

He was approaching Weldon now and he put all other considerations out of his mind as he entered its outskirts. It was a small, pleasant market town, or had been before the developers got their hands on it in the sixties when the tangle of narrow streets behind the Town Hall had been demolished to make way for a new shopping precinct. Better from the point of view of the traffic, he supposed, as he circled round it, looking for somewhere to park. Perhaps an improvement for the inhabitants as well who now had a spanking new supermarket and a Marks and Spencer's, and a multistory car park, which he finally drove into, having given up hope of finding anywhere else to leave the car. But soul-less all the same. A wire shopping trolley abandoned at the bottom of the ramp seemed to sum it up.

He remained sitting in the car while he took out of his pocket

Vaughan's envelope addressed to the bank and Kyle's report on it which he hadn't yet had the opportunity to read. Only Vaughan's prints were on it, it said, and those were so smudged from contact with his coat that no more than two were identifiable. It was therefore impossible to say if anyone else had handled it. As the envelope was sealed, no saliva tests could be made on the flap.

So much for that, Rudd thought, as he put both the report and the envelope away. It was another bit of evidence which, like the glasses, hadn't amounted to anything much. There was still the letter itself, of course, he added to himself as he turned into the covered shopping centre where Vaughan's bank was situated.

But even that hope was short-lived. The manager, who opened it in his presence, passed it back across the desk with the comment, "There's no reason why you shouldn't look at it, Inspector."

Rudd scanned it quickly. It was one of those printed forms supplied in every book of cheques which has to be submitted before a new one can be acquired. Vaughan had filled it in by hand and had scrawled across the top "To be collected on Tuesday." Presumably he had realised he was running short of cheques and had completed it in a hurry, intending to get it in the post in time to reach the bank before he called there himself early the following week; hardly an urgent enough reason to make him get dressed and leave the cottage at half-past one in the morning. All the same, small enough though it was as evidence, it was a breakthrough in the investigation that might be crucial in building up a case against Vaughan's killer.

"Would you mind if I kept these for the time being?" Rudd asked, and when the bank manager nodded agreement he slipped both the form and envelope into his wallet. Kyle could now complete his saliva tests on the gummed flap and the stamp, which might add another brick to his edifice. God knows he could do with it. The rest of it was a mere scaffolding of theory and supposition.

"About Mr. Vaughan?" he began.

"I'm afraid I can't tell you very much about him," the bank manager said apologetically. "His account was transferred from one of our London branches last January. To date, it's been satisfactory. That's all I can say."

It was only to be expected, Rudd thought as he shook hands and left. Bank managers, like doctors, have their professional responsibilities to their clients to consider. Anyway, at this stage of the investigation, it wasn't all that important. Besides, he had Vaughan's own account book and bank statements if he needed to look into the man's finances.

After inquiring of a passer-by, he found the bookshop behind the shopping precinct in a part of the town that had remained relatively untouched. Boutiques and a delicatessen stood side by side to an old-fashioned newsagents and a grubby-looking tea-and-sandwich bar with steamy windows, although its days seemed to be numbered judging by the estate agent's sign that hung above it.

The shop itself was set back a little way from the pavement behind its own flag-stoned frontage and Rudd stepped onto it to look through the window, past the display of books propped up on stands to show their covers, into the interior.

Two women were inside; one, who was wearing a navy-blue mackintosh and who had her back to him, he assumed to be a customer, while the other, who was serving her, was in the act of ringing up money in the till and handing over change.

As he watched, she finished serving and glanced up, catching sight of him at the window. Anxious not to appear too curious, Rudd moved towards the door in time to hold it open for the customer, who was on the point of leaving. She smiled shyly at him to thank him and he caught a fleeting impression of an attractive, middle-aged woman with dark hair that was just beginning to go grey.

"Miss Shand?" Rudd asked as he stepped inside the shop and closed the door behind him although he knew, from Neave's description of Hilary Shand, that it was unlikely. This woman was short, plump and plain, with big round glasses perched on a tiny nose and a lot of slippery brown hair bundled up untidily on the top of her head.

"No, I'm Stella Maxton, Hilary's partner," she replied. "Did you want to see her personally? I'm afraid she's out at the moment."

"Will she be long?"

"I shouldn't think so. She's gone to the station to pick up a box of books that's being delivered by rail. You can wait if you like."

There was the easy air of cheerful assurance about her of the fat woman who is quite at home in her body which Rudd liked and which prompted him to continue the conversation. It was possible, too, that she might know something about Hilary Shand's relationship with Vaughan, although he doubted if he'd persuade her to talk about it if she did. For all her relaxed manner, there was a shrewd, intelligent look in her eyes and he realised that she had already summed him up the moment he walked through the door. All the same, it was worth a try.

"I've called about a friend of hers, Mr. Vaughan," he continued. Her reply surprised him.

"Patrick?"

"You knew him?" he asked quickly.

"Yes, but what's happened?" she countered, picking up at once his use of the past tense.

"I'm afraid Mr. Vaughan was killed sometime last night in a road accident," he explained.

"I'm very sorry to hear that." Her expression of regret was quite perfunctory, though her next remark was more revealing, showing a genuine concern for Hilary Shand. "You're from the police, aren't you?" she asked, and then, barely giving him time to introduce himself, she added, "I don't understand, Inspector, why you need to talk to Hilary."

"Mr. Vaughan had a visitor sometime yesterday evening whom we'd like to interview," he replied. "I wondered if Miss Shand had called on him."

"I see."

Two words only and yet the tone of voice in which they were spoken told him a great deal; that Stella Maxton knew of Hilary's affair with Vaughan; that she disapproved of it; and that she had no intention of saying anything about it to him or anyone else.

"Then it couldn't have been Hilary," she stated firmly. "She was in London with me yesterday and we didn't get back until quite late."

It was Rudd's turn to give nothing away, however interesting he found that particular piece of information, which of course he'd have to check with Hilary Shand when she returned. Meanwhile he was more concerned to keep the conversation going and to get Stella Maxton talking about Vaughan, whom she had obviously met.

"You knew him?" he asked, repeating the question he had already asked.

"Yes, quite well. He came into the shop fairly often."

"To buy?"

She looked amused.

"Occasionally. More often just to talk when he was at a loose end with nothing much else to do. I think also he was angling for us to put on a display of his books but I wasn't very keen on the idea."

"Why was that?" he asked curiously.

"He wasn't all that well known as a writer—well, I suppose, of his type, he was better than average. I'd place him somewhere about the middle—too literary to be really popular and not quite good enough for the high-brow reader. A lot of his earlier stuff was out of print and anyway, as you can see for yourself, we haven't got enough room for the books we can sell." She indicated the crowded shelves and display stands. "I'm afraid Patrick took his own work more seriously than I did. He very much wanted to be accepted as an important novelist."

"How often would he come in?"

"A couple of times a week usually, when he was in Weldon."

"Didn't you find that a bit of a nuisance?" he hinted.

"Sometimes," she agreed, "when we were busy."

Rudd, who had propped himself up against the counter in the attitude of an interested listener, decided to try a more direct approach. There was a frankness about Stella Maxton that he thought would respond to a straightforward request for information, but he took care to arrange his face into his artless expression, the honest copper appealing for help.

"I must admit I'm curious about him, Miss Maxton. I find him a bit of an enigma and I'd like your opinion."

"Why? Do you usually get so involved with the people whose deaths you're investigating?"

Blast! he thought. She's a damned sight too quick off the mark. The flattery, concealed though it was, would have worked on most people but evidently not on her, and he hastened to retrieve the situation.

"Not always, but in this case I've heard so many different comments made about Mr. Vaughan that I'm intrigued to know which is correct."

"Such as?"

He chose a couple of words at random which Kitty Fulton had used.

"Charming. Amusing."

She laughed, showing excellent teeth.

"I would imagine that was said by a woman."

"Yes, it was," he admitted, surprised by her perspicacity.

"What other things were said about him?"

"Less flattering and made by a man this time," he replied. "I was told that he was inquisitive about other people and it was sometimes resented."

It was a paraphrase of what Neave had told him and he watched to see her reaction. Her expression immediately took on a look of slight distaste, as if the remark had touched off some answering disfavour.

"Yes, he was inquisitive, Inspector, though the people he talked to in the shop seemed flattered on the whole by his attention, because, as you've already said, he could be charming and amusing. And, of course, once they knew he was a writer, they were interested to talk to him."

"Customers, you mean?" he asked.

"Yes, people who came in to browse. If Patrick was in the shop at the same time, he'd chat to them. They were mostly middle-aged women with plenty of spare time who were pleased to spend some of it talking to him." She frowned as if the memory of it still displeased her. "I didn't really mind. Except on a Saturday, we're hardly ever busy enough for it to have mattered . . ."

"And yet you didn't like it?" Rudd prompted her, for she had paused.

"It's hard to say why," she replied. "It's just that sometimes I had the feeling that Patrick was using them for his own ends. You know how some people, especially women who are a bit bored, tend to exaggerate their hardships? Well, Patrick seemed to have a knack of playing on this tendency, drawing them out to talk about their problems. At times, I was dubious about his motives. I felt that he was enjoying their self-pity and little tales of woe. I'm probably making too much of it. Most of the time, he'd discuss books or architecture, subjects that interested the individual he was talking to, but even then I felt it was a bit glib the way he could slip into almost any subject. But when he got them talking about themselves, there was a quality about it that I can't exactly describe except that their dissatisfactions seemed to confirm something self-congratulatory in him. Can you understand that? Almost as if he preferred people to be unhappy. They weren't aware of it themselves. Looking on as an outsider, I was conscious myself of it at times. Destructive is perhaps too strong a word to use, although I think he was capable of it." She gestured with her hands to indicate the meaninglessness of words and smiled in apology. As she spoke, it crossed Rudd's mind that she was referring obliquely to Vaughan's affair with Hilary Shand. "But there was a ruthless, tricky quality about him. To put it another way, I felt he resented other people's happiness and wanted to deflate it."

"Was he a bitter and disillusioned man, would you say?" Rudd asked, remembering the other comments Kitty Fulton had made about Vaughan.

"Oh, yes, underneath the charm, I'm sure he was, but he kept it well hidden," Stella Maxton said in quick agreement. "And very insecure as well. He didn't like it if anyone wasn't willing to be charmed, although he pretended not to mind. But he'd get back at them later with some disparaging remark which he'd make in private either to Hilary or me. You know the kind of thing? 'Oh, him? The man with the National Health teeth and the passion for science fiction?' We both tried to discourage him but it wasn't easy. If we showed our disapproval, he'd treat us as a couple of stuffy spinsters with no sense of humour. Either way, we couldn't win."

"So Miss Shand shared your dislike for him?" Rudd asked, but he could see he had gone too far.

"I wouldn't say I disliked him, Inspector," Stella Maxton corrected him. "That also is too strong a word. As for Hilary, you can ask her yourself. She's just arrived."

She nodded towards the door through the glass panel of which Rudd could see a blue Mini drawing up outside, its parking lights flashing, and a woman getting out and lifting a large cardboard box from the back seat. There was no time to register her appearance. Stella Maxton had opened a door behind the counter and was saying, "If you'd like to wait in here, Inspector, I'll send Hilary in to speak to you."

It was done so briskly and efficiently that there was no time to protest before he found himself ushered inside and the door closed behind him.

He looked about him. It was a small back room equipped as an office, with a desk, a couple of chairs and a filing cabinet. Two mugs and an electric kettle standing on top of a low cupboard suggested it was also here that the women would make tea or coffee for themselves, a small domestic detail which, he felt, allowed him a brief glimpse into their shared lives.

From the other side of the door, he could hear their voices; first Stella Maxton's and then Hilary Shand's, he assumed; quieter, nothing more than a murmur. He couldn't hear what either of them were saying, though he could guess what it was. Stella Maxton was telling Hilary Shand of his visit and why he had come.

It was a damned nuisance. He would have preferred to confront her himself with the news of Vaughan's death and, had it been a straightforward murder case, he would have insisted on it. But under the circumstances of a supposed accident, he could do nothing except wait.

It didn't take long. A few minutes later, the door opened and Hilary Shand entered hesitantly.

"Miss Shand?" Rudd said pleasantly. "I'm Detective Inspector Rudd. Won't you sit down?"

While he was speaking, he took in her appearance. Like Shand, she was slightly built and small-featured with the same quiet, diffident air that, in her, took the form of a girl's awkward gawkiness, an impression that was heightened by the navy-blue skirt and cardigan she was wearing over a white blouse, rather like a school uniform, and the way her hair was scraped back from her face, revealing a wide forehead and large, dark eyes. But there was a difference. Shand's expression had been earnest, the face of an anxious, kindly, conscientious man. In her, Rudd sensed a more complex intelligence and a greater capacity for passion.

As she crossed the room to sit down, he saw that, in profile, she was much more attractive. There was a purity about its outline that reminded him of the fine-drawn features of a medallion, while the loop of dark hair at the nape of her neck, which in full-face wasn't visible, gave the whole head a delicate balance.

It was a pity, he thought, that she made so little of herself. There was a conscious drabness about her, as if she had deliberately set out to minimise her appearance, and he wondered what Vaughan had seen in her. That fleeting moment of beauty perhaps when she turned her head? Or her mouth, which with its long upper lip had the defenceless look of a child's?

"You've heard about Mr. Vaughan?" he asked her gently.

"Stella told me," she replied.

There was no obvious reaction, only a faint contraction of the shoulders as if she were flinching away from pain.

"I'm sorry. I believe he was a friend of yours?"

"I knew him quite well. I'd met him first at Mrs. Fulton's and after that he used to call in here fairly often."

"So Miss Maxton told me. Did you ever meet him in the village? Or call in at his cottage?" She seemed about to deny it and he added in the same gentle voice, "Your car was seen on Tuesday evening, Miss Shand, driving away from the gatehouse."

"By my father?" she asked quickly. Her concern was obvious and revealed, he thought, a good deal about her relationship with her father.

"No," he assured her. "By someone else who isn't likely to gossip."

"So my father doesn't know?"

"No." It seemed better for her sake to say this, although Rudd himself suspected that Shand was aware of the affair. There seemed no point in adding to her distress. "You were very friendly with Mr. Vaughan?" he added quietly.

"We were lovers." She stated the fact quite simply, with no false modesty or overt sign of tension, almost in the same tone of voice that she might have said, "We went for a walk."

"For how long?"

"Several weeks."

Rudd decided to leave it there. There would be plenty of time later to probe more deeply into her relationship with Vaughan once he had established how far she was involved in his death.

"I believe you were in London yesterday evening?"

"Yes. Stella and I drove up there to see a book exhibition and afterwards we went to the theatre."

"What time did you get home?"

"I'm not sure exactly. We drove up in Stella's car. I left mine outside her flat. I suppose we arrived back about midnight but I stayed at Stella's afterwards for coffee. It must have been about half-past twelve when I left."

"You'd have to pass Mr. Vaughan's cottage on the way?"

"Of course."

There was no reaction here either, only the simple affirmation of the fact.

"Which would be about one o'clock?"

"Perhaps a little before that."

She was still answering his questions with the same simplicity and directness. Either she was innocent of Vaughan's death, Rudd concluded, or she had herself under perfect control. She was sitting straight-backed in the chair, her hands clasped in her lap, her features quite calm but with a composure that was too disciplined to be altogether natural. It was imposed, he realised, as if the expression had been learnt by rote like a lesson and reproduced with the same lack of emotion. Neave had said that she'd once had a nervous breakdown and he wondered if the experience hadn't schooled her to withdraw to some dark, secret place behind her face, presenting to the world only its closed, rigid exterior.

"Did you happen to notice Mr. Vaughan walking up the road as you drove past?"

"No, I didn't."

"Or anything unusual about the cottage? A car parked outside, for example?"

She must have looked, he thought. No woman would pass her lover's house without giving it at least a glance.

"I didn't see one but I noticed there was a light on at the back. It was shining out onto the bushes."

It must have been the kitchen light, Rudd thought. It had still been burning when he and Boyce arrived at the cottage after Vaughan's body was discovered.

"You didn't stop to call on him?"

"No."

"Why not, Miss Shand? After all, if you and Mr. Vaughan were . . ."

He left the sentence unfinished, reluctant to put into words the exact nature of their relationship. It was partly, he realised, prudery on his part. Faced by her careful composure and that odd amalgam of schoolgirl and spinster, any term would have seemed too explicit. He was aware also that her self-control was too finely balanced. A few more turns of the screw might destroy it. It was apparent in her mouth, her most vulnerable feature. The top lip was drawn slightly upwards in a small, nervous spasm, although the rest of her features retained the same calm immobility.

"I had no reason to call. The relationship was finished."

"When did you realise this?"

"On Tuesday. Nothing was said. There was no need for it. I knew Patrick wouldn't want to see me again."

It was said in the same flat tone of voice in which she had admitted they were lovers, without any rancour or bitterness and yet Rudd found it hard to believe that she had accepted the ending of the affair with so little emotion. As if aware of his thoughts, she added, "Both of us knew it wouldn't last. There was no question of marriage. Neither of us wanted or expected it. It wasn't that kind of romance."

She placed a small, deliberate stress on the last word, ironic and self-mocking, which made him look at her with a new respect. There was a quality of strength in her that he hadn't seen before; a resilience of spirit that lifted her out of the ordinary. It convinced him, too, that, had she wanted to, she could have killed Vaughan. In her own way, she had as much drive and purpose as Mrs. Fulton; less overt perhaps but nevertheless present. And a much more obvious motive.

She was certainly intelligent enough to carry it out. Whoever had killed Vaughan had gone about it quite cleverly. Apart from a few mistakes, it was almost a perfect murder, carefully thought out beforehand.

He'd have to discuss it with Boyce, even though, as he thought it, he realised he would be constructing yet another theory and that this wasn't the answer.

It was simpler than that. It had to be. Somewhere along the line he had missed out on some trivial and yet vital aspect of the case which, if only he could grasp it, would mean the rest would fall into place. Meanwhile, all he could do now was to continue the interview, using the few facts that seemed relevant.

"When you used to visit Mr. Vaughan, did you ever see a notebook on his desk? It was fairly large with a stiff, red cover."

"Yes, I have seen it. It was his journal. He mentioned it once. He used it for his writing. He'd make notes in it about the characters of the book he was working on, background material, that sort of thing. I think he also used it as a kind of diary; not so much about things that happened day to day but general comments about people and events; anything that caught his attention." Her expression suddenly sharpened and she showed the first real sign of concern. "Have you read it? Is there anything in it about me? Did Patrick mention our affair?"

"No, we haven't . . ." he began but she didn't give him time to finish.

"When you find the person who knocked Patrick down, there'll be a trial won't there? Could the journal be read out in court?"

He could see the fear behind the questions. She was worried that Shand would learn about her and Vaughan.

"Oh, no, Miss Shand," he reassured her. "In a hit-and-run case like this, the only evidence used would centre round the accident itself." Unless, of course, he added to himself, we can prove it's murder and you, Miss Shand, were the person guilty of it. "Besides," he continued, "the journal appears to be missing at the moment."

This comment also evoked no reaction in her except a look of quick relief. "Is it? I think Patrick usually kept it in the top drawer of his desk when he wasn't using it."

"Then I expect we'll find it if we need it," he replied comfortably and started to get to his feet.

"May I ask you something, Inspector?" Hilary Shand said suddenly.

"Of course."

"How exactly did Patrick die?"

"I wish we knew that ourselves," Rudd replied with perfect truth. As there seemed no reason why she shouldn't know some of the facts, he added, "It appears he was walking towards the post box at the Cross sometime last night when he was knocked down. We found a letter in his pocket which suggests this was why he had gone out." It seemed a good opportunity to ask a question of his own. "Can you tell me, Miss Shand, if Mr. Vaughan was in the habit of taking walks late at night?"

"I don't know, Inspector. I never usually stayed after eight o'clock in the evening."

It was said with the same ironic tone of voice that she had used before.

He rose to go, remarking as he buttoned up his raincoat, "Don't bother to get up, Miss Shand, I'll see myself out. And thank you for answering my questions so frankly."

She remained in her chair and the last glimpse he caught of her as he closed the door behind him was of her sitting there, feet and knees primly together, her hands still clasped in her lap, and only her thin shoulders, bowed under the navy-blue cardigan, betraying any sign of her sense of loss at Vaughan's death.

Stella Maxton, however, showed her concern as soon as he reentered the shop.

"How is she?" she asked quickly.

"She seemed all right," Rudd replied. "Quite calm."

"All the same, I think I'll make her some coffee," Stella Maxton replied.

It was the kind of sensible, practical suggestion that he might have expected from her but, as she moved towards the office, he stopped her.

"Miss Maxton, may I ask a favour of you?" he asked, his voice carefully casual.

"Of course."

"I wondered if you could let me have a list of the customers Mr. Vaughan was in the habit of talking to, those he knew quite well."

She hesitated and looked dubious.

"I'm not sure . . ." she began.

"I may not need to contact them at all," he reassured her. "But in case I do, it would be useful. One of them might have called on Mr. Vaughan earlier in the evening."

"I see."

She still sounded unwilling to comply.

"It's a question of establishing the time Mr. Vaughan left the cottage and was knocked down. It could be crucial evidence."

"Oh, very well," she conceded. "But it could take time. There were about five or six people, mainly women as I said, who knew Patrick well. In fact, you may have noticed one of them leaving the shop as you came in—Mrs. Doulton."

"Her address?" Rudd asked.

"I can't tell you offhand. It's somewhere quite close, not in Weldon itself but only a few miles outside the town. She's a housekeeper-companion, I think. About twice a week she comes into Weldon shopping and she quite often calls in here. Then there's Miss Bannister and the canon's widow. . . . Look, the easiest thing for me to do is to draw up a list of their names and addresses from the order book, or failing that, I could check in the telephone directory. I really can't stop to do it now." She glanced towards the closed office door. "Perhaps you could call in again in a couple of days' time to collect it."

"Better still, would you mind phoning it in?" he suggested. "I'll give you the number." As he wrote it down on a piece of paper, he added, "If I'm not in my office, the sergeant on duty will take a message."

"Very well." She took it and placed it on the counter, then looked at him and smiled. "By the way, Inspector, while you were talking to Hilary, the thought occurred to me that you and Patrick are very much alike in some ways. You, too, have the knack of getting people to talk and you listen in exactly the same way, with your head on one side, looking interested and encouraging. Now if you'll excuse me . . ."

And having delivered this parting shot, a small punishment, he felt, for his having persuaded her to supply him with the list, she opened the door and entered the office, where Rudd could hear her saying in a cheerfully offhand voice, "Coffee, Hilary? I'm longing for a cup myself."

There was nothing he could do except make his own exit as quickly and with as much dignity as he could, although, once outside, he lingered on the pavement long enough to examine Hilary Shand's Mini, which was still parked at the kerb.

There was no sign that it had been involved in an accident. The front grille and both bumpers were unmarked and, anyway, one glance at the wheels was enough to tell him that their base was too narrow to fit the width of the skid marks that had been left behind on the road.

Besides, he wasn't sure now how much it mattered because, if he was right, the motive for Vaughan's murder was so entirely new and unexpected that it threw quite a different light on the whole case.

10

"Blackmail?" said Boyce incredulously. Rudd had joined him in the far corner of the saloon bar in the Red Lion, discussing the case in lowered voices. Even so, the sergeant managed to put a wealth of expression into the word. "What the hell put you onto that?"

"Something Neave and Stella Maxton told me about Vaughan —his curiosity about other people," Rudd replied. "When Neave mentioned it, I didn't take all that much notice. But when Stella Maxton made the same comment, it seemed significant. And yet neither Shand nor Mrs. Fulton said anything about it, which struck me as odd, especially in her. She must have known Vaughan fairly well. According to her, he made a bit of a nuisance of himself, dropping in uninvited in the evenings for a chat, and to cadge a free drink, too, I suspect."

"Well, she's definitely out of the running," Boyce interrupted. There was a stubborn belligerent look about the set of his chin. The encounter with Rudd that morning still rankled and he was inclined to be uncooperative. "Don't forget I checked her car and there wasn't a mark on it; and if you're going to ask about the wheelbase, you needn't bother. It nowhere near fits the width of those tyre marks on the road. So on that evidence, she couldn't have killed Vaughan."

"Neither could Hilary Shand," Rudd reminded him. He had already given Boyce a brief summary of his interview with both her and Shand.

"But she had motive and opportunity." Boyce sounded argumentative. "She even admits herself she drove past the cottage at roughly the time Vaughan was killed."

"And saw nothing except a light on at the back."

"That's what she says."

"It still doesn't get away from the fact that her car couldn't have been used to run Vaughan down," Rudd persisted.

It silenced Boyce but only for a moment.

"Couldn't she have borrowed another car?" he suggested. "Or hired one?"

His voice had the eager note of someone clutching at straws.

"It's possible, I suppose," Rudd admitted grudgingly. "But I don't see how she managed the timing. She'd have to return the car to wherever she borrowed it, presumably in Weldon, collect her own and then drive home. It would add on roughly another hour after the time Vaughan was killed. I agree, a woman could have faked those skid marks. Someone like Hilary Shand might very well be nervous about braking too fast on a wet road, but why did she put through those phone calls to Neave and Cotty? That part doesn't make any sense at all. They establish the time of death too precisely and that's the last thing she'd want, if she had to drive back past Vaughan's cottage on the way home from returning a hired car. She'd have run the risk of being seen by either Neave or Cotty, who'd be at the scene of the accident by then. But it's worth checking, I suppose," he added without much enthusiasm. "We'll do the rounds of the car-hire firms and meanwhile I'll try to find out from Shand what time she came home, if he knows. I've got to see him again anyway. I deliberately didn't ask to examine his car when I saw him this morning because I thought we'd go back there sometime and pay him a more official visit. As I told you, I'm not convinced by the reason he gave for calling on Vaughan the other evening. It sounded cooked up to me and I'm fairly certain Mrs. Fulton was in on it. Which brings me back to her. She had as much opportunity to kill Vaughan as Hilary Shand. Her house is only a short distance from the cottage and she knew him well enough to persuade him to leave on the pretext of posting that letter, if that's what happened, but I'm not too sure about that anymore. I can't see Vaughan bothering to get dressed and go with her, or anyone else come to that, simply to post off an application slip for a new cheque book. And I can't see him changing his clothes in front of her either. But, leaving all that aside for the moment, if I'm right about the blackmail angle, then she could have had a motive for wanting him dead. That notebook of Vaughan's is missing, which certainly looks suspicious."

Boyce shifted defensively on his chair, as he had done when Rudd had first mentioned it.

"All right, I agree we didn't find it in the search," he replied, "but couldn't Vaughan have got rid of it himself?"

"Why?" Rudd asked. "It was there on Thursday evening when Shand called on him. He noticed it lying on top of the typewriter; and Mrs. Fulton, who seems to know something about Vaughan's writing habits, told me he worked from notes, although she didn't mention the notebook specifically. But when I questioned Hilary Shand about it, she was quite definite about seeing a square, red-covered book among Vaughan's papers. In fact, she said she thought it was a journal in which he made general comments as well as notes for his novels. Now we've guessed that Vaughan was working on his latest book and, from the rings on the desk surface, it seems likely that he was typing part of it out yesterday evening before he died. So, assuming he used it for reference, why destroy it? And even if for some unlikely reason he wanted to, how and where did he get rid of it? There were no ashes in the grate to suggest he burnt it, were there? Nor any torn-up paper in the dustbin?"

"Kyle looked in the bin," Boyce said, as if wanting to deny any responsibility for that part of the search."

"And he found nothing?" Rudd insisted.

"Only a couple of empty gin bottles and some tins, that's all."

"Which suggests someone else removed it," Rudd continued, "and that smells to me not just of murder but blackmail as well. It ties in, too, with what I've found out about Vaughan and, oddly enough, it was Stella Maxton who put me onto it. When I was talking to her, it suddenly occurred to me, Tom, that she was the only person I'd so far interviewed who was being anywhere near objective about him, apart from Neave, and even Neave's account was coloured by a kind of inverted snobbery. To him, Vaughan was a Londoner, a writer, an intellectual; someone Neave didn't understand and didn't want to understand. He was worried, too, that his death involved people in the village who were important locally, such as the Shands and Mrs. Fulton. Afterwards, when I interviewed them, I realised they weren't exactly being honest either but for quite different reasons. All three of them had something to hide about their relationship with Vaughan. Only Stella Maxton seemed prepared to be objective, but even her attitude wasn't exactly unbiased. She didn't like Vaughan very much, partly because she knew about his affair with Hilary Shand and didn't approve; partly because he made a nuisance of himself by dropping in at the shop. But at least she was intelligent enough to make some kind of balanced judgement about him."

He didn't like to add that it was Stella Maxton's comparison of Vaughan with himself that had given him the first real clue to Vaughan's personality. It was too self-revelatory and he was in no mood for confession. Besides, he didn't think Boyce would appreciate the implications behind the parallel. But, as he continued speaking, he was uneasily aware that what he said of Vaughan might be equally applicable to himself.

"Vaughan had this ability to get under the skin of other people, especially women who were vulnerable in some way. He seemed to be able to sense their needs, flattering them by his attention and getting them to talk about themselves. It was probably physical attraction as well, though I doubt if any of the women would admit to it or even realised it themselves."

There, at least, Rudd thought wryly, the comparison with Vaughan broke down. The image of himself that he projected was avuncular rather than libidinous; a deliberate choice that protected himself against God knows what complications; he didn't care to examine that too closely.

"Certainly Vaughan must have possessed a strong sexual magnetism," he continued. "We can guess that from his affair with Hilary Shand. She didn't strike me as being naturally promiscuous. She knew, too, that Vaughan had no intention of marrying her. She was honest about that, if nothing else. And yet, he managed to get her into bed with him. It's relevant as far as her part in the case is concerned, but, at the moment, I'm more interested in the other women that Vaughan managed to charm—middle-aged women, like Mrs. Fulton, or the others that Vaughan chatted up in the bookshop, especially people who had something to lose."

"Money?" Boyce suggested. "Do you think Vaughan was putting the squeeze on someone?"

"Perhaps. It's worth checking. I'll get Hazlett from the Fraud Squad to go through Vaughan's accounts. According to Mrs. Fulton, he didn't make a lot of money from his books, which he was bitter about, but I think he would operate in a more subtle way. From what we found in the cottage, he didn't have much in the way of possessions but Stella Maxton said it was recognition as a writer that he was looking for. I was thinking more of reputations. Supposing Vaughan found out something disreputable about a person living in the village or in Weldon; someone who wouldn't want that secret to be generally known. It's possible. Stella Maxton also said he could be destructive. It would have fed his sense of power and superiority. Anyway, it's worth following up. She's going to send me a list of people that Vaughan was in the habit of chatting to in the bookshop which we can follow up."

"I suppose it's worth a try," Boyce said grudgingly. "What else wants doing?"

"You've finished searching the cottage?" Rudd asked.

"Yes, that's cleared. I left Kyle and Marsh to turn over the kitchen and the garage while I checked Mrs. Fulton's car. They'll put in a report later."

"And the garden?"

"Stapleton and his men gave it the once-over after they'd finished at the accident site this morning. I had a word with him before he left. They found nothing to interest us, although Stapleton came across with something you might like to know. It's negative evidence but I suppose it's worth having."

"What was it?" Rudd asked quickly.

"There was nothing at the scene of the accident that could have caused Vaughan's head injury," Boyce explained. "Stapleton was quite positive about it. He told me he got his men to search a good length of the verge as well as the ditch and the hedge but all they found was wet grass and a few broken twigs."

"So Neave was right about that," Rudd said, half to himself.

"Seems like it," Boyce replied. "How do you think Vaughan got it then? By striking his head on the car that ran him down?"

"It's possible," Rudd said. "But until I get Pardoe's report, we won't know exactly how it happened. If it was on the car, we ought to be able to find some evidence on the bodywork. There might even be traces of paint on the wound itself. If so, it'll give us the colour of the car we're looking for which will narrow the field. I only hope it doesn't come to a full-scale search of every damned car in the area."

"Could it?" Boyce asked. The prospect seemed to fill him with gloom.

"It may have to be done. If I'm right about the blackmail angle" —and as he said it he saw Boyce pull a small, disbelieving face —"then we'll have to check on everyone that Vaughan had any contact with, which could involve most of the people in the village and a good few from Weldon as well. Which reminds me. I must ask Mrs. Fulton for the names and addresses of the guests she invited to a party in order to introduce Vaughan into the village. It was there the Shands first met him. Even then it's not going to be easy. We don't know who else Vaughan may have met. He's been here nearly a year so he could have made a lot of contacts. Stella Maxton's and Mrs. Fulton's lists will help but I doubt if it'll cover everyone. Added to that, of course, we've got the problem that we can't make it an official murder hunt; not at this stage, anyway, and people may not like us nosing about."

Influential people, he added to himself. Like Mrs. Fulton, who had already shown her resentment of his inquiries. The interview with her still rankled; not that he thought she'd follow up her implied threat of contacting Davies, and, even if she did, he could easily explain the situation to the superintendent. There was enough evidence to support his theory that Vaughan's death wasn't accidental; none of it, though, hard facts, only circumstantial. But what he disliked most was the prospect of having to justify himself to authority like some raw, inexperienced inspector hauled up before his superiors to give an account of his actions. He had been too long in the force to accept that kind of official interference, even though he was willing to admit that his reaction was unjustified. He was, after all, part of a team, which necessitated a hierarchy, a chain of responsibility that reached way above him to the chief constable himself; and anywhere along it, rank could be pulled.

He did it himself at times, he realised. Take Neave as an example. As a local bobby he was even further down the heap. Or Kyle. Even Boyce himself. Rudd liked to think that he had a good working relationship with his sergeant but he remembered with a pang of self-contempt the look on Boyce's face when he had snapped back at him after the interview with Mrs. Fulton. He had been passing the kick down the line, a piece of behaviour that he didn't care to recall too clearly.

He was uncomfortably reminded, too, of Stella Maxton's comparison of himself with Vaughan. It was possible that he found some perverse pleasure in the power he had over people. He wasn't sure. But he was certainly conscious of an increasing sense of frustration and irritability that he could no longer properly control. Part of it was physical tiredness. Sitting opposite Boyce now, he felt the exhaustion soak down into the marrow of his bones. Part of it was the case itself. It was all so bloody negative and yet there were more than enough lines of inquiry he could follow up. The trouble was, as soon as he began them, they all seemed to peter out, leaving him with more questions unanswered.

There was one other aspect of the case that he couldn't quite reconcile himself with, which he had been aware of for the first time during the interview with Hilary Shand—that all of the suspects were as much victims as Vaughan himself. Vaughan had entered their lives as an outsider, and had deliberately disrupted them. He thought of Hilary Shand, her shoulders bowed under the schoolgirl navy-blue cardigan and that fleeting moment of beauty he had glimpsed in her profile; Mrs. Fulton's sudden, extraordinary eagerness to explain her relationship with Vaughan; Shand, too, sick with an anxiety that Rudd could only guess at, and God knows how many more besides; decent people whom Vaughan had used and whose happiness he had probably threatened.

The difficulty was that, in following through the investigation, he would have to assume Vaughan's role, and the thought filled him with antipathy. Vaughan's victims would become his victims and he would have to go about the task with the same destructive inquisitiveness that Vaughan had employed. It would be sordid work following that kind of trail and he had no sense of joy in the hunt, only a weary realisation that he would be fulfilling that part of himself which he shared with the dead man.

Boyce, who had been watching him, felt his own resentment drain away at the sight of the inspector's face. He looked so damned tired, he thought, and defeated, sitting there, his crumpled mackintosh folded across his knees and his head sunk low on his chest.

"The other half?" he suggested brightly, pushing forward the empty beer glasses with his elbow. It was a clumsy attempt at reconciliation but the only one he could think of on the spur of the moment.

Rudd looked up.

"No thanks, Tom. We ought to be making a start, I suppose."

He sounded anything but eager.

"What's on the books then for this afternoon?" Boyce asked, trying to inject some enthusiasm into his voice.

"Get someone to do the rounds of the car-hire firms," Rudd replied. "Not Kyle or Marsh. They've done more than their fair share." He thought briefly of Kyle's strained features and red-rimmed eyes. "Barney and Roper can handle it. Tell them I want a list of anybody, men and women, who've hired a car recently. And while they're about it, they can call in on the garages in the area, too. I want to know of any vehicle that's been brought in for repair. If the car that killed Vaughan was damaged, the owner may take it to be fixed. Meanwhile, I'd like you to have a word with Neave, who's doing a house-to-house at the Cross; find out if he's come up with anything interesting. After that, I want you to check up on a road accident for me. It happened about fifteen years ago, in or near Broadstairs."

"Shand's wife?" Boyce asked quickly.

"That's right."

"You think there might be a connection?"

"I don't know. Possibly not. God knows there're enough people killed on the roads every year. But I want it followed up all the same. Shand's hiding something, exactly what we may find out when we go to see him tomorrow morning, and before we do, I'd like to know a bit more about his background. Two people connected with him have been killed in car accidents, or what look like car accidents, which may or may not be coincidence. But Shand could have had the opportunity to kill Vaughan. He was alone in the house until round one o'clock, if we accept Hilary Shand's account as being correct, and that would have given him just about enough time to knock Vaughan down and get home before his daughter returned. Admittedly, he'd be running it fine but it's possible."

"Motive?" Boyce asked.

"I'm not sure about that. He could have found out about his daughter's affair with Vaughan and disapproved of it but whether that's a strong enough reason for murdering him, I don't know. There's some connection, too, with Mrs. Fulton that I haven't got to the bottom of yet. When I called on Shand this morning, I was convinced he already knew about Vaughan's death and there's only one person who could have told him—Mrs. Fulton. No one else knew, except Neave and Cotty, and they'd hardly warn him."

"Well, we'll know one way or another when we examine his car tomorrow morning," Boyce pointed out.

"True enough," Rudd agreed, but in his present pessimistic mood he didn't hold out much hope for such an easy conclusion. Vaughan had been murdered—he was still convinced of that, but exactly how, he was no longer quite so certain. Boyce's theory about hired cars wasn't the answer, although he'd have to go through the motions of following up that line of inquiry. No, the solution had to be much simpler. Perhaps that was the problem. It was so damned simple that he hadn't taken any notice of it but had simply run his eye over it, without realising its significance.

"What about you?" Boyce was asking. "Where will you be this afternoon?"

"I want to call on Dr. Cotty on the pretext of getting him to make a statement. It'll have to be done sooner or later, anyway. But I'm hoping to get him to talk about Hilary Shand. He treated her when she had that nervous breakdown and I'd like to find out a bit more about it. I doubt if I will, though. He didn't strike me as the sort of person who'd enjoy a chat at the best of times, and, as a doctor, he'll be even less keen to discuss one of his patients with me. But it's worth a try."

"So you still think she may be in the running as a suspect?" Boyce asked, and Rudd felt his exasperation return. The sergeant had the annoying habit at times of wanting all the t's crossed and the i's dotted, as if the inspector were deliberately holding back information.

"I'm not counting anyone out at this stage," Rudd replied. "It's too early for that. Vaughan's been dead for only twelve hours." He was conscious that his tone was too abrupt and he added more kindly, "They'll all get their fair share of the limelight, Tom—the Shands,

Mrs. Fulton and anybody else we can turn up. We're not at the end of the case by a long way."

If we ever reach it, he thought sourly. There was always the chance, of course, that nothing would ever come of it. It wouldn't be the first time it had happened. Vaughan's death could easily go on the files as another unsolved inquiry—a supposed hit-and-run accident that he didn't have enough evidence to take any further, let alone charge anybody with murder.

"And after that?" Boyce asked.

"After what?" Rudd repeated, rousing himself. Wrapped up in his own thoughts, he had lost the drift of the conversation.

"When you've finished seeing Cotty."

"Oh, I'll be at the office, if you want me. I ought to make a start on some of the paper work."

It wasn't strictly true. There was one other call that he intended to make which he didn't want Boyce to know about. It was partly Boyce's own fault. If he hadn't been so disparaging about the blackmail motive or quite so triumphant about dismissing Mrs. Fulton, Rudd might have confided in him. But it was a long shot; too long perhaps, although worth a try all the same. Rudd just didn't want the sergeant round to pull one of his I-told-you-so faces if nothing came of it.

The visit he planned was to Harry Acton, for many years a reporter on the local paper, the Essex *Gazette;* now retired and living in Barnsleigh. Harry would know, if anyone would, of any scandal about the Fultons. He had always covered the elections as well as running a column of political news and comment.

Had he known of Rudd's intention, Boyce would probably have disapproved, which was another reason why Rudd hesitated to tell him about it. And in many ways, Boyce would be right. Muckraking had its dangers. Harry might be retired but he was still a newspaperman at heart and Rudd didn't like the idea of seeing a headline in the *Gazette* the following week reading "MP's Widow in Police Inquiry." That could really set the cat among the pigeons and might lead to an even more uncomfortable interview with Detective Superintendent Davies.

It was a risk, though, that he was prepared to take. Vaughan's killer had to be found, for, like Cotty, he had his own professional standards and a sense of pride in his work which nothing, not even offical disapproval, was going to stop him from seeing out to the end. If necessary, he'd even be willing to jeopardize his own chances of promotion. Better to remain as he was, a comparatively humble detective inspector, than be afraid of sticking his neck out.

It was a decision, he realised, that was emotional rather than rational, but, having made it, he knew it was the right one for him. Oddly enough, it was a relief to have it clarified. That, at least, was one aspect of the case that needn't bother him anymore.

He began briskly to button up his raincoat.

"Come on," he said to Boyce. "Time to get moving."

They walked together onto the forecourt of the Red Lion into the thin rain, and just before they parted for their separate cars, Rudd touched the sergeant's arm briefly.

"I'll see you later, Tom," he said.

As an attempt at reconciliation, it was as clumsy and as inadequate as Boyce's and yet he seemed to respond, for as he walked away he turned and raised his hand in a small but friendly gesture of farewell.

11

Dr. Cotty's house was close to the centre of the village, just beyond the cluster of shops and period cottages on the sharp S bend that formed its nucleus. It was a trim, detached Edwardian house of red brick, set back from the road behind a high bank of shrubbery and a gravelled drive wide enough to take several cars. A single-storeyed, flat-roofed surgery had been attached to one side with its own separate entrance. A sign beside it announced in black letters "Morning Surgery 10–12 A.M. Evening Surgery 6–8 P.M."

It was probable that Cotty was out on his afternoon calls, a fortuity that Rudd hadn't considered until that moment. All the same, he tried the door and, finding it locked, peered curiously through the glass panels. The small waiting room beyond was what he might have expected, having met Cotty. It was austerely clean, furnished with banquette seats covered with a shiny, black plastic material and facing one another across a low table on which some magazines had been lined up with mathematical precision. There was nothing on the cream-painted walls to distract the eye except a large "No Smoking" notice and a poster giving instructions for mouth-to-mouth resuscitation, although someone, perhaps Cotty's receptionist, had placed a pot of bright yellow chrysanthemums on the ledge of the hatchway leading into the office. It had a jaunty, defiant look.

Stepping back, Rudd walked on towards the front door and rang the bell. It was answered by a small, fragile-looking woman: Cotty's wife, as he discovered when he asked to see the doctor.

"I'm afraid my husband's out visiting a patient," she replied, inviting him into a long, gloomy hall with a vista of closed doors.

"Will he be long?" Rudd asked.

He spoke gently. There was a diffident, nervous air about her that brought out a protective instinct in him. She looked ill, too, he thought, her face worn down to the bone so that it was possible to see the shape of the frail skull that had the delicate, hollow look of a bird's. But she must have been pretty once. Her blue eyes still retained some of their beauty, though they seemed too large, as if all her engery was centred in them, leaving the rest of her features drained of life.

"I don't know how long Edwin will be," she replied.

"Is he in the village?" Rudd continued. If Cotty was making a local house call, he might return shortly and it would be worth waiting for him.

"No, he's driven over to Haddon to see a private patient. She's an elderly lady and usually keeps him rather a long time. I've no idea when he will be back. Is it important? Perhaps I can take a message?"

"It's not urgent but perhaps you could tell him that Detective Inspector Rudd called about his statement?"

"About Patrick Vaughan?" she asked.

"You've met him?" Rudd was surprised.

"Only once, at Kitty Fulton's. She gave a party at Coppins soon after he arrived to which Edwin and I were invited." As she spoke, Rudd remembered Shand mentioning the fact that the Cottys had been among the guests. "I was so sorry to hear that he'd been killed. I thought him such a charming man and so interesting to talk to. We discussed poetry, I remember."

Her voice and eyes brightened at the memory of it and Rudd could imagine that Vaughan must have inspired in her the same animation. He certainly had the power to charm, as both Kitty Fulton and Stella Maxton had mentioned, in order to draw out this shy, diffident woman.

"I'll certainly tell my husband that you called," she was adding.

"I'll try to see him another day," Rudd replied and, thanking her, walked back to the car.

It was a damned nuisance that he hadn't been able to talk to Cotty but it couldn't be helped. There was no guarantee anyway that Cotty would be willing to discuss Hilary Shand with him.

He had more hope of Harry Acton, whom he knew enjoyed a gossip, although, in his case, Rudd was more concerned not with getting him to talk but preventing him from finding out too much about the case.

Barnsleigh, where Acton now lived, was about ten miles away, a straggling village with a good pub, the Coopers' Arms, which according to Acton, was the only reason he had chosen to retire there. His bungalow stood almost next door to it, a low building with a disproportionately large tiled roof under which it seemed to squat as if seeking shelter from the rain. An overgrown garden fronted it, and as Rudd pushed open the gate and walked down the path, he reflected that retirement hadn't changed Acton all that much. Places had never mattered much to him and he had an extraordinary gift of creating squalor round him. Rudd remembered meetings with him in various saloon bars over the years, and how, in the space of half an hour, Acton would manage to cover the table with spilt beer, crushed cigarette packets, burnt matches and the miscellaneous contents of his pockets, which he would empty in the search for a telephone number or an address scribbled down on a scrap of paper.

Physically, he hadn't altered much either, Rudd noticed, as Acton opened the door to him. He was still a shambling untidy bear of a man with a head of shaggy grey hair and a beer belly slung low under a bulging waistcoat that was scattered with cigarette ash.

"Good God!" he exclaimed. "What in the hell brings you to this neck of the woods?"

"I was passing," Rudd replied, lying pleasantly, "and I thought I'd drop in for old time's sake."

Acton looked at him with small, shrewd eyes before jerking his head as an invitation to enter and Rudd followed him into a sitting room furnished mainly with books and papers, as far as he could see. They lay everywhere, on the floor and window-sills, some still in cardboard boxes, as if Acton had only just moved in. Rising above the chaos, like small islands of conventional comfort, were two sagging armchairs and a coffee table on which stood a pack of beer cans and an overflowing ashtray.

"Sit down," Acton said, sweeping an armful of books from one of the chairs. "Have a beer."

He tore the metal ring from one of the tins before Rudd had time to protest, tossing it negligently to join the others already littering the hearth, where a gas fire was hissing viciously.

Rudd perched himself carefully on the edge of the seat, avoiding the deep hollow in the centre where the springs had given way.

"So," Acton asked, lowering his bulk into the other chair, "you're paying me a social visit, are you?" His huge, mottled face looked amused. "Come off it, Jack. You've never once called me up unless you've wanted something out of me. What's it this time?"

"All right," Rudd admitted. There seemed no point in trying to keep up the pretence. "I'm looking for information, Harry, but before we start I want your promise that anything I say will be strictly between the two of us."

Acton pursed his lips doubtfully, weighing up the proposition. "What's in it for me?"

"Nothing at this stage, but there might be a story in it eventually. But I'm not telling you anything until I have your guarantee that you won't get in touch with the *Gazette* the minute my back's turned. Come on, man," he added as he saw Acton was still hesitating. "You've had enough out of me in the past. Remember the Larson case? You scooped the London dailies on that one. I reckon you owe me a good turn."

He was conscious as he spoke that he was using Acton in much the same way that Vaughan had manipulated others, although Acton was a lot less vulnerable than the middle-aged women Vaughan had managed to charm.

"And you say there might be a story in it?" Acton asked, his eyes still on Rudd's face.

"Possibly," the inspector replied cautiously.

"A good one? Front-page material?"

Rudd tried to hide his smile. And he had been worried about using Acton! Good Lord, the man was a past master at it himself and could teach him a few tricks. He put the beer can down and began getting to his feet.

"As there doesn't seem to be much use staying, Harry, I'll push off. Nice to have seen you . . ."

"All right. You win," Acton said abruptly. "I give you my word. What's it you want to know?"

"Anything you can tell me about Kitty Fulton," Rudd replied, resuming his seat.

Acton raised his eyebrows.

"Richard Fulton's widow? Lord, don't tell me she's in schtook with your lot. What's she been up to?"

"Nothing. Her name cropped up in connection with a case I'm working on, that's all, and I'm curious about her."

"I assume you don't want the usual stuff. You could have got that from the *Gazette* files. So what are you looking for?"

"Whispers," Rudd replied. "Back-stairs gossip."

"About her? Then you're out of luck. I've heard nothing and I wrote most of the reports about her and Fulton before he died. If you're hoping for an affair, I can't help you. Kitty Fulton was happily married and that wasn't a publicity stunt either. She worked damned hard for Fulton, too, when he was MP; not just on the hustings but on the boring bits as well, opening fetes, serving on committees, pounding round the doorsteps drumming up a few more votes, the nitty-gritty of politics that a lot of Westminster wives can't be bothered with. He had her to thank for a lot of his popularity."

There was a vehemence in Acton's voice that Rudd couldn't

account for, but it was clear that, whatever had caused it, he had drawn a blank as far as Kitty Fulton was concerned.

"What about Fulton himself?" he asked. If the wife had nothing to hide, perhaps the answer lay in the husband's past.

Acton shook his head.

"Sorry, can't help you there either. He came from an old, established, county background which pleased a lot of the constituents; Tory, of course, with a lot of emphasis on local issues—farming interests, protection for the small businessman, that sort of thing. Nothing very new in my opinion but that's what the voters seemed to want. He was especially hot on law and order, which should be up your street. Right of centre, of course, but not so far to the right that you couldn't see him for reactionary dust. As a matter of fact, he was very approachable."

"Yes," Rudd agreed. "I met him once. I was impressed."

"Pity he died," Acton admitted.

"I was going to ask you about that. I remember you covered it for the *Gazette* but I've forgotten some of the details. It didn't happen at Coppins, did it?"

"No, in London. He had a flat near Westminster which he used when Parliament was in session, although he'd go home most weekends. Kitty was with him when he had that last heart attack. They'd evidently been out to some official function together and he complained of feeling tired when they got back. She found him dead in the morning."

"So Cotty, the local doctor, wasn't called in?"

"I shouldn't imagine so, though he may have treated Fulton when he was at Coppins. I do know he'd been seeing a London heart specialist since he'd had that first attack two years before and it was the specialist who signed the death certificate. Of course, there was a lot of fuss about it at the time. I did a feature on it for the *Gazette.*"

"Yes, I remember reading it," Rudd said. "So you don't know anything about him that didn't get into the newspapers? No other woman, for instance?"

"No," Acton replied. "And no boy friends either."

"What about his financial affairs?"

"No funny business there that I've heard of either. He inherited quite a lot of money when his father died and Fulton was a shrewd businessman. It was all carefully invested, so Kitty was left comfortably off."

"And the children?"

"They had three, two boys and a girl. I don't know much about them except for the eldest son, James. He's the member for a Sussex constituency; a chip off the old Fulton block as far as I can see, but a bit more to the centre than his father and less parochial; into foreign affairs and European economics. He'll probably make the Cabinet one of these days. I've met him a couple of times and he struck me as being one of the new breed of politicians, highly professional and well-informed but lacking his father's wit and charm. But perhaps I'm prejudiced. I prefer someone with fire in his belly and a flag to wave, whatever the colour.

"If you want to know about the other children, I can't help you much. Helen, the daughter, is married to a surgeon, and the younger son, Geoffrey, is a barrister. I haven't seen either of them for years, not since the days when they used to be good for a front-page picture in the *Gazette*, competing at some local gymkhana or a Young Conservative tennis tournament."

"And that's all you can tell me?" Rudd asked, trying to keep the disappointment out of his voice. He had hoped for more.

"Sorry I can't come up with anything juicier," Acton replied. "Believe me, if there was anything in Fulton's background, I'd've found it out. I trailed round after him for twenty bloody years from one political meeting to the next and I'd've been grateful for anything out of the ordinary to make a headline. You know me, Jack. I've got small respect for the establishment at the best of times and Fulton was no exception." He looked at Rudd, his eyes very bright in their pouches of flesh. "Now Kitty was a bit different. Plenty of fire there, all right, and courage. I admire that. A good-looking woman, too. What's she like now? I haven't seen her for years."

"Still good-looking," Rudd replied, remembering the strong, vigorous face and dark eyes, although he would never have imagined that Acton was capable of such susceptibility.

"And what's she up to these days? That is, apart from getting herself involved with you?"

"Busy with village affairs," Rudd replied, ignoring the hint to explain his involvement with Kitty Fulton in more detail. "On the parish council, governor of the local school. That sort of thing."

"God! What a waste!" Acton exclaimed. "She should have gone in for politics herself. She'd've made a damned good MP if she hadn't been so occupied with pushing Fulton's career."

"You're going?" Acton asked as Rudd got to his feet. He heaved himself out of his own chair and accompanied the inspector to the door.

"I might call on Kitty one of these days," he remarked with a grin and added, deliberately echoing Rudd's words, "for old time's sake."

"Don't meddle," Rudd told him sharply. "It won't do any good, Harry, and you might muddy the pool."

"So it is a serious case?"

"It could be," Rudd conceded grudgingly.

"Serious for Kitty?"

"I don't know. It's too early to say."

The smile disappeared from Acton's face and the heavy folds of flesh sagged downwards, giving him the melancholy, long-jowled look of a Great Dane.

"Anything I can do to help?" he asked.

"Yes," Rudd said promptly. "Keep it out of the papers for as long as you can."

Thank God, there would be no headlines in the *Gazette*, he thought, as he walked to his car through the ruined garden. Acton might be loyal to his profession but, if he was right, his affection for Kitty Fulton would take precedence. The inspector no longer felt any guilt either at using Acton. The man had his own set of values, too deeply rooted for anyone else to manipulate or suborn.

Boyce was waiting for him when he got back to his office, sitting sprawled out in a chair, his tie loose and his shoelaces undone. He struggled to get to his feet as Rudd entered but the inspector waved him back.

"Don't bother," he told him, as he took his seat behind the desk. "We've both been too long on our feet. How did you get on with Neave?"

He sounded better-humoured, Boyce noticed with relief. Almost like his old self.

"The house-to-house at the Cross didn't produce anything useful," he replied. "Neave interviewed everyone living there but not a single one of them saw or heard anything last night. I had a look round there myself before coming back here. There's a lay-by a couple of hundred yards from the phone box so whoever put through those calls could have parked the car there and walked to the kiosk. But I did have a bit more luck with the other inquiries." He produced a notebook and flipped over the pages. "About Vaughan's next of kin —I found the name and phone number of his solicitor in his files and rang him up. It seems Vaughan drew up a will at the time his divorce was going through, leaving everything to his mother. There wasn't much in the way of money, mainly the copyright on his books. There's a cousin, too, who was named as one of the executors. Apart from them, he didn't seem to have any other relatives. Do you want their addresses?"

"Yes. Copy them out, will you, Tom? I'll get in touch with their nearest police stations tomorrow. Someone will have to go and tell them of his death." He was thankful not to have the task himself. Faced with other people's grief, he always felt inadequate. "What about Shand's wife?"

"I struck it lucky there, too. I spoke to an inspector who'd been one of the PCs involved in the case. It was a straightforward road accident; no chance of any funny business. Mrs. Shand was evidently driving home alone from a shopping expedition and was trying to overtake a lorry on a hill when she met a van coming in the other direction. She braked, skidded off the road into a tree and was thrown through the windscreen, although she lived for another two or three days. Apart from the evidence of the two other drivers, the police managed to get a statement from her before she died in which she admitted it was her fault. Do you still think it could be significant?"

"I don't know," Rudd admitted. "I'll keep an open mind on that one until we know a bit more about Shand's involvement with Vaughan. What's that?" he added, as Boyce placed a large envelope on the desk.

"That manuscript of Vaughan's with Kyle's report on it. You told him you wanted it quickly so he dropped it in this afternoon."

"Ah, yes," Rudd said, remembering. In the scurry of the day's activities it had almost slipped his mind. "What about the other reports?"

"Give them a chance," Boyce protested. "They've been up most of the night. None of them have had time to put anything down on paper but I'll chivvy them to produce something tomorrow. And before I forget, Barney and Roper reported in a short while ago. They haven't finished the rounds of the car-hire firms and garages yet but they'll start on it again in the morning. Is that the lot?" he added, stifling a yawn. "Or can I go home?"

"Yes, you can push off, Tom. There's nothing much else you can do today. I'll meet you here at nine o'clock and then we'll drive over to Chellfield together to see Shand. After that, God knows . . ." He broke off and sat hunch-shouldered at the desk. Boyce, seeing his expression, began edging his way towards the door. But his curiosity got the better of him and he paused to ask, "By the way, was Cotty able to come up with anything interesting about Hilary Shand?"

"No. He was out when I called. I'll try to see him tomorrow, after we've interviewed Shand."

"If you want my opinion," Boyce said, "you don't need to look any further than her."

And with that parting shot, he left.

Rudd was glad to see him go. He didn't want Boyce hanging about the office, ruminating on the case against her yet again. Of course, he could be right and, if pushed hard enough, Neave would probably agree with him. After all, he had been too eager to defend her, which suggested that he had considered the possibility of her guilt. It could also account for his conviction that the voice on the telephone had been a man's. Cotty hadn't been nearly so adamant about that piece of evidence. He wondered whether to see Neave again when he drove to Chellfield the following morning; not that he thought Neave was being deliberately obstructive, just too susceptible to the kind of unspoken influence that people like the Shands could wield in a place like Chellfield.

But at the moment he was more concerned with reading Kyle's report and, leaning across the desk, he picked it up. It was detailed, he noticed with approval. Kyle had not only given a synopsis of the plot but had supplied a summary of the characters as well and it was these that interested him the most. The story was set in a secret government weapons-research centre based near a small town, where Bruno, the main character, escaping from an unhappy marriage, had applied for a job as a physicist. Just how far Vaughan had identified himself with Bruno was difficult to tell. Bruno was a loner, a man with a keen and incisive mind, who felt himself alienated from his colleagues and the work in which they were involved; an anti-hero, as Kyle had described him, deliberately avoiding any emotional commitment and despising the petty squabbles and interdepartmental jealousies of the other characters. Women found him intriguing, especially Hester Stewart, the beautiful and intelligent woman in charge of the centre's library. It was the name and the bookish background that gave Rudd the clue to her real identity, but there was no doubt in his mind. Hester Stewart was Hilary Shand, transmogrified into the enigmatic heroine, long-legged and slim, whom Bruno, despite his cynicism about love, nevertheless took to bed, "trying," as Rudd read in Kyle's quotation from the original manuscript, (copied out, he felt, with a relish beyond the normal call of duty) "to find between her thighs the dark oblivion of his own despair."

He nearly laughed out loud. Read out of context, the quotation had a self-conscious, literary ring about it that struck him as humorous, although his amusement quickly turned sour.

In God's name, what had Vaughan been at? Had he really seen

her like that or had the reality been so painfully prosaic that Vaughan
had been forced to transform it into this travesty of the living woman?
He remembered Hilary Shand as he had seen her only that morning,
that faint wincing of her mouth as he had spoken of Vaughan's death
and the impression of all too genuine emotion held back by a
willpower that was stretched to breaking point.

He felt the bitter taste in his mouth thicken as he read Kyle's
account of the last character—Eliot Charteris, the middle-aged head
of the research centre, one-time Oxford don, fussy, pedagogic,
priggish, and hopelessly in love with Hester Stewart.

It was a cruel travesty of Lewis Shand; altered, of course, but
nonetheless recognisable in the physical description. Even Shand's
interest in local history had been made use of, although Charteris's
obsession was archaeology; not all that much different, in fact, and
easily compared.

But what was much more evident was the hatred that existed
between the two men. It came over even in Kyle's notes. Charteris
had loathed Bruno, and Bruno, in turn, had despised the head of
research; and the reason for their mutual dislike wasn't difficult to find
—Hester Stewart, whom Charteris loved with the single-minded
passion of a man who would be willing to commit murder for her
sake.

Rudd laid the report down on his desk. He was dealing with
realities, he told himself, a far cry from Vaughan's highly charged,
literary view of life. But all the same he couldn't help wondering if
Vaughan hadn't unwittingly supplied a motive for his own murder in
the pages he had been typing only a short time before his death, and
that in Eliot Charteris, alias Lewis Shand, he might also have named
his own killer.

Hilary Shand drove home from Weldon, passing the cottage
where Patrick had lived. Somewhere along this road, he must have
been killed, she supposed, although she had no idea exactly where it
had happened. There was nothing to mark the place out; no police cars
or warning signs; only the grass verges with the high hedges and trees
that backed them and, in front of her, lit by her headlamps, the
expanse of tarmac polished black by the rain.

The cottage itself was in darkness and almost lost in the
thickening twilight. She turned her head briefly to glance at it, with an
involuntary movement. Over the months since she had known
Patrick, this twice-daily sideways look at the place where he lived had
become a habit on her journeys to and from work. In time, she would

force herself to stop doing it. Anyway, it would become pointless. Someone else would occupy the gatehouse and his death would become an established fact.

Indeed, now that the first shock of the news had passed, she no longer felt any need to mourn him or even to consider too deeply the circumstances of his death, as if all of it were already in the distant past.

After Rudd's departure that morning, she had gone about her work in the bookshop, grateful that Stella had referred to him only in passing with the simple statement, "I was sorry to hear about Patrick."

"Yes," was all she had said in reply.

Later, perhaps, they would discuss it at more length, but she doubted if she would ever be totally frank, not even with Stella, about the exact nature of the relationship. After all, what could she say about it? On one level it was so utterly trivial—an affair that had meant very little to either of them apart from the sexual involvement. In many ways, she hadn't even liked him very much as a person.

But beyond the mere physical desire that she had felt for him, there were other needs that she was incapable of explaining to anybody, an inexpressible longing for God knows what. She wasn't sure she could put it into words. It seemed to exist only in negatives —emptiness, loneliness, lack of purpose, a void that she had never expected Patrick to fill.

The part she dreaded most was facing her father. She still didn't believe that he knew about the affair but even so Patrick's death would impose a restraint between them that she wasn't sure she knew how to handle. How should she behave? What words would she use? It would have to be referred to by one or the other of them. After all, it couldn't be totally ignored.

In the end, she spoke first. Coming in through the front door, after putting her car away, she saw Lewis at the far end of the hall in the brightly lit kitchen, turning away from the stove to look towards her. With her back to him as she hung up her coat, she found the courage to ask, "Have you heard about Patrick Vaughan?"

"Yes, a Detective Inspector Rudd called this morning to tell me about it. Did he come to see you?"

His voice seemed strained but not unusually so, perhaps nothing more than a natural reluctance to discuss a sudden death.

She bent forward slightly to look into the square mirror that was set just a little too low in the oak hallstand as she took off her head scarf and tidied her hair.

"Yes, he came to the shop just before lunchtime." Her own

voice, she thought, sounded steady enough. "He seemed to think it was a hit-and-run accident."

There was a silence which neither of them wanted to fill. The rest of it, Lewis Shand thought, was better left unsaid: the inspector's inquiries into his own visit to Vaughan earlier that evening; Kitty's warning that it could be murder; the suggestion that Vaughan had had another visitor on the night he died. Certainly there was no question of even alluding to Hilary's affair with Vaughan.

"Supper's nearly ready," he said at last, turning away from the doorway. "I prepared it early. I have to go to a meeting this evening."

She followed him into the kitchen.

"The Antiquarian Society?"

"Yes. I've promised I'd present a paper."

Thank God, he thought, the conversation had moved on. He knew that Hilary would be unlikely to refer to Vaughan again. That much, at least, he could count on. Like him, she had always been reticent about discussing her feelings; one quality that she did not share with Marion.

"Anything I can do?" she asked.

"If you could lay the table," he suggested. "And afterwards . . ."

"Oh, of course, I'll wash up. You can leave all that," she replied, and he felt suddenly very close to her in that half-articulated exchange in which there was no need for him to explain himself too precisely.

They ate at the round table under the fringed hanging lamp that concentrated its brightness on the cloth and their hands moving among the plates and dishes, so it was difficult to see her face or read its expression.

It was only when the meal was nearly over that she referred again to Patrick's death but so obliquely that he wasn't sure if that was the intention behind the question.

"Do you ever think about Mother?" she asked suddenly.

He looked across the table where she sat in the shadows.

"Sometimes," he replied.

"A lot?"

"Not as much as I used to." He paused and then continued awkwardly, "I suppose as time passes . . ."

"Yes," she agreed. "I was thinking that only the other day. I can hardly remember her anymore."

She was reaching across the table to collect up the used plates and cutlery, rattling them together on the tray in one of those little bursts of energy that he knew was designed to put an end to the conversation. He had done it himself enough times.

"Hadn't you better hurry?" she added, carrying the tray towards the door. By the time he went into the hall to put on his coat and scarf, she was already in the kitchen, the hot water gushing into the sink.

He called good-bye to her, waiting a few seconds to give her time to reply, before stepping out into the rain.

12

"So you think Vaughan's manuscript could be evidence?" Boyce asked.

It was the following morning and they were in the car driving towards Chellfield.

"It might be," Rudd replied cautiously.

"But it's only a book," the sergeant objected. He lifted one hand from the wheel and gestured downwards, dismissing all of literature in that one small, disparaging gesture.

"Even books have to be based on some form of reality," Rudd replied. He was torn between amusement and exasperation at Boyce's philistinism, so smugly and massively negative. "Vaughan had to find his characters from somewhere. He'd change them, of course. Apart from the risk of libel charges, a village headmaster and his unmarried daughter are hardly the stuff from which Vaughan's type of highly charged novel is made. But even so there could still be a germ of truth left in them. After I'd gone through Kyle's notes yesterday evening, I read the manuscript for myself and, out of all the characters, Charteris came over as one of the more convincing, especially in his relationship with the girl. I felt Vaughan was describing something he knew at firsthand; the way Charteris watched her, for example, and the obsessive interest he took in the girl's affair with the hero, like a kind of voyeurism."

"Sounds kinky to me," Boyce remarked.

"It was kinky," Rudd replied. "It was meant to be."

It was pointless, he realised, to try explaining to Boyce the flavour of that third unfinished chapter on which Vaughan had been working just before he died. He had been gripped by it almost against his will. There had been no compassion in it. Vaughan had felt nothing but contempt for the man, and yet, in spite of it, Charteris had seemed to Rudd a tragic figure. Or had he been reading into the character some of Shand's qualities? It was difficult to be objective or even to disentangle in his own mind what was real and what was imaginary. Yet he had remained convinced of one thing: Shand's

141

relationship with his daughter had provided Vaughan with a nucleus of reality from which Charteris had been created, and in that tiny core might lie the answer to his own inquiries.

"All right," Boyce was saying. "I can see the motive." He spoke grudgingly, as if not entirely persuaded. "Shand's one of those possessive fathers who doesn't like the idea of his daughter having a boy friend."

It only approximated the truth but Rudd let it pass. If Vaughan had been right, then Shand's true feelings were as far removed from that description as trying to play Bach on a tin whistle.

"I can see also that he could have had the opportunity," Boyce continued. "The daughter's out for the evening. It's only a few minutes' drive to Vaughan's place. It couldn't have taken much more than a quarter of an hour to kill Vaughan, fake the accident, put through those phone calls and be safely home and in bed before she got back. He was taking a hell of a risk, though. He couldn't have known the exact time she'd turn up."

"I agree, but from his point of view it could have been a chance worth taking. And don't forget, Tom, he'd count on her silence. Even though she might suspect, she'd never give him away. If the relationship's as close as Vaughan's book suggests, he'd know that. Besides, with Vaughan dead, who else did she have? No one."

"What about the two glasses? Why didn't he take those?"

"He didn't need to. He'd be prepared to admit calling on Vaughan earlier in the evening. But supposing, during that first visit, Vaughan taunted him with the fact that he was having an affair with his daughter? It's possible. If we accept that Vaughan's manuscript was based at least partly on the truth, then there was no love lost between him and Shand. We know, too, from what Hilary Shand's partner, Stella Maxton said, that there was a streak of malice in Vaughan. It could have been the reason why Vaughan told Shand that he and Hilary were lovers. Shand leaves but he can't get the idea out of his mind that he might lose her to Vaughan, even though Vaughan had no intention of marrying her. He may have remembered already losing his wife in that car accident and that gives him the idea of how to fake Vaughan's murder. So he returns to the cottage that night, knowing that Hilary won't be home until late.

"Up to that point, I'm on fairly safe ground; at least, I think I am. It makes some kind of sense anyway. It's only after that it begins to get tricky. The question is, how did Shand persuade Vaughan to leave the cottage? Knowing the enmity that existed between them, I can't see Vaughan agreeing to go with Shand in his car, let alone getting out of it a little way up the road to let Shand run him down. Then there's the notebook . . ."

"I was going to mention that myself," Boyce put in. "Shand would hardly tell you he'd seen it on Vaughan's typewriter if he'd walked off with it himself."

"Which could knock him off the list of suspects," Rudd added. "Anyway, we'll know one way or the other soon enough. We're coming into Chellfield now. When we get to his house, I'll keep him talking while you check his car. And remember, as far as he's concerned we're investigating an accident and the inspection's simply routine."

"Right," Boyce agreed as he drew up in front of the school, its playground deserted and an empty, Saturday look about its closed doors and windows.

Lewis Shand wasn't aware of their arrival until a heavy, double knock at the front door announced the presence of visitors. The interruption annoyed him. He was washing the kitchen floor, a task he could easily have left to Mrs. Tyler, the daily help, who would be coming on Monday morning to clean the house. Shand's decision to do the task himself was only partly a natural fastidiousness about a dirty floor, soiled by wet footprints and mud brought in from the garden. It took his mind off the conversation he had had with Hilary the previous evening, which still disturbed him. He was sure that she had been indirectly asking for his help in coming to terms with Vaughan's death, perhaps, too, with David's desertion, and he felt he had failed her. Why hadn't he had the courage to be more frank with her? For the first time in their lives, they might both have been open with one another about their real feelings and yet he had allowed the opportunity to slip away. It might never come again.

He was troubled, too, by Hilary's confession that she could no longer remember her mother, which had shocked him deeply. He had always imagined that Hilary had preserved some clear recollection of her even if his own memory had grown dim over the years, and, even at the meeting of the Antiquarian Society, he had found himself recalling little details of the past which involved, not his own relationship with Marion, which God knows had lasted nearly sixteen years, but Hilary's too; events that he could not believe she had forgotten: Marion brushing out Hilary's hair with long sweeps of the brush until it crackled before plaiting it into the long, loose pigtail she had worn as a schoolgirl; and one vivid scene earlier still, of her walking hand in hand with the child down the garden and then lifting her up in her arms to smell the lilac flowers. Did none of it remain?

That day in the garden had come back to him in one of those moments of almost total recall when details he had thought were lost returned with a sharp, clear outline, as if time had no relevance. He had seen the garden with its long strip of lawn and the concrete path that ran the length of it beside the washing line and the two figures, mother and child, poised together, the woman's arms extended while the child reached upwards with its face towards the pale mauve tassels that swung with the breeze just beyond her reach. Finally, he had joined them and, catching hold of a branch, had bent it down for her. The fragrance of the flowers, he remembered, had been mingled with the scent of the creosoted boards in the fence, warmed by the sun.

Did she really have no recollection of that either? It seemed impossible and he was suddenly aware how little, in fact, he knew of her.

She had already gone to bed when he returned from the meeting, another deliberate withdrawal, he felt, and, in the morning, although they had met and talked over breakfast, she had held him at arm's length by asking him too brightly about the paper he had presented, almost like a stranger who is afraid to let the conversation lapse into silence. Then she had left for work.

He had been trying, too, as he washed the floor, to think over the implications of his visit to Kitty's that afternoon. It was obvious that they would discuss Vaughan's death, which he had no desire to do, any more than he had wished to discuss it with Hilary. And yet, paradoxically, he longed to tell her everything: not just his love for her but all his fears and anxieties concerning Hilary; her affair with Vaughan, the fact that the police had interviewed her at the bookshop, and that Rudd knew that she had driven past the cottage late last night, possibly at about the time that Vaughan had been killed. But he was no longer certain that he could rely on Kitty's strength to sustain him. She, too, was afraid.

He was filled with a sudden overwhelming hatred for Vaughan. That bloody man! Even dead he still seemed to dominate their lives, spreading his poison to foul every relationship that had once seemed to be settled and secure. But he felt none of the nausea he had experienced when he had seen Hilary's car parked behind the cottage. This time his rage was strong and positive. It seemed to clear his mind of many of his doubts and uncertainties so that when the double knock came at the door and he answered it to find Rudd standing on the doorstep, accompanied by a tall, broad-shouldered man, Lewis Shand was able to face them with a new assurance.

Rudd was aware of the change in the schoolmaster's attitude and wondered what had caused it. The flustered, nervous air had gone and he looked much more assured.

"Yes?" he asked sharply in the tone of voice of someone interrupted in the middle of something important.

As Rudd introduced his sergeant and made his formal request that Boyce might be allowed to examine Shand's car, he watched his face closely. But Shand showed no sign of anxiety, only faint exasperation.

"It's in the garage," he said, addressing Boyce. "I suppose you can manage by yourself."

"It's simply a routine check," Rudd explained as he followed Shand inside the house. "We shall be examining all the cars in the area."

"All?" Shand repeated. There was a note of irony in his voice that Rudd didn't much care for. "Is that usual in an accident inquiry?"

"It has been known to happen," Rudd replied cautiously. Shand hadn't invited him to sit down this time and he stood awkwardly, feeling oddly on the defensive. It wasn't a very auspicious beginning to the interview, he felt. He had hoped to get Shand talking about Vaughan and, in the process, sting him into a more personal reaction than the polite, guarded account he had given yesterday but Shand seemed prepared to take the initiative, a possibility that he hadn't bargained for. And yet Shand's new assertiveness was in itself interesting. It was a side of his personality that Rudd hadn't seen before, although he realised it must always have been present. After all, Shand was a headmaster, accustomed to using his authority. He was showing it now and Rudd was aware that, pushed far enough, Shand might indeed have been capable of murdering Vaughan. He'd certainly have the intelligence to carry it through, while, at the same time, he would lack that cold-blooded objectivity needed to make him aware of the small mistakes that Vaughan's killer had overlooked. Were they the same person? The mental picture he had built up of the murderer could quite easily fit Shand in his present mood, and, if Rudd was right, he didn't have to search for a motive. Vaughan had already supplied it.

His instinct told him to let Shand have his head. Something had angered the man and he might very well reveal more than a formal interview could uncover. So he remained passive, his expression noncommittal, inviting Shand to take charge of the interrogation.

His next question was more significant than Rudd had dared hope.

"I believe you called to see my daughter yesterday? Was that also routine?" Shand asked sharply.

So he did know about the affair between her and Vaughan, Rudd thought. It was the only explanation for that particular choice of attack.

"It's part of my duty in an investigation of this nature to check on anyone who was known to the deceased," Rudd replied, deliberately taking refuge behind the formal phraseology that gave little away.

"I thought I'd made it clear to you yesterday that my daughter hardly knew Vaughan."

It was time, Rudd decided, that Shand was given a small, sharp shock.

"Oh, I think they were better acquainted than that," he pointed out. "Mr. Vaughan was in the habit of calling at the bookshop fairly frequently."

It was clear Shand hadn't known this for he remained silent, and Rudd noticed that the two patches of dull red had returned to his cheeks.

"Besides," the inspector continued pleasantly, "I understand your daughter drove home past Mr. Vaughan's cottage on the night he was killed. I hoped she might have seen something that could be useful to our inquiries."

"And did she?"

Shand made no attempt to disguise the eagerness and anxiety in his voice and that, too, was revealing. Whatever Hilary Shand had said to her father about the police investigation, it was obvious to the inspector that she had not discussed it with him in detail and that Shand was still largely unaware of exactly how far she was involved in the case. It told him a great deal about their relationship and he was suddenly conscious of the gulf of reserve that must exist between them. They were very alike in many ways, both basically shy people who would find it difficult to discuss their feelings openly and yet he supposed their affection for each other must be deeply felt. In a way, he could sympathise. Every one of his own relationships had been limited by the same reserve. It was one of the main reasons why he had never married. Even though he had been in love on one or two occasions, he had always lacked the nerve to make the final commitment because it would have meant putting into words what, ridiculously, he had felt to be an essentially private emotion, not to be shared with anyone else. And it was too late now.

"No," he replied, in answer to Shand's question, "your daughter noticed nothing unusual."

Shand, who had recovered some of his former assurance, was quick to take advantage. "I take it then that there will be no need to question her further?"

"I can't guarantee that," Rudd said quietly. He could see the way Shand's mind was working and he half expected Shand's next remark, spoken in the stiff, formal, slightly ridiculous accents of the pedagogue which Vaughan had caught so exactly in Eliot Charteris's conversation.

"I fail to see, Inspector, why my daughter should be harassed in this matter. She has given you a statement. That should surely be enough."

"I have no intention of harassing anybody . . ." Rudd began, but Shand didn't give him time to finish. Like many other shy people who have learnt to assert themselves, he was ready, once having got the taste for it, to pursue it to the limits. Besides, he was fighting, not on his own account, but on his daughter's.

"I think I should warn you that, should it continue, I am quite prepared to take the matter to a higher authority."

A leaf out of Kitty Fulton's book, Rudd commented to himself, and wondered if Shand hadn't got the idea from her, which would suggest that they had got their heads together over the case. It could be awkward if they chose to make a joint complaint about his conduct of the case. Kitty Fulton on her own was a big enough local gun. Backed up by Shand, the headmaster who was also a fellow parish councillor, they could really raise the dust between them.

It was obvious that he'd made a bad mistake in allowing Shand to take the initiative. He'd lost out on that hunch and there was no longer any point in trying to continue the interview. It was better to bow out now before he antagonised the schoolmaster even further. Anyway, he could always return to the offensive later when he'd heard Boyce's report on Shand's car.

But Boyce had found nothing. That much was obvious as soon as Rudd let himself out of the front door. Boyce was dusting off the knees of his trousers and, as he straightened up, he made a small, shrugging movement with his shoulders, expressing negation.

"Not a mark on it," the sergeant explained as they got into the car. "And the wheelbase doesn't fit either."

"Damn," Rudd said softly.

"So what happens now?"

"We go to see Cotty," the inspector replied, deliberately ignoring the other implications behind Boyce's question. But he turned them

over in his own mind as he sat beside the sergeant on the short drive to
the doctor's house.

Shand had been afraid, but not on his own account. All his
anxiety had been directed towards his daughter, which could suggest
that Shand knew, or suspected, that she was more deeply involved in
Vaughan's death than he dared admit. He certainly knew that she and
Vaughan had been lovers. There was no doubt of that now in Rudd's
mind. But had Shand, knowing that she had been out in her car on the
night that Vaughan was killed, jumped to the same conclusion as
Boyce and merely assumed that she was responsible? If that were the
case, then it didn't necessarily follow that she was guilty. Shand,
whom Rudd guessed would probably always fear the worst, could
have allowed his anxiety to cloud his judgement. On the other hand,
he knew his daughter better than anybody else, with the possible
exception of Cotty, who had treated her, and would be aware that she
might be capable of murder if pushed too near the edge of hysteria.

Cotty might confirm this, if only he could be persuaded to talk,
Rudd thought, as Boyce swung the car into the driveway in front of
the doctor's house. This time, it seemed, the inspector had better luck
and Cotty was at home. At least a black Humber, which he assumed
belonged to the doctor, was parked at the side of the house opposite
the entrance to the surgery.

"Wait here," Rudd told Boyce brusquely as he got out and
walked towards the front door. The interview was going to be tricky
enough as it was without the presence of the sergeant complicating it
further and he already felt keyed up in readiness for the encounter,
although, as Mrs. Cotty opened the door to him and invited him
inside, he tried to appear bland and smiling.

She had evidently been anticipating the visit because she
remarked, "My husband said he'd speak to you in the surgery when
you called again," as she preceded him down the hall and opened a
door at the far end which led directly into a large, square, modern-
looking office, as clean and as anonymous as the waiting room, which
Rudd had glimpsed when he had called the day before.

Cotty was seated behind the desk and rose to his feet as the
inspector entered, indicating a chair drawn up facing it, which was
obviously placed there for his patients' use. Rudd sat down. It was an
uncomfortable, metal-framed chair with a straight back and a slippery
seat of moulded plastic, hardly the kind on which to relax and
encourage a tête-à-tête. Anyway, one glance at Cotty's face was
enough to tell him that the doctor was in no mood for a friendly chat.
He was wearing horn-rimmed spectacles which gave his thin, stern

features a look of added severity and he had planted one hand, fingers outstretched, on the cover of a medical report which lay in front of him, as if to remind the inspector that he had been interrupted in the middle of important business.

He came straight to the point.

"I believe you wanted me to make a statement," he remarked.

"At your convenience," Rudd replied. "Although I'd be grateful if you could call in at my office sometime in the next few days."

He spoke with deliberate casualness, in order to play down the official nature of the visit, and, in an attempt to add to the informality of the occasion, tried crossing his legs. But the chair wasn't designed for so negligent a posture and, as he felt his buttocks lose purchase on the unyielding surface, he was forced to uncross them quickly and assume a more upright pose.

Cotty, who was consulting an appointments book, appeared unaware of his momentary discomfiture.

"Tuesday afternoon?" he suggested, looking up briefly over the top of his glasses. "I appear to be free then."

"That'll suit me," Rudd agreed cheerfully. "Drop in anytime."

"I prefer to make an exact appointment," Cotty replied stiffly. His tone of voice suggested that, even if Rudd's timetable was undemanding, his own was far too full to allow such offhand flexibility. "Three o'clock?" he added, pen poised over the page.

"Very well," Rudd replied and watched as Cotty noted it down in a small, niggling hand: "Insp. Rudd. 3 P.M. Statement."

"And is that all?" Cotty continued, closing the book and laying the pen aside.

"There were a couple of aspects of the case I'd like to discuss with you while I'm here," Rudd said. It was heavier going than he had imagined. Given half a chance, Cotty would show him the door and that would be the end of it. As he spoke, he thought hastily what other features he could possibly mention which might lead him onto the subject of Hilary Shand. It was going to be a question of improvising as he went along, at the same time watching for the slightest sign that Cotty might unbend far enough, if not to gossip—that was too much to expect—then at least to be a little more human and indiscreet.

"I believe you said Mr. Vaughan wasn't one of your patients?" Rudd begin.

"That is correct."

"But you had met him socially?"

"Yes. I'd been introduced to him at Mrs. Fulton's. She gave a small party not long after he arrived in the village." Cotty's voice was clipped, merely stating the facts.

"What sort of person was he?" Rudd asked, and added obsequiously, "I'd value your opinion as a professional man."

It had some effect. Cotty considered the question for a moment with a grave, judicious air.

"He gave me the impression that he was a heavy drinker; not an alcoholic, but a man who needed the stimulant."

"Yes?" Rudd said encouragingly and waited, head cocked, for the doctor to continue.

"I really can't think of much else to add," he replied, "except he was obviously intelligent and well-read."

It was said grudgingly, as if Cotty had dredged up the comment from some deep recess at the back of his mind.

"You talked to him at the party?" Rudd insisted. It was like getting blood out of a stone, he added silently to himself, although he might have anticipated the lack of response. Cotty was an unimaginative man with very little curiosity about human nature, unlike Vaughan.

"He talked mainly to my wife," Cotty replied, and added with more warmth, "She shared his enthusiasm for Donne. A seventeenth-century poet," he went on, in case Rudd should be ignorant of the facts. "Metaphysical, or so I'm told. I rarely read poetry myself."

It confirmed what Mrs. Cotty had already told him about her own meeting with Vaughan and added another small touch to the picture he had built up in his mind of that occasion: Cotty standing at her side, stiff and silent, listening politely but taking little part in the conversation.

It provided, also, a useful introduction to the subject of Hilary Shand, although Rudd still trod warily.

"I believe he also met Miss Shand at the same party?" he suggested.

Cotty's expression immediately closed over.

"She was certainly there, with her father," he replied, the clipped tone returning to his voice.

"You weren't aware that she knew him quite well?" Rudd continued. "That, in fact, they were very friendly?"

"No, I wasn't," Cotty replied. "And I fail to see why it should be relevant."

"If Vaughan was murdered, it could be highly relevant," Rudd pointed out.

Cotty took off his glasses and laid them down carefully on top of the folder. Without them, his eyes were bleak and regarded Rudd with a look of cold distaste across the desk.

"Is this the purpose of your visit, Inspector? Are you trying to say that you think Hilary Shand is guilty of deliberately running Vaughan down and killing him?"

It wasn't at all how Rudd had hoped the interview would develop but at least the subject was now out in the open and he could speak with greater frankness.

"There are aspects of Vaughan's death that I'm still not entirely satisfied with," he replied, "although at the moment I'm accusing nobody. But Hilary Shand's relationship with Vaughan could have given her a motive. She might also have had the opportunity. I'm not sure, however, if she'd be capable of it. When I spoke to her yesterday, she struck me as someone highly strung who was living on her nerves. I'm curious to know just how far she might go if she lost control."

"I assume from that remark that you know about her breakdown?" Cotty asked sharply.

"I was told about it," Rudd replied.

"Then you'll probably also be aware what caused it. She had been overworking at college; not uncommon, especially in someone as conscientious as herself. A pity, of course, but she may have been under additional strain at home. You're aware that her mother died when Hilary was quite young?"

"Yes, I knew that," Rudd replied. "And I knew about the strain from overwork. But I'd heard there was another reason as well—a broken love affair which was probably the main cause for her breakdown. Or so the rumour goes."

Cotty made an abrupt, impatient gesture with one hand, eloquent of contempt for village gossip. There was a pause and then he seemed to come to a decision.

"You must realise, Inspector, that I cannot go into any detail with you about Miss Shand's medical history and that anything I do say is strictly confidential?" He waited for Rudd's nod of agreement before continuing. "But, having treated her, I can state quite categorically that she is quite incapable of any act of violence, however distressed she might have been. Her breakdown took the form of a passive withdrawal and loss of interest in life; not hysterical or excitable in any way. I treated her with antidepressants in the usual way. In fact, left to herself, she might have recovered in time. She is a young woman with a great deal of quiet common sense and personal integrity. However, there was always the danger . . ." He stopped abruptly and began again. "I prefer in such cases to help the patient to a quicker recovery."

What had he been about to say? Rudd wondered. That there was a chance that Hilary Shand might have attempted suicide? It would fit in with the loss of interest in life that Cotty had mentioned. But how significant that might be to Vaughan's murder Rudd felt incompetent to judge. If Hilary Shand was capable of self-violence then it could imply, whatever Cotty might say about her passivity and withdrawal, that the potentiality for destruction might, under other circumstances, be turned away from herself towards another person. It was hardly the sort of question to put to Cotty but Pardoe might know and Rudd made a mental note to discuss it with the police surgeon as soon as he had the opportunity.

Cotty was rising to his feet.

"I'm afraid that's all I'm prepared to say on the matter," he said in the hard, decisive voice of a man who has no intention of changing his mind.

"Thank you for being so frank with me," Rudd replied as he followed the doctor to the door. Almost as an afterthought he added, "By the way, there was one other small point. Neave seemed sure that the voice he heard on the phone was a man's. You weren't so convinced, Dr. Cotty. I wondered if he could have been mistaken."

The doctor's face took on the look of deep disfavour that Rudd had seen when he had raised the same query on the night Vaughan's body had been discovered; probably for the same reason, that he felt it called into question his professional reputation.

"I have no reason to go back on the statement I made to you at the time," he snapped. "In my opinion, the voice was far too indistinct for anyone to make up their mind about it so definitely. I could be mistaken, of course. So, too, could Neave. He has a tendency to jump to conclusions, not always the right ones. I can only add that I didn't recognise the voice and I have no idea who telephoned me."

So it was still stalemate on that one, Rudd thought as he walked back to the car; with the question remaining unanswered as to whether Neave might subconsciously be shielding Hilary Shand; or come to that, whether Cotty, who was obviously of a stubborn turn of mind, was refusing to back down and admit he was mistaken.

"Any luck?" Boyce asked as Rudd climbed into the passenger seat beside him. He sounded bored and slightly aggrieved at having been left outside to wait in the car.

"Just a small injection to keep me going," Rudd replied,

grinning. "I did get him talking about Hilary Shand but it was like a forceps delivery."

"I'm surprised you got anything at all," Boyce said.

"I wrung something out of him; not a lot, but he did say that, when he treated her after the breakdown, she was passive and nonhysterical; hardly the type, in other words, to commit murder."

"Is that the way you see her?" Boyce asked as he turned the car out of the drive and headed back towards the village.

"It's hard to say," Rudd replied. He tried to recall the impression he had received of Hilary Shand when they had sat together in the tiny office behind the bookshop. There had certainly been a docile, quiescent air about her which he had felt at the time hadn't been entirely natural but had been inculcated into her; self-imposed, perhaps, but more likely a product of her upbringing. He could imagine Shand, kindly and gentle though he might be, setting great store on good manners and polite behaviour. But the affair with Vaughan suggested another side to her nature and, besides, as he talked to her he had been aware himself of inner emotions, banked down but still alive under the dead coals that were heaped over them.

"I'll ask Pardoe about her," he added. "He may be able to explain the clinical aspects of a nervous breakdown. I've got to see him anyway about his report on Vaughan's injuries. Until we know more about them, including that crack on the head, we can't be sure exactly how he died."

"And after that?" Boyce asked.

"We plod on, I suppose. We get Barney and Roper to finish checking the car-hire firms and the garages. We interview all the people who knew Vaughan, which we can make a start on as soon as I get that list from Stella Maxton. And, by the way, Tom, that reminds me, I shall have to see Mrs. Fulton again sometime and get the names and addresses of the people she invited to that party. Cotty mentioned it just now which jogged my memory about it. After that, we ask a lot of questions and hope to God someone comes up with a few more positive answers because all we have at the moment amounts to not much more than damn all—suspicion of murder, three possible suspects and not one scrap of hard evidence to pin on any one of them."

And, at the same time, he added to himself, we keep our fingers crossed that Shand and Kitty Fulton don't chuck a bloody big spanner in the works by issuing a formal complaint about the way I'm conducting the case.

Almost without thinking, he added, "Don't you sometimes feel, Tom, that you'd rather have gone in for something else?"

"Now and again," Boyce agreed. "Especially on the days when it seems all kicks and no ha'pence. But I'm not sure I'd want to throw in my badge." He gave Rudd a curious, sideways look. "What about you?"

"I must admit, like you, I'm sometimes tempted."

"But you can't be serious!" Boyce protested. "Come off it! It's meat and drink to you."

"Is it? I sometimes wonder if I wouldn't have been better off going in for something restful like road mending."

"Of course it is." There seemed no doubt in Boyce's mind. "You've only got to see yourself at the start of a case. One sniff at the evidence and your ears go up like a bloody pointer's. You know," he went on, in a little burst of confession, "I've sometimes envied you that ability to get really stuck into an investigation, even the routine stuff that bores me solid. Anyway, with the chance of promotion coming up, you'd be mad to chuck it all up now."

"I suppose so," Rudd replied. There was no point in saddling Boyce with his own personal worries about that aspect of the case. It was better kept to himself.

"Besides, what would you do if you did resign?"

"That's the problem," Rudd admitted. "There's not much else open to me at my age."

Except working for a security firm, he thought, and he didn't much fancy that idea. It would be exchanging one life-style for another very similar one which didn't offer nearly as much scope. At least, as a policeman, he had the advantage of changes of routine. A day spent in the office on paper work could be superseded by a new case the following morning involving on-the-scene investigation, interviews with witnesses and consultations with people like Boyce and Pardoe whose company, he realised, he would miss more than he cared to admit.

All other doors had been closed to him long ago; or, at least, he had refused to recognise the fact that he might have opened them. For there had never really been much choice as far as he was concerned. He was a policeman. It was as simple as that. He had never wanted to be anything else. Some decisions are not consciously made; they are inevitable.

So it seemed, if the crunch came, he thought wryly, he'd accept it, even the loss of promotion, with as much grace as he could muster.

He'd swallow his pride somehow, take whatever disciplinary measures were handed out and continue in the force until he had to retire.

After that—but he didn't like to think too far ahead, although he supposed vaguely that he'd find something to do to keep himself occupied, as Harry Acton had done. Perhaps, like him, he'd find a small house somewhere not too far from the local pub where he'd drop in for a drink and a gossip in the evenings. He'd dig the garden and maybe even take up some of his schoolboy hobbies that he no longer had time for, like fishing. He'd read and watch television and make a point of going through the newspaper from cover to cover, following up any cases that were sensational enough to get press coverage.

But, dear God, how dull it would all seem! Like sitting in the audience after you've been up there on the stage; the excitement and the action no longer experienced at firsthand.

He wondered if Harry Acton felt the same. In many ways, their jobs were similar. Acton, too, cut off from the bustle and activity of a newspaper office, must be aware of a loss of purpose and drive which had been the centre of his life for more than forty years.

I ought to see him more often, Rudd thought guiltily; make a point of dropping in from time to time. It was something that he should have thought of doing before. After all, they had shared a lot in the past; in fact, he supposed, they were friends, a realisation that hadn't occurred to him until that moment. Certainly they had a great deal in common that they could talk over together.

But not yet; not until the case was over and Kitty Fulton's part in it had been finally resolved one way or the other.

Boyce was saying something that he hadn't quite heard, absorbed as he was in his own thoughts.

"What was that?" he asked, rousing himself.

"I said, do you think we've got time for a swift half before we go back to the office?"

"Oh, I think so, Tom," Rudd replied. "In fact, I'll do better than that. I'll treat you to a pint and a ploughman's at the first likely looking pub on the way."

13

After lunch Lewis Shand walked to Coppins through the wood, as he had done on the previous occasion when he called on Kitty and seen Hilary's car parked behind the gatehouse. This time it was not so much to avoid passing the cottage; with Vaughan dead, he no longer regarded it with quite the same repugnance, although he felt that some of the man's influence must still linger about the place. It would be a long time before that particular ghost was laid. However, he was more concerned that afternoon with postponing the interview with Kitty. He still hadn't made up his mind what he was going to say to her. The new-found assurance with which he had faced Rudd earlier had quickly evaporated, leaving him once more floundering in the old morass of fears and anxieties.

The weather did nothing to raise his spirits. The wind had dropped and a drab, dead, grey atmosphere had closed down under a low sky, heavy with undischarged rain, which hung just above the treetops, coating every twig and blade of grass in a film of dull moisture. Even his footsteps were absorbed into the wet ground and there was no movement of bird or animal in the undergrowth to disturb the stillness. The place might have been abandoned to the elements of cloud and water.

Kitty must have been waiting in the hall for his arrival for she opened the door to him the moment he rang the bell, drawing him inside and bundling him out of his coat, at the same time asking in a voice that was harsh with impatience, "What happened? Has Rudd been to see you? What did he say?"

"Not a lot," Lewis Shand replied. He followed her into the drawing room, where he sat down gratefully. The walk had tired him and he felt chilled to the bone. The room seemed less welcoming than usual or perhaps it was his own inner lack of joy that robbed it of its warmth and glitter. A fire burned in the hearth but it had not been lit very long and a few small flames flickered uncertainly round the heap of coals. There were no lamps alight either to give a burnish to the gilt and silver, while outside the long sash windows the bare outlines of the trees and bushes seemed to huddle together in the wan afternoon light.

Kitty, too, seemed aware of the cold. She had taken a seat at the end of the sofa nearest the fire and sat hunched over her arms, regarding him with ill-concealed exasperation.

"But he must have said something, Lewis!"

Lewis Shand took off his glasses and pressed his thumb and forefinger wearily against the bridge of his nose. He felt worn down already by the force of her personality and her overwhelming need for reassurance. But how could he set her mind at rest when his own was in such a turmoil? He couldn't even remember anymore exactly what Rudd had said. It all seemed curiously distanced and nebulous, overlaid by an indefinable sense of menace so that the most innocuous questions acquired, in retrospect, a new and dangerous significance.

He was aware suddenly that Kitty had risen to her feet and had moved to the little table, although, without his glasses, she appeared only as a blurred shape, larger than usual, her outline softened as she bent down. It wasn't until he heard the chink of the decanter that he realised what she was doing and he hastily put on his spectacles again as she came towards him and thrust a glass into his hand.

"My dear man, drink that," she told him. "You look exhausted."

"At this time of the day?" he protested.

She smiled down at him with that old, teasing affection that was too familiar for him to resent.

"Just this once. I'm going to have a whisky, too, and you're surely too much of a gentleman to let me drink alone." As she resumed her seat, tucking her feet up under her as if more relaxed, she added, "I'm so sorry, Lewis. I'm too impatient. Richard was always warning me about it. It's just that since Patrick's death I've been so dreadfully on edge."

"I know," Lewis Shand broke in. "It can't have been easy for you, Kitty."

"Nor for you either," she pointed out.

"I've been afraid," he confessed. The words seemed to be spoken without his volition, as if the fears themselves had become articulate.

"For yourself?" she asked. "But I don't understand why, Lewis. I know you called on Patrick the evening before he died and I'm sorry that I had to tell Rudd about it. As I explained on the phone, he knew someone had visited him; I don't know how. I thought if I tried to cover it up it would only make things worse. . . ."

Her distress and bewilderment were too painful to witness and he interrupted her again to reassure her.

"It didn't matter, Kitty. I wasn't worried about that."

There was a silence and he looked up with a shy, almost furtive glance over the rim of his spectacles to find her gaze still fixed on him, sharper now and more attentive.

"Then it's Hilary," she said, stating the fact quite flatly. It seemed the only explanation. Lewis would never be frightened on his own account. As he ducked his head away, avoiding her eyes, she added in the same direct manner, "You've found out about her and Patrick."

"You already knew?" he asked in disbelief.

"I saw them together a few weeks ago in Weldon. They were going into the White Hart, for lunch I imagine. I guessed from the way they looked at each other that they were . . ."

She hesitated, finding it impossible to say the word "lovers" out loud; it seemed totally inappropriate. Lewis, who appeared to be unaware of the reason for her hesitation, took advantage of the pause to ask, his tone accusatory, "Why didn't you say anything to me about it?"

"I didn't want to distress you, my dear. Besides, it seemed none of my business." Then in a softer voice she asked, "How did you find out?"

"That Tuesday evening when I first called on him. I told you he was out but that was a lie, Kitty. He was there with Hilary. I saw her car parked behind the cottage."

"And yet you went back to see him on Thursday? For God's sake why, Lewis?"

"Because you asked me to," he said simply. "You were worried; I could see that. I wanted to help and there didn't seem anything else I could do." He heard her draw in her breath but he hurried on. Now that he had started, it was impossible to hold back the flood of words that came pouring out. "But don't you see? It could give her a motive for wanting him dead. Vaughan would never have married her and I think she wants affection so desperately, especially since David left her. I can't give it to her, Kitty; not the way she needs it. I love her but I can't *tell* her. I don't know why. It was the same with Marion. It's all held back somewhere here." He placed his clenched hand against his chest. "And what makes me so terribly afraid is that she could have done it. She was out until quite late on the night Vaughan was killed. Rudd knows it, too. He went to see her yesterday morning at the shop. Supposing it wasn't an accident, Kitty . . . ?"

"But Hilary couldn't have done it!" Kitty cried. "For God's sake, Lewis, you don't really believe that?"

"I don't know," he replied dully. The peak of emotion had passed and he felt himself losing momentum, sliding down into the trough on the other side where even fear no longer possessed the same sharp edge of terror and he was left with only a sense of exhausted despair. "I think she might." He looked up again and met Kitty's eyes. "You see, my dear, she once tried to kill herself and that's why I'm afraid."

It was the final confession and he found it easier to make than he had imagined. In a strange way, it no longer mattered anymore. After all, it was so easy; there was no sense of guilt or shame, only relief, as if he had hacked his way out through a great tangled undergrowth of lies and secrecy with one clean blow. He couldn't understand why he hadn't done it years ago.

Kitty was holding out her hand towards him and he went to sit beside her. She still clasped his hand, beating it gently against her knee in an oddly soothing rhythm as if she wanted to convey, in that soft, repeated contact, all the strength and comfort of her affection, as a mother might console a child. They sat in silence for a moment, and then, giving his hand a final pat, she broke the grasp.

"I'm so glad you told me, Lewis, because it makes what I want to say to you so much easier. I can tell you now the reason why I wanted Vaughan out of the cottage." She got up abruptly and went to stand by the fireplace, her elbow resting on the mantelshelf in an attitude that Lewis Shand had grown familiar with over the years. It was Kitty's declamatory stance, which she adopted whenever she wished to be in command of a situation and demand attention. It was also, he saw now, a defensive pose as well, as if by standing there with her feet firmly planted on the carpet, the heavy marble mantelpiece solidly behind her, containing all its array of possessions, the French gilt clock, the pieces of T'ang porcelain, the family photographs in their silver frames, she was asserting for her own sake as much as anyone else's her authority and her invulnerability as mistress of it all. "Secrets!" she said suddenly and laughed. "How ridiculous they are when we've known each other for so many years! And especially when we've both been trying to hide the same guilt from each other. I don't understand why we should think of suicide as such a shameful thing, Lewis. I suppose it's because we feel we must have failed somebody we loved that we try to cover it up. I know that's how I feel about Richard. Now, don't interrupt me," she said brusquely as Lewis Shand started to speak. "If I stop now, I won't be able to go on and then I'll never find the courage to tell you the truth, although I'm not even sure myself what it is and that makes it worse. I only know that ever since Richard died I've had this terrible fear that he might have taken his own life. You know, of course, that he died in London. We'd been out to a reception and got back to the flat quite late. Richard was exhausted. Ever since his first heart attack, he used to get very tired by the evening. The specialist had ordered him to rest more but it wasn't easy with all his commitments, although he did try to cut down on some of them. It used to make him very despondent at times that he couldn't cope as well as he'd used to. That evening he seemed particularly depressed. We spoke about the future and he said that perhaps he ought to retire from politics for good. I tried to cheer him up by talking about all the things we could do together if he had more free time—the holidays abroad, the old friends we could visit, how we could have the grandchildren to stay here at Coppins more often. But it was no use, Lewis, he wasn't listening properly.

"After a while, he said he'd go to bed and I agreed to sleep in the spare bedroom so that he could get a good night's rest. The next morning, I went in to wake him and found him dead. On the bedside table was a glass of water and a bottle of sleeping pills that he'd been prescribed some time before. He must have taken it from the bathroom cabinet. But it was empty and the terrible thing is I don't know how many tablets were left in it."

So that explained her unwillingness to take the pills that Cotty had left for her, Lewis Shand thought. No wonder she had become angry when he had tried to persuade her.

Out loud, he asked with a decisiveness that surprised even himself, "Did he leave a letter?"

"No, there was nothing."

"Then, Kitty, you must take my word for it that Richard didn't kill himself."

She looked at him with wide, dark eyes.

"How can you be so sure?"

He couldn't explain why; he just knew it with total conviction. Richard Fulton wouldn't have bowed out of life without some kind of final gesture. There was too much of the showman in him, although he could hardly tell Kitty that. But Lewis Shand, who had seen Fulton on so many occasions, witty, urbane, holding the centre of attention, recognised for the first time other qualities about the man that, to his mind, made suicide an impossibility. He was surprised Kitty herself hadn't been aware of them: that small, hard centre of ruthlessness and complete self-assurance, the lack of humility, well disguised but nevertheless present, which had helped Fulton to get to the top and stay there; the consciousness of his own rightness; none of these qualities suggested to Lewis Shand that Fulton would even contemplate self-destruction.

Besides, ridiculous though it seemed, Fulton had been too articulate not to have left behind some explanation, if only to justify his action. He was too accustomed to handling language, manipulating it sometimes, Lewis Shand had felt, to die without taking the opportunity for one last finely turned phrase. Even Hilary, with her reluctance to express her real feelings, had left a note; not to him, and the fact still hurt him, but a short general statement, addressed to no one in particular. The principal of the college had given it to him to read as he sat in her study; a half sheet of file paper, he remembered, containing only a few words: "I don't see any point in living anymore."

But above all these other considerations, Richard Fulton had been too fond of Kitty to leave her so cruelly in the dark. He might have been a selfish, self-centred man but he had never been consciously unkind.

"I just know," he told her, and added wryly, "Don't forget, I have had some experience."

"Oh, Lewis, I'm so sorry," she began.

"Don't be," he replied. He didn't want her pity and he gestured with one hand, thrusting it away. "How did Vaughan find out?" he added. Just as she had guessed about Hilary, he knew without having to be told that this was what had happened.

"Not from anything I told him directly, Lewis. In fact, even now I'm not sure exactly how he knew. He used to come here some evenings to talk, I think when he was lonely and bored. At first, I didn't mind too much. I enjoyed his company. We chatted about books and the theatre; his work, too, which I found interesting. And then gradually, as the weeks went by, we got onto more personal topics. He began by telling me about his marriage, which had broken up, and, in turn, I spoke about Richard and the children. He seemed genuinely interested, as if he really understood." She stopped and then went on more passionately, "I'm a fool about people, Lewis! It's something I've learned about myself. I'm so damned naïve! No, don't shake your head at me, my dear. It's perfectly true. Oh, I'm all right on committees and that sort of thing when I'm dealing with people I'm not involved with personally. I can handle them quite well. As Richard used to say, put me in the chair with an agenda in front of me and I'd manage anybody. You're aware of it yourself. You must be

You've seen me at work on the Parish Council bossing everybody about and getting my own way a lot of the time because that's what I'm used to. But I was never very good at close relationships, not even with Richard and the children. For some reason, I can't stand back and look at them dispassionately. But you can. I've seen you do it. You suddenly go quiet and I know you're listening quite objectively to what's being said, almost like a stranger. And you saw through Vaughan right from the beginning."

"I never liked him," Lewis Shand agreed. "I thought him malicious."

"There you are, you see!" Kitty exclaimed. "I didn't realise that until it was too late. In fact, I still don't understand him properly. I saw the charming side of him first and you must admit that he could be very amusing. And then, later on when he used to come here alone for a drink and to talk about himself and his problems, I suppose I was flattered that he confided in me. It seemed natural to talk about myself in the same way. And he took the trouble to listen, which few people do, even one's own family. I suppose over the months I knew him he must have started to put together little things I'd said, remarks which weren't really indiscreet but which added up. You know how it is."

Lewis Shand nodded, encouraging her to continue, although he said nothing. The thought of the relationship between her and Vaughan filled him with a sad, lost feeling; not exactly jealousy but a sense of regret at missed opportunities, of conversations in which he had not taken part and laughter that he had not been asked to share. Kitty's remark that Vaughan had listened to her hurt him the most. He felt it as a personal criticism and he was aware, with a sudden pang, that there must have been occasions when he had failed her in the same way that he had failed Hilary.

"I didn't realise what he was doing until one evening about a fortnight ago when we were discussing Graham Greene," Kitty was saying. "Patrick asked me if I'd ever read *The Heart of the Matter*. I said, no, I hadn't, and he replied that he thought I ought to. So I borrowed a copy from the library in Weldon. Do you know the book?"

"Yes," Lewis Shand replied. He remembered it well and could see why Vaughan had suggested it. Put very simply, the plot concerned Scobie, a middle-aged police officer, who decided to commit suicide. By pretending to be suffering from angina, he persuaded his doctor to prescribe sleeping tablets which he saved up until he had enough for a fatal overdose, knowing that when he was found, it would be assumed that he had died from a heart attack. The details of the story didn't fit all of Richard Fulton's circumstances but there was enough there for Kitty to have made the comparison.

It was a cruel thing to do but, knowing Vaughan, in keeping with his character. It had all the stamp of his personality, the malice, the intelligence, the clever manipulation of events, even the literary background.

"But for God's sake, why?" he cried out.

"My dear Lewis, I'm not sure myself. We never discussed the book afterwards or referred to Richard directly. But he knew I'd read it and he knew, too, that I'd made the connection. There wasn't any need for it to be put into words. After that, he started dropping in practically every evening, sometimes quite late and when he'd already had too much to drink and I didn't dare send him away. I was terrified that if I did, he might talk. It's a small place and gossip soon spreads. It wasn't that I minded for myself so much but I wanted to protect Richard's reputation. People looked up to him and suicide seemed such an awful stigma. And then there were the children. . . . No!" she said suddenly, her voice rising, "I'm not being honest. I did mind for myself, very much. I loathed the very thought of other people's pity. And I felt they'd think that I'd let Richard down in some way, as if I hadn't cared for him enough. That was the hardest part to bear. Suicide seemed so bloody destructive, not just of his life but of all the things we had shared, the love, the companionship, the years we'd spent together."

"Perhaps that's why he did it," Lewis Shand said quietly.

"I don't understand," Kitty replied. "Explain it to me, Lewis."

"It was a kind of iconoclasm."

"I still don't understand."

"A breaking of images."

"Oh, I know what the word means," she said impatiently. "Don't be obtuse, Lewis. I just don't see how it applies to me."

"Very well, Kitty. To put it crudely, I think Vaughan wanted to cut you down to size."

He was shocked to find, as he said it, that the expression gratified some small iconoclastic need in himself and he continued hastily, "Have you read any of his books? Then you'll see the same quality in them. He was one of those people who can function only in a balance; in order to go up in his own or other people's estimation, someone else had to go down. What will happen now?" he added. "You'll stay on at Coppins, of course?"

Her answer surprised him.

"I'm not sure what I will do."

"But surely, Kitty, now that Vaughan's dead . . ." he began in protest.

"I feel it's all spoilt, as if he'd trailed some sort of filthy slime over everything."

As she spoke, she looked restlessly round the room.

"Yes, I know what you mean," he agreed in a low voice.

She came immediately to sit by his side.

"I'm so selfish, my dear. I hadn't realised that what he did to you and Hilary was far worse. At least my world's left relatively intact. You must have minded a great deal about her and Patrick."

"It was the lies she told that hurt the most," he replied. It cost him a lot to say this and his distress must have shown in his face because she touched his hand again in a quick gesture of sympathy before she went on, speaking briskly in her lady committee member's voice that he knew so well.

"Lewis, you won't mind if I speak to you frankly as an old friend? You must let her go. There's no other answer."

"But I've never wanted to keep her," he replied. "We live our own separate lives. She's been free to leave any time she likes."

"That's not quite true and I think you'll realise that yourself if you're honest. Your anxiety for her is like a millstone round her neck. How can she be free when she has to carry that burden about with her every day of her life? She'll never leave while she knows you worry so much about her."

"But where would she go if she left?" he asked.

"Oh, Lewis, you're doing it again!" she exclaimed with amused exasperation. "To a flat of her own in Weldon? Perhaps to share with that partner of hers? Does it matter where she goes? Can't you see it's her problem not yours? She must make her own decisions without having to keep glancing over her shoulder to see whether you're concerned on her behalf. Besides, she'll survive. She's a lot tougher than you give her credit for. I'm surprised you aren't aware of it yourself; after all, you saw through Patrick clearly enough. Try to see her with the same objectivity."

Was Kitty right? Lewis Shand wondered. For the first time, he realised that Hilary's affair with Vaughan could have been a protest against himself, an attempt to live her own life and find the kind of freedom of which Kitty had spoken. If that were true, then he was much to blame for the lies and deceit that had accompanied it.

"I think my first priority is to look at myself objectively, not her," he replied drily. "I suppose I have always been totally self-centred where Hilary's concerned."

"But I didn't mean it in that way!" Kitty cried in quick protest.

"No, my dear, I didn't think for one minute you did. I'm making that judgement of myself, not you. I need her. I should be a very lonely man if she left; more lonely than ever if you leave, too. I have few friends. I don't think I ever learned the knack of making them."

"And if I agreed to stay?" Kitty asked.

She was making a bargain with him, he realised. Hilary's freedom for her continued presence at Coppins, and he didn't know whether to be amused at her audacity or angry at her presumption. She had been right about herself; she was extraordinarily naïve where close relationships were concerned. It hadn't even occurred to her to consider what his reactions might be to that sort of suggestion.

He realised, too, that he would never tell her now that he loved her. In fact, he wasn't sure anymore that he did; not in the way he once had. He could see what his life with her would be like, if he ever found the courage to propose marriage to her and if she accepted him, which he doubted. He didn't possess the same ruthlessness as Richard Fulton, which had provided the checks and balances in their relationship. Kitty would run his life for him with the same bustling efficiency with which she organised the Parish Council or his own school management committee; in a kindly manner, of course. He would be well looked after; it would be a very comfortable life in many ways, but not his own.

Alternatively, they could go on as they had before, which seemed on reflection much the better option. He'd call in from time to time and there would be whisky by the fire, or sherry in the garden in the summer; conversation that was centred round village affairs or their own particular interests; the Antiquarian Society on his part; on hers, her grandchildren. It would be, to use Vaughan's words, bucolic and bloody boring. But then Vaughan had never understood the satisfaction of small pleasures or the excitement that can be engendered by even the most trivial events.

"I don't think it's a matter of my choosing," he replied, smiling. "Hilary will leave home if she wishes. I have no intention of standing in her way."

It was, he could see, now he had made up his mind, only a matter of time before it would be finally achieved.

"That's settled then!" Kitty said with a pleased air at getting her own way. "It's the best thing that can happen, Lewis, believe me. She'll get over Patrick. It was only a passing infatuation, because nothing will persuade me that she really loved him."

"But does Rudd believe the same?" Lewis Shand reminded her

and saw by her startled expression that she had forgotten the real reason for his visit there that afternoon.

"Of course he doesn't! That's quite ridiculous!" she exclaimed.

"He made it quite clear that he may have to interview her again."

"Even if he does, it needn't mean she had anything to do with Patrick's death."

She was trying to reassure him, he realised, with the same brisk, no-nonsense air that he used himself to the children in his charge, persuading them that although they might have fallen over, they hadn't really hurt themselves.

"And if it really is murder?" he asked, choosing the word that she had first used to him.

"Then the police will find out who did it," Kitty replied. "That's their job. And if there's any nonsense about the way the case is conducted, I'll get in touch with Rudd's superiors. We simply can't allow him to blunder about making stupid mistakes. You can back me up, Lewis. Perhaps we could get a few more people, like Major Barry, to sign an official complaint, especially if Rudd starts checking on everybody else's car in the village."

"He's no fool," Lewis Shand said quietly.

"Then he'll make sure he doesn't arrest the wrong person," was her reply.

It was pointless continuing with the conversation, he thought. Kitty had persuaded herself that everything was going to be all right and nothing was going to make her aware of the true nature of the situation, certainly not Hilary's part in it. Perhaps, having confessed her fears about Fulton's death and being reassured that they were groundless, she assumed the whole inquiry would have the same satisfactory outcome. It would all turn out for the best in the end, because she wished it to be so.

"I must go," he announced, getting to his feet.

"Must you?"

"There are one or two things I must do," he replied vaguely.

"Then I mustn't keep you any longer."

As they both stood, they were aware that the grey light outside the long windows had darkened and that the rain had begun to fall again, large drops that pattered against the glass, collecting and merging together into thin streams through which the outlines of the trees appeared broken and disjointed.

"Did you bring the car?" she asked him.

"No, I walked."

"Then I'll run you home in mine. You'll get soaked to the skin in this downpour. Wait while I get it and put on a coat."

She returned in a few minutes, buttoned up in her serviceable Burberry raincoat, her hair covered with a scarf.

"The car's outside," she told him.

They began the journey in silence. It wasn't until the cottage came into sight at the end of the drive that she referred to Patrick Vaughan and, in doing so, made him realise that she hadn't entirely dismissed his death from her mind.

"You know," she said unexpectedly, "I had as much motive for killing him as Hilary. Had that occurred to you, Lewis?"

He shifted uncomfortably on his seat.

"It had crossed my mind," he confessed.

"Do you believe I did it?"

"No, of course not, Kitty."

He was convinced of that now, although he didn't like to admit that at one time he had been as much afraid for her sake as for Hilary's.

She had drawn the car to a halt at the gates while she looked to see if the road was clear before taking the right-hand turn towards Chellfield and, as they waited, they both glanced sideways at the cottage, standing in its drenched garden, a dead air already about its closed windows as if the place had been uninhabited for months.

"I could have killed him at one stage," she continued. "I was desperate enough. And, after all, I had the opportunity, better perhaps than anyone else. I think that was in Rudd's mind when he called the morning after Patrick was found dead. Don't forget either that I had a motive."

"Rudd wouldn't have known that," he pointed out as they turned into the main road and headed for the village.

"No," she agreed.

"And anyway, Kitty, you could apply the same reasoning to myself. With Hilary away from home, I had just as much opportunity and equally as good a reason."

Her astonishment was genuine.

"To protect Hilary? Oh, Lewis, how absurd! Knowing you, it's quite out of the question."

In some ways, it was flattering, he supposed, to be thought incapable of murder, but he wasn't at all sure that Kitty's remark didn't imply a certain inability on his part to act decisively. Perhaps it was justified. To murder must take the kind of courage and sense of purpose which he had never possessed; an aspect of it that had never occurred to him before.

"What on earth did Rudd say to give you that idea?" Kitty was asking.

"Nothing much," he replied. "I was probably reading too much into his question. He asked me, of course, about the visit I paid on Vaughan the evening before he died; why I'd gone to see him, what was said, how long I'd stayed." Even now he couldn't bring himself to tell Kitty that he had suspected Rudd hadn't been convinced by the reason he had given for calling on Vaughan. "He seemed more concerned with trying to establish the time of death. He wanted to know in some detail what Vaughan had been doing before I arrived. I suppose he was trying to find out if Vaughan had settled down to do any writing after I'd left. It was rather an odd experience," he added. "I'd glanced at the desk when Vaughan first showed me into the sitting room and noticed what was lying on it, mainly because I was surprised to see how tidy it all was. But I hadn't realised until Rudd started asking me about it how much in fact I could remember. I suppose it's part of a policeman's skill to draw out that kind of information. There was a jar of pens and pencils, I remembered, and a red-covered notebook lying on top of the typewriter, that's how I knew he hadn't been doing any typing before I arrived, although I suppose he could have been writing up notes. It looked rather like a diary."

While he was speaking, they had drawn up outside the school-house and he opened the passenger door, adding, "Won't you come in for tea, Kitty?"

Her face looked up at him and he was shocked to see how old and tired it was. He felt guilty that he had talked too much in his eagerness to minimise his interview with Rudd and had wearied her. Perhaps after all he had maligned her by thinking that she had been too sanguine about the police inquiry into Vaughan's death. It had frightened her as much as it had frightened him, but he was still convinced that she had no real cause for concern, unlike Hilary. In Rudd's eyes, she had no motive, however desperate she had been when Vaughan had discovered her secret. And what a burden to carry round! She had spoken of Hilary's but Kitty's was far worse. It was six years since Fulton had died and in all that time she had never once disclosed her true feelings about his death, which had taken courage and the kind of resolution that he had only glimpsed before but never properly appreciated or admired.

"No thanks, Lewis, I ought to get home," she said shortly and drove off at once, leaving him standing at the gate in the rain, surprised at the abruptness of her departure.

A little way up the road, Kitty Fulton turned the car into the entrance to the council estate and put the hand brake on, although she left the engine running. The purse that contained her keys was in the glove compartment and she snatched at it impatiently, pulling at the catch, which for a few maddening moments refused to open. The bunch of household keys, thank God, were inside, including the spare Yale to the front door of the cottage. She had kept it as a precaution in case she ever needed to let herself into the gatehouse in Vaughan's absence, handing over to him only the one set.

What a fool she'd been to imagine she was in the clear! Patrick had told her that he made notes when he started a new novel—she remembered passing on the information to Rudd—but it had never crossed her mind that he might have recorded them in a permanent form. She had imagined they were the kind of quick memorandum that she herself made, jotted down on a scrap of paper and then thrown away.

But supposing, she thought, he had taken it into his head to keep a diary—Lewis had described the book he had seen as being like one —in which he had written down an account of their conversations together or, worse still, what he had found out about her anxieties over Richard's death? She no longer believed that he had killed himself. Lewis had assured her on that and she could see, now that she had brought her fears out into the open, that they were absurd, like shapes in the dark to a child that resolve themselves into quite ordinary objects once the light has been switched on. Thank God for Lewis's common sense, which had made her realise it.

But that wasn't the point. The frightening possibility remained that the notebook might contain information which, if read by the police, could give her a motive for murdering Vaughan. And once that was out, she could be subjected to the kind of cross-examination in which nothing would remain secret any longer. Richard's reputation could still be smeared by the suspicion of suicide. And what would the children think if they ever found out? Her own guilt at allowing herself to imagine the worst was more than she could bear.

There was a chance, however, that the notebook hadn't yet been found. Rudd had said that they had searched the cottage, looking for the name and address of Vaughan's next of kin, which had involved, she imagined, going through his letters and personal papers. But they'd hardly take the trouble to read through a whole notebook connected with his writing, though that didn't guarantee that they might not return at a later date to make a more thorough search. After all, Rudd still had the keys and could let himself into the place any time he liked.

She had exactly the same opportunity. Assuming the notebook was still in the cottage, on the desk or in one of the drawers, all she had to do was find it and scan through it quickly. It wasn't as if she need tamper with any evidence. If it contained nothing relating to herself or Richard, she could put it back where she found it. If, on the other hand, there was any damaging reference—well, then, she'd have to decide what to do about it when the time came, but she knew she'd already made the decision. She'd take the damned thing away with her and get rid of it. It was as simple as that.

Putting the car into gear, she drove back through the village towards Coppins, turning into the drive and parking the car just inside the entrance under the trees. With the key in her hand, she walked back the short distance to the little wicket gate that led into the front garden, noticing with disfavour how neglected the garden had become since Vaughan had lived there. She wouldn't let the gatehouse again, she decided. She's rather allow it to fall into ruin than run the risk of finding another tenant like Patrick. But perhaps that was a foolish decision. After all, it was a comfortable little cottage, which Lewis might like to live in after he'd retired and had to give up his house. She was sure he'd agree once she suggested it to him, because he'd see how very pleasant it would be for both of them to live so near to one another when they were too old to keep making the journey backwards and forwards to their separate houses.

The cottage smelt cold as she let herself in at the front door; a chill air poured down the narrow hall to meet her, and the sitting room seemed quite dark, its curtains not properly pulled open, so that the light could hardly enter through the small diamond panes. She drew tham back on their rods and, turning back towards the room, noticed, as Rudd had done, the dust on the furniture and the coffee stain on the carpet near the desk. The desk itself looked suspiciously empty, although the typewriter was still there and the mug of pens and pencils that Lewis had mentioned. There was, however, no sign of the manuscript or the notebook, but she noticed immediately, on its clear surface, the whitish rings where Patrick had stood a damp glass. The sight of them angered her. How dare he treat her possessions in such a cavalier fashion! Her own children, even when quite small, had been brought up to value good furniture. As it was, the whole top would have to be stripped down and repolished.

She began tugging open the drawers and searching through their contents but they contained nothing except packets of typing paper and a few odds and ends, a stapler, a spare typewriter ribbon, some plain sticky labels.

The only other place where it seemed likely Patrick might have put the notebook was the bookcase and she turned towards it, a little daunted by the task of searching through the shelves. As she did so, she heard a small click as the back door was opened, followed immediately afterwards by the sound of footsteps crossing the kitchen, and she realised, in a sudden agony of panic, that in that tiny place there was no time for her to get out of the room to the front door before her presence was discovered.

14

Rudd and Boyce returned to headquarters, both of them in a better mood, having stopped on the way for a pub lunch, and Rudd was further heartened to see, on entering his office, that the reports had started to come in and were already piling up on his desk. Normally he disliked paper work; it was the routine part of his job which he dealt with only because he had to, but that afternoon he welcomed it. It meant that the investigation which had started so inauspiciously in the rain on a roadside in the small hours of the morning had settled down to the normal, steady pattern of accumulating evidence, which he was accustomed to.

He flicked through the reports quickly. Stapleton's was there on the search of the area where Vaughan's body had been discovered as well as the one on the gatehouse garden; so, too, was Kyle's on the envelope found in Vaughan's pocket, neatly typed out this time instead of hastily written down on a scrap of paper. Rudd laid it on one side in readiness to add to it his own account of the interview with Vaughan's bank manager. Below it was a thicker pile of typewritten pages, clipped together at the corner, which, at a cursory glance, he saw was a detailed description of the room-by-room examination of the cottage itself, compiled, he suspected, by Marsh, judging by the vagaries of the punctuation and the official style of the few sentences that caught his eye. "Having completed our investigation of the lounge, we proceeded to the kitchen where . . ."

It looked like dull reading and he wished Kyle, who had a more literary bent, had written it, although he could hardly blame the young constable for passing up the task. Kyle already had his hands full with the report on the envelope and Vaughan's manuscript.

And that was all. There was nothing from Pardoe, but Rudd shuffled pages, wondering if it had become mixed up with the other reports. He was just reaching for the telephone to speak to the police surgeon when the door opened and Pardoe himself entered.

"Your report?" Rudd reminded him.

"I know, I know," Pardoe said irritably. "That's what I've come

173

about. In fact, I called to see you this morning but you were out." His tone of voice implied that the inspector had been away gallivanting on some private pleasure but Rudd was too used to his manner to take offense. "It's all written down here," he added, taking a cardboard folder from under his arm and slapping it down on the desk. "You can read it later but I wanted to see you in person about one or two details in it. Firstly, though, the clothes. They've gone up to forensic for the experts to examine them, although, in my opinion, it'll take time to get anything from them that's of any use to you. They were wet through and covered with mud. Next, the general injuries to the body —I still haven't had time to make a detailed examination but I can tell you this—all of them were caused by crushing—crushed pelvis, crushed spleen—well, I needn't go on. You've got the picture and you can read up the details for yourself."

"So it looks as if he went under the car," Rudd commented, half to himself.

"What you make of it is your business," Pardoe retorted. "I'm simply giving you the medical facts as I found them. But yes," he added, relenting a little, "I'd agree with you there. What I really came to talk to you about, however, is the head injury. It's down in the report but it makes such odd reading that I thought I'd better explain exactly what I mean so that there's no confusion."

"Odd?" Rudd repeated.

"In the sense that there's nothing I can say about it except for the wound itself. As I told you before, it's superficial; in fact, the skin's barely broken. It'd bled quite a lot but that's nothing to go by. Scalp wounds, even minor ones, often do. There was, by the way, no sign of any neck injuries, which is what I would have expected if he'd struck his head on the car and been flung onto the side of the road by the impact, if that's any help. And that ties in with what I found, or rather failed to find, in the wound itself—no flakes of paint, no rust, no wood splinters or particles of metal, or anything else, come to that. In other words, Vaughan didn't receive that injury by hitting his head on any part of a car or on some object that happened to be lying about at the time. In fact, I can't tell you what caused it except it must have been about an inch wide."

Rudd was silent for a moment. As far as he could see, Pardoe's statement could mean only one thing—Vaughan had been murdered. Any lingering doubt he might have had was no longer tenable in the face of the medical evidence he had just heard. For there seemed only one explanation that would fit it—someone had struck Vaughan over the back of the head and then had deliberately run him over as he lay on the ground before moving his body onto the verge. All the other theories put forward by Boyce, which had seemed too complicated to make proper sense, were now invalidated. The solution was much simpler than that. There had been no need to persuade Vaughan to get out of the car. He was already unconscious, knocked out by the blow on the head, which had probably happened within a few seconds after he had entered it. Or even in the cottage itself, Rudd thought, as the idea suddenly occurred to him. That theory would simplify the case even further. The problem lay in what weapon had been used that left no evidence in the wound, unless, of course . . .

"Something like a poker," he suggested to Pardoe, "or a metal bar of some kind, wrapped in plastic?"

"I came to the same conclusion myself," Pardoe replied. "It'd have to be the heavy-duty stuff, of course. The thin sheeting that's used for plastic bags might have torn, unless he used several layers of it."

And that confirmed his own suspicions, Rudd added to himself, that the murder had been premeditated. Whoever had killed Vaughan had gone already armed with the weapon. You don't expect to find a plastic-wrapped poker or iron bar ready to hand if you lose your temper and strike out at someone in the middle of a quarrel.

"Well, I'll get off," Pardoe was saying briskly.

"Before you go," Rudd put in, "there's something I'd like to discuss with you first."

"About the medical evidence?" Pardoe asked.

"No, but it's connected with the case. You've been in general practise, George. Have you ever had any experience of someone suffering from a nervous breakdown?"

"A few," Pardoe replied. "What is it you want to know?"

"The kind of behaviour pattern you might expect to find in the patient."

"That's a tall order," Pardoe said, perching himself on the edge of Rudd's desk. "The term itself covers a multitude of clinical symptoms—hysteria, depression, anxiety neurosis and so on. You name it and even doctors will slap the label 'nervous breakdown' on it. I'd need to know a lot more about the patient and the symptoms that were shown."

"A woman, now in her late twenties but probably nineteen or twenty when it happened. Intelligent. Conscientious. Mother died when she was about eleven. Anxious, overprotective father. Sheltered upbringing, I should imagine," Rudd said, describing Hilary Shand in a few brief sentences. "A broken love affair was probably the main cause, although she may have been studying too hard as well. I spoke to her doctor and he described her as being withdrawn and apathetic. There's a possibility of an attempted suicide as well."

"It sounds typical," Pardoe replied, "but I shouldn't rely too much on what her GP told you. If she came from the sort of sheltered background you describe, she may have an exaggerated respect for authority, which means she might have presented the apathetic symptoms not only to her family but to her doctor as well, who'd be a surrogate father in her eyes."

"You mean she'd hide any aggressive tendencies?" Rudd asked.

"Anxiety is often attributed to repressed anger," Pardoe pointed out.

"So the anger could have been released and turned outwards onto someone else?"

"It's possible."

"To the extent of murder?"

"That's possible, too, although from my limited experience it's more likely to take the form of a sudden rage that's directed towards one or more members of the family, followed by suicide. I've dealt with a couple of cases like that. One was a man who killed his wife and children and then himself. The other was a woman but the pattern was exactly the same. Interesting case, that," Pardoe continued, warming to the subject. "She wasn't much above five feet four but she managed to batter to death her father and her husband, both big men, with a spade; a bit like a modern, English Lizzie Borden. Amazing what strength even a small woman can produce when she's hysterical."

"Have you ever come across a case of a premeditated murder under those circumstances with no suicide following?"

"No, but that doesn't mean it couldn't happen," Pardoe replied. "The longer I'm in this business the less I seem to know. Anything's possible. As the North Country saying goes, 'There's nowt so queer as folks.' Is that all?" he added. "I've still got some tests to complete on that corpse of yours. Knowing you, you'll be clamouring for a detailed report in a couple of days' time."

"Yes. Sorry," Rudd said distractedly, his thoughts elsewhere.

After Pardoe had gone, he sat for a few minutes at his desk, mulling over the implications of what Pardoe had told him before sending for Boyce, who listened in silence to the summary of the medical evidence and Rudd's explanation of the facts.

"I agree it's a better theory than the one I came up with," he admitted when the inspector had finished. "But it still doesn't quite add up."

"Why not?" Rudd asked quickly. He had hoped Boyce would point out any holes in it. It was one of the reasons why they worked so successfully together.

"Well, for a start, why did Vaughan get dressed again? If the murderer knocked him out, as you now think, in the cottage, why wait for him to get changed out of his dressing gown and slippers?"

The same thought had occurred to Rudd as he had been explaining his theory to the sergeant, and the answer he'd come up with seemed as simple as the theory itself.

"Vaughan didn't get changed. I think whoever killed him changed the clothes himself. He'd have to if he was going to make it look like a road accident. Vaughan would hardly go wandering off up the road in the pouring rain wearing a dressing gown and slippers. But let's start at the beginning again, Tom. The murderer calls on Vaughan fairly late on Thursday evening. Vaughan's already had a bath—we've got Shand's evidence on that and I see no reason to disbelieve him—and from the look of the stuff lying about on the desk, he's settled down to work on his book. He's interrupted in the middle of it by a knock on the door and he lets the visitor in. It's someone he knows; it must have been because he invites the caller into the sitting room. What happens next is pure guesswork because we don't know exactly when Vaughan was attacked. It may have been straightaway. There may have been some discussion first, possibly about the threat that Vaughan was holding over his killer, because I still think blackmail was the motive. There's the missing notebook, which backs up that theory. Anyway, leaving that aside for the moment, the murderer knocks Vaughan out, strips off the dressing gown, which he throws down on the sofa, leaving the slippers on the floor beside it. It explains why they were found in the sitting room instead of the bedroom, which I said at the time seemed odd. He then dresses Vaughan in the clothes he'd been wearing earlier, which were probably still lying about, adding the raincoat and boots to make it look as if Vaughan had got ready to go out and, as a final touch, slips that letter into his coat pocket. It was probably on the desk, ready for posting, though I think Vaughan didn't intend mailing it until the following day. The envelope itself backs up that theory. Kyle found only two clear prints on it, which suggests that the murderer deliberately smudged the surface so we wouldn't find any evidence of it having been handled twice. Even if he'd been wearing gloves, we'd've still found the marks. As it was, he hoped we'd think it was smeared by contact with Vaughan's pocket, a clever touch, that.

"The rest is comparatively plain sailing. He carries Vaughan out to his car, which he'd probably left parked behind the cottage where it wouldn't have been seen, having first taken the notebook, which was either on the desk or in one of the drawers. It could have been about this time that Hilary Shand drove past. She spoke of seeing a light on at the back."

"So she's definitely out of the running as a suspect?" Boyce put in.

"Not necessarily. I deliberately said 'could have been.' At the moment, I'm simply summarising the evidence as we have it, assuming everyone's innocent, including her, Shand and Mrs. Fulton. But that doesn't mean that any three of them couldn't have done it, including someone else whose name hasn't yet cropped up. But they can't all be guilty and if we assume one person's guilt, it stands to reason that any statements made by the others must have some truth in them. We can look at the individual cases later, including Hilary Shand's. It's possible she could have murdered Vaughan for the reason we've already discussed. I asked Pardoe about nervous breakdowns and he made it clear that there's no cut-and-dried behaviour pattern. Cotty may have seen her as apathetic but that doesn't mean she couldn't have behaved hysterically or even violently at times, an aspect of her symptoms that she might have repressed in front of Cotty or even Shand. Given that possibility, she can't be dismissed from the case."

"Wouldn't she have found it difficult enough to change Vaughan's clothes, let alone get him outside and into a car?" Boyce asked. "He'd be unconscious and a dead weight."

"Vaughan wasn't a very big man and besides it's surprising what a determined woman can do when she has to. Pardoe pointed that out to me. She's strong, too, in spite of the fragile air. She managed to lug quite a heavy box of books out of her car while I was at the shop. But I'd rather leave all that on one side for the moment, Tom, and get back to the broader issues. The murderer, whoever he or she was, had got Vaughan in the car. The rest, as I've said, was relatively easy. All he had to do was drive a little way up the road, dump Vaughan, run over him, causing the crushing injuries that Pardoe spoke of, and move the body onto the grass verge before faking the skid marks, which, as I pointed out at the time, could have been made by someone nervous about driving too fast on a wet surface; and that could fit any one of them, Mrs. Fulton, Hilary Shand or Shand himself. None of them struck me as the daredevil kind who'd risk slamming on the brakes at fifty miles an hour."

"There's one thing you've forgotten," Boyce interjected, "and that's the telephone calls."

"I know," Rudd replied with a hint of his former irritability. "I was coming to those. I still don't see why any of the three of them, or anyone else come to that, should go to the trouble of ringing up Cotty and Neave. That part still doesn't make a lot of sense. I know it adds a touch of authenticity to the faked accident and that could have been the reasoning behind it, but it would have been a damned sight more intelligent to leave the body there to be found later the next day. By then the skid marks might have been obliterated and we wouldn't have been able to establish the time of death so precisely. After all, it was perfectly feasible that the driver involved could have panicked and simply driven off without reporting it, as in any other hit-and-run accident. Like the skid marks and the letter planted on Vaughan, it was a mistake which I'm surprised the murderer made. The rest of the crime was carefully planned, with very little left behind in the way of evidence; certainly not in the cottage. There was no indication that Vaughan had been knocked out first. From the look of it, I'd assumed he'd walked out of the place."

"There was one thing," Boyce pointed out. "I don't know if you noticed it. I did, but I didn't think all that much of it at the time—that stain which looked like coffee on the carpet by the desk."

Rudd, who had forgotten it, looked across at Boyce sharply. "You think it could have been blood?"

The sergeant shrugged.

"I don't know, but if that's where Vaughan fell after being knocked out, it's possible the head injury bled a little onto the carpet before the murderer realised what was happening. A quick wipe with a damp cloth would have got rid of a lot of it but still left a stain. Forensic will be able to tell from the fibres."

"You were there when the sitting room was searched," Rudd said. "Who examined the carpet?"

Boyce looked uncomfortable.

"I'm not sure," he replied, sounding on the defensive. "I know I was going through the desk and parcelling up any stuff that looked likely as evidence. Kyle and Marsh checked the rest of the room." He nodded towards the papers lying in front of the inspector. "It'll probably be in their report."

Rudd picked up the sheets and turned the pages rapidly. At least Marsh had had the sense to subdivide the statement under headings so that he didn't have to scan the whole bloody lot before he found the relevant section. There was a great deal under "Lounge" but no mention of the stain on the carpet apart from the laconic comment that it was there; nothing, in fact, to suggest that either he or Kyle had checked to see if it was still damp or that it might have any importance to the investigation.

"They were tired." Boyce offered the remark hesitantly, and then, seeing the inspector's expression, wished he had kept his mouth shut.

"That's no excuse," Rudd snapped. "We were all bloody tired."

He was angry as much with himself and Boyce as with the two constables. Someone should have kept a tighter control over the search, if not himself then the sergeant; it was their joint responsibility, although he realised that the ultimate blame could be laid only at his door. He himself should have pointed out the stain and made it clear that he wanted it examined. Instead, he had let his glance pass over it before dismissing it from his mind. At least Boyce had remembered it and had had the sense to remind him of it.

This realisation only increased his exasperation, and, as he continued to scan the report, running his eyes down the subdivisions, "Bedroom," "Kitchen," "Garage," he was further infuriated by Marsh's punctuation. In God's name, hadn't anybody taught him the proper use of the apostrophe? One sentence in particular caught his attention: "The garage doors were locked but, having acquired the key from Sergeant Boyce, we proceeded to examine it's interior."

Boyce, who was watching the inspector's face closely, hardly daring to move on the uncomfortable wooden chair on the far side of the desk, saw his expression go stony and waited, breath held, for the outburst. But when he spoke, Rudd's voice was quiet and formally polite, a sign, the sergeant realised, of worse to come.

"Would you ask Marsh and Kyle to come and see me?" he said, and Boyce retreated hastily, leaving Rudd staring down at the last page of the report.

They entered awkwardly, standing stiffly to attention in front of the desk, and, from the fixed glaze about their eyes, concentrated on a point on the wall behind Rudd's head. It was obvious that Boyce had warned them what to expect. He stood a little to one side of them, as if disassociating himself from whatever further error they had committed, which Rudd had found in the final section of their statement.

"Who searched the garage?" Rudd asked, leaning back in his chair while he surveyed the pair of them.

The two men exchanged sideways glances, the rest of their features remaining immobile.

"I did, sir." It was Kyle who spoke, and for a second his pleasant, nondescript face took on the guilty, frightened look of a schoolboy hauled up in front of the headmaster.

Rudd turned his attention to the other constable, a heavier built young man whose full lower jaw gave him a stolid, obstinate look.

"What were you doing, Marsh?"

Marsh's eyes didn't move from the spot behind the inspector's head.

"I was checking the kitchen, sir." He paused, and then added in a sudden rush of words, "But I did go out with Detective Constable Kyle when the garage was first unlocked. We had a look inside and decided that, as there wasn't much in there except for a few odds and ends, it didn't need the two of us to turn it over."

It was extraordinary, Rudd thought, that on paper Marsh should show such an exasperating talent for officialese when his speech betrayed none of the same jargon, even when faced with an irate detective inspector. Or perhaps sheer nerves and the compulsion for confession had reduced him to his natural vocabulary. It was clear, too, that he was anxious to accept part of whatever blame was about to fall and not let it all descend on Kyle, a point in Marsh's favour, which, despite himself, made Rudd more kindly disposed to the heavy-jawed and humourless constable.

"Did you take a look at the garage?" Rudd asked, turning unexpectedly to Boyce, who, caught unawares, replied too quickly.

"No, sir. If you remember, I left the search early to check Mrs. Fulton's car."

True enough, Rudd admitted to himself, and added silently that for this, too, he was entirely to blame. He had wanted too much to be accomplished too quickly, always a bad mistake in any investigation. Boyce had had enough on his hands with the search, without the added burden of extra duties. As for Kyle—well, one look at his face was enough to tell Rudd what kind of pressure he had been subjected to. Not only had he taken part in the search, but he had been responsible for examining the envelope found in Vaughan's pocket and reading his manuscript as well. It had been too much to expect of him and the man looked ready to drop in his tracks, his hands, held at the regulation distance from the seams of his trousers, visibly trembling.

"So none of you thought to have a look at Vaughan's car while you were at it?"

The dumbfounded silence that followed gave him the answer.

"Right!" he said with official curtness. "Then that'll have to be done straightaway. You two, wait for me downstairs"—addressing the constables—"and, Sergeant, I'd like a word alone with you."

As Marsh and Kyle withdrew, Rudd added in a more human voice, indicating the chair, "For God's sake, sit down, Tom. You look shaken rigid."

"I am," Boyce confessed. "It didn't cross my mind . . ."

"It didn't cross mine either," Rudd interrupted. But it should have done, his voice implied. "But let's leave the recriminations aside for the moment. The point is, if I'm right, we've been wasting our time checking up on car-hire firms and garages. You'd better pull Barney and Roper off that at once. If I'm wrong, we can put them back on the job on Monday, but I'm pretty damned sure it won't be necessary. Vaughan was run over by his own car, in his own garage. It's as simple as that. All the killer had to do was move his body afterwards a few hundred yards up the road before dumping it and faking the skid marks."

"Using Vaughan's own car?" Boyce asked.

"Probably. We'll know that when we've checked the wheelbase. It could account, too, for the fact that he didn't dare drive too fast. It was a car he wasn't used to and he wouldn't know how the brakes would react to being slammed on suddenly. Once he'd got rid of the body, he had simply to return Vaughan's car and collect his own before driving to the Cross to make those phone calls. At least, that's what I assume happened. He wouldn't dare risk returning Vaughan's car later because he must have guessed that Cotty and Neave would turn up shortly afterwards and he had to make sure he was safely off the road and out of sight before they arrived. But you realise what this means, Tom?"

"They're all back in the running."

"Exactly. Shand, his daughter and Kitty Fulton; any one of them could have done it, besides any other of Vaughan's friends and acquaintances. I'll check at the desk as we go downstairs to see if Stella Maxton's phoned that list through yet. While I'm doing it, will you alert the breakdown team that they'll probably be needed to tow Vaughan's car back here? We'll take a look at it ourselves first, just to make sure we're not letting another theory run away with us."

"Right," Boyce said, and as they left the office, he added, "I take it Marsh and Kyle are coming with us?"

"Yes, they can make themselves useful jacking up the car," Rudd replied promptly.

There was no message from Stella Maxton, Rudd discovered when he asked the duty sergeant. It was a damned nuisance now that the rest of the case was shaping up so satisfactorily, but it couldn't be helped. Nor could the hang-dog expressions of the two constables who were waiting uneasily downstairs. Rudd put them into the back of the car, where they sat in silence during the drive to Chellfield. Rudd and Boyce hardly spoke either and the only sound for much of the journey was the steady ticking rhythm of the wipers as they swept the windscreen free of the rain, now falling heavily once again.

"Park round the back out of sight," Rudd told Boyce as they turned into the gates of Coppins. "I don't want it known what we're up to."

The sergeant eased the car through the opening that led into the garden behind the cottage and drew up in the narrow gap alongside the garage where the overhanging bushes and trees screened it from both the drive and the road. They all got out, Rudd feeling in his pocket for the bunch of keys that Boyce had found hanging in the kitchen on the night the cottage was searched, and, as he unfastened the padlock and removed it from its hasp, Kyle and Marsh, with the eagerness of men anxious to be seen doing their duty, opened back the double doors.

Rudd stepped inside. As Marsh had said, there wasn't much in the garage apart from some old tins of paint on a shelf and a few gardening tools propped up in a corner. And the car itself, of course. It was a battered grey Vauxhall, with a dented boot and a rim of rust running round the edge of the bodywork. Rudd peered in at the driver's window, taking care not to touch anything. The interior was empty, although he noticed the ashtray was full of cigarette stubs, some of which had fallen out and lay scattered about on the floor.

He turned and beckoned to the two constables, who stepped forward smartly.

"You know the drill," he told them. "Jack it up and then Sergeant Boyce'll have a look under it. We'll test it for prints later at headquarters if we need to, but meanwhile I don't want your dabs all over it. Understood?"

Rudd and Boyce stood watching as Marsh and Kyle took off their coats and, using the jacks they had brought with them, raised the car off the garage floor. When they had finished, Boyce bent down to peer under it, and then, with a resigned shrug, removed his own jacket and, spreading out an old rug that he'd had the foresight to supply himself with, lay down full length on his back and wriggled cautiously backwards and forwards until the upper part of his body was underneath the chassis.

For a moment there was silence, and then Rudd heard him give a grunt of satisfaction, his legs began to struggle once more and he slowly re-emerged, the inspector helping him to his feet.

"Found anything?" Rudd asked eagerly, unable to conceal his impatience.

Boyce grinned.

"Enough," he replied, opening his hand to reveal what was in it. It wasn't much but, as Boyce had said, it was sufficient. On his palm lay a few pieces of hard mud and a circular ring of metal broken open where the fastening should have been.

"Exhaust clip," Boyce said succinctly.

"I know that," Rudd replied, a little exasperated by the sergeant's habit, which he had noticed before, of explaining the obvious. He turned to address Kyle and Marsh: "Wait in the car, will you? I'll give you a shout when I need you."

As they walked off, Boyce continued, "And that's not all. Apart from the clip and the lumps of mud which must have been jolted off at the impact, there's some scraps of plastic caught up underneath the chassis as well. I didn't remove them. I thought forensic would want to have a look at them first."

"Plastic?" Rudd repeated. He was silent for a few moments until he heard the car doors close and he knew the constables were out of earshot, then he added, "Well, we know now how Vaughan was killed. He was carried out unconscious from the cottage, laid down crossways on the garage floor, wrapped in plastic sheeting, probably so that no oil would drip onto his clothing, and then the murderer simply drove the car over him, which would account for the crushing injuries that Pardoe found. The rest of it, dumping the body and faking the skid marks, was as I've already described. Get through on the car radio, will you, Tom? I want the breakdown team out here straightaway. And while you're at it, check again to see if Stella Maxton's phoned that list in yet. We may need it."

He broke off suddenly, signalling to Boyce to keep silent, and, as they both listened, they heard the sound of a car approaching, the engine changing note as the speed was reduced and the gears re-engaged down into second. Wheels crunched on the gravel of the drive and the noise of the engine died, to be followed a few seconds later by the sound of a door slamming and determined footsteps walking hurriedly away.

"Someone's going round to the front of the cottage," Boyce said in a whisper.

"And letting themselves in by the sound of it," Rudd added as the front door clicked shut. "We'll give whoever it is a couple of minutes start and then I think I'll surprise them."

With the back door key in his hand, he crossed the concrete apron and narrow strip of lawn and, mounting the step, inserted the key in the lock and turned it softly before stepping inside the kitchen. As he did so, he was aware of subdued noises coming from the sitting room which were immediately silenced. Whoever was there had heard him enter. It robbed him of the element of surprise, but in that doll-sized cottage it could hardly be avoided, and with a few rapid strides he crossed to the door that led into the hall before the intruder could slip away by the same route he had entered.

Or rather she, Rudd corrected himself, for he had already guessed the identity of the person. There was only one candidate who was likely to possess a key to the cottage and that was Mrs. Fulton, so it came as no surprise to him, as he opened the door into the sitting room, to find her standing beside the bookshelves, looking guilty and frightened, although he was careful to assume an expression of shocked bewilderment at finding her there.

"Mrs. Fulton!" he began but she over-rode him.

"I thought, as I was passing, that I'd check the cottage," she explained, speaking too quickly in her eagerness to justify herself. "Patrick had borrowed one or two books which I thought I'd take back with me."

"And some papers, too?" Rudd suggested pleasantly, moving forward into the room and nodding toward the desk, whose half-open drawers suggested that she had already searched through those. He was smiling as he spoke. The pleasure of witnessing her alarm and consternation more than made up for any lingering sense of grievance he might feel towards her for her treatment of him at their last meeting. The tables were now very neatly turned and it was he who had the advantage. But he was equally gratified, and also amused, to see how quickly she recovered her poise. Harry Acton had been right. She was a courageous, strong-minded woman.

"I was looking for Patrick's copy of the lease," she replied. Her voice was brisk, no longer anxious or overeager. It was the woman of affairs who was speaking now, crisp and to the point. "I suppose you didn't find it yourself when you searched the cottage? My solicitor may need it when he deals with the tenancy."

Top marks for nerve, Rudd thought, and sheer, bloody audacity. For an excuse thought up on the spur of the moment, it had the ring of authenticity.

"It may be in Mr. Vaughan's files," Rudd replied, as if he had

believed every word of what she had said. "We took them away with
us. I'll get my sergeant to go through them and return the lease to you
if it can be found."

"Thank you," she replied and gave him a small, gracious bow of
the head, acknowledging his co-operation but still too *de haut en bas*
to be entirely to his liking, and he couldn't resist asking, "Have you
finished, Mrs. Fulton? Or is there anything else you'd like to look for
while you're here?"

It was said too politely for her to object to the remark, although
its implications weren't lost on her. He saw her tighten her lips as she
replied, a cold edge to her voice, "No, thank you, Inspector. There is
nothing else."

Neither of them spoke as he escorted her out of the cottage and
through the front garden to where her car was parked in the drive. He
even stood waiting in the rain as she drove away, hoping that the
implications of that weren't lost on her either. He was seeing her off
the premises in exactly the same way that she had shown him the front
door of Coppins.

Tit for tat, he thought. It was a bit childish but all the same he
was in a jaunty, confident mood as he rejoined Boyce.

"That was Mrs. Fulton," he explained.

"I know," Boyce replied. "I saw her car go past. What was she
doing in the cottage?"

"My guess is she was looking for Vaughan's notebook," Rudd
replied cheerfully.

"And you let her go?" Boyce sounded shocked.

"There was no reason to detain her."

"But if she was searching for the notebook, it could mean she
had a motive for murdering Vaughan," Boyce protested. "You said
yourself it could tie in with the blackmail angle. He must have known
something about her which she was afraid he'd written down . . ."

"That's the whole point, Tom," Rudd put in. "She was *looking*
for it. But we know that whoever killed Vaughan must have taken it.
So it can't be her. She's one suspect we can definitely cross off the
list."

"Well, yes, I suppose so," Boyce agreed, but he still didn't
sound too sure. "All the same, she could have had a reason for
wanting Vaughan dead."

"Of course she had," Rudd agreed. "Vaughan must have found
out something about her she didn't want generally known. But we're
not likely to find out now what it is. The secret's safe."

And was likely to remain so, he added to himself. In many ways he wasn't sorry, although natural curiosity made him wonder what it was. Certainly it was nothing that Harry Acton had discovered in the twenty years he had followed the Fultons round the county reporting on their affairs—but Vaughan had evidently managed to worm it out of her in the few months he had been in the village, which suggested that Vaughan was a damned sight more clever and subtle than Acton, and Acton was no fool.

"Did you get in touch with headquarters?" he continued, getting back to the job at hand.

"Yes, the breakdown team's on its way," Boyce replied. "And that list you wanted has come in, too." He searched his pockets and produced a scrap of paper. "I copied the names and addresses down. There's about six in all. Sorry about the handwriting," he added as he handed it over to the inspector. "It's a bit of a scrawl but I think you can just about make it out."

Rudd read it through quickly. At first glance, none of the names meant anything to him. They were mostly women's, although there was one man's, a Rev. Charles Ainsworth, retired, he gathered from the abbreviated form of the word that Boyce had scribbled down in brackets after it. Nor were any of the addresses familiar either, all of which, with one exception, were in Weldon. It was this exception that caught his attention and reminded him briefly of another address he had heard somewhere else during the investigation, a mere scrap of information that for a moment he couldn't place.

At the same time, the name connected with it rang a faint bell at the back of his mind. Mrs. Jean Doulton. Not a very unusual name and yet he was sure he had heard it before. And then he remembered where: in the bookshop, of course. Stella Maxton had mentioned it when she had referred to the customer Rudd had passed briefly in the entrance, the pleasant, middle-aged woman who had smiled at him as he held the door open for her.

And, as he remembered her face and voice, he was able at last to place the other face and voice which had eluded him, and, with that recollection, the last pieces dropped into place.

What a fool he'd been not to see it before! It had been in front of him all the time in Vaughan's manuscript, as well as the notes that Kyle had made; down there in black and white for any idiot to read who had one iota of imagination.

Boyce, who had seen his change of expression, asked excitedly, "You've found something?"

"Vaughan's murderer," Rudd replied simply, and told him.

For a moment, Boyce looked at him with disbelief.

"But that's not possible!" he said at last.

"It's got to be," Rudd replied. "It's the only answer that makes any sense of all the evidence. For the time being we can only guess at the motive, although I've got a damned good idea why Vaughan had to be killed. But come on, Tom. We're not home yet. There's a phone call I've got to make first and a very short visit to pay on a lady called Mrs. Doulton. After that, it ought to be in the bag."

He strode over to the car, where Kyle and Marsh were still sitting out of the rain, and jerked open the rear door.

"Out!" he told them briskly. "There's a breakdown team on the way. You can hang on here and give them a hand to get Vaughan's car towed away when they arrive. You'll have to beg a lift off them as well or find your own way back by bus. Sergeant Boyce and I are taking the car. And while you're waiting, you can make yourselves useful by collecting up some of the fibres from that stain on the sitting-room carpet. The back door's open. Make sure you lock the place up afterwards. Here are the keys."

They scrambled out, he and Boyce taking their seats in the front of the car, and as the sergeant backed and turned into the drive, Rudd caught a final glimpse of them, two subdued and huddled figures standing in the rain, too bewildered by the sudden turn of events to seek shelter inside the cottage, although, in his present mood of jubilation, Rudd found it difficult to feel much sympathy for either of them.

15

Boyce stayed in the car while Rudd made the two calls. For the first, there didn't seem any point in getting out of the car into the rain. It was a phone call and they drove into Weldon to the police station so that Rudd could make it in the privacy of one of the offices. After about five minutes, he emerged, looking pleased.

"That's one bit of evidence nicely parcelled up," he remarked as he got back into the car. "But the last part isn't going to be so easy, I'm afraid."

They drove next to a village on the outskirts of Weldon and this time Rudd asked Boyce to remain behind.

"I don't want the visit to look too official," he explained.

They had parked at the roadside opposite a large, white-painted house, and the sergeant, leaning forward to peer curiously after the inspector, watched him walk up the drive and knock at the front door. A woman opened it. There was a brief conversation on the porch and then the woman stood aside to allow Rudd to enter. They both disappeared inside and the front door was closed.

Boyce sat back, prepared for a long wait.

In fact, the visit took less time than he had expected. In just over ten minutes the front door opened again and the inspector came out, accompanied by the woman. After a few final words, they parted and Rudd began walking rapidly towards the car.

"Tricky," he said briefly, anticipating Boyce's question, as he got into the front passenger seat. "But I don't think I showed my hand. I hope to God I didn't. If I did, she's only got to make one phone call and the cat's out of the bag. Drive back to Chellfield, Tom. You know where we're going next. I'll fill you in with the details on the way."

It had stopped raining by the time they reached the village and a pale sun was struggling to shine through the last remnants of cloud that were being whisked away by a rising wind. It reflected back from the puddles and the wet surfaces of the road and pavements, giving them a thin, silvery dazzle that was painful to the eyes.

Cotty's Humber was standing in the driveway when they arrived, parked this time in front of the house so that Boyce was forced to take his car round to the side and leave it opposite the surgery entrance. As they got out, Cotty himself appeared at the glass door leading into the waiting room, as if he had heard the car and had come to meet them. He gestured to them to enter and they followed him into his office, leaving damp footprints from the gravel across the immaculate floors.

"Well?" he said brusquely, turning to face them. He had taken his place behind the desk and Rudd thought how ill he looked, his skin grey and papery dry, his lips drawn tight with that look of deep disapproval that Rudd had seen on his face the night Vaughan's body was discovered.

As if by common consent, all three remained standing. Then Rudd glanced briefly at Boyce, who, already prepared, stepped forward and spoke the official words of caution.

"Edwin Cotty, you are not obliged to say anything unless you wish to do so, but anything you say may be put into writing and given in evidence."

Cotty remained impassive through this recital. He was leaning forward to listen, his hands resting on the desk, only the chalky whiteness of his knuckles betraying any sign of tension. Once Boyce had finished, he stood upright and looked directly at Rudd.

"You know, of course, how I did it." It was said in the same abrupt voice that Rudd had heard before, a mere stating of the facts. All the same, Rudd felt that something more was needed than a simple affirmation.

"Yes, we do, Dr. Cotty. I've checked with the supervisor at Weldon telephone exchange this afternoon. You asked for an alarm call to be made to your number at one A.M. on the morning Vaughan was killed. The exchange keeps records of such calls so it was easy enough to verify that fact. I think you altered your own clock so that when the phone rang and woke up your wife, as you knew it would, the time appeared to be one-thirty. You left the house, telling her that you'd received a message calling you out to an accident but, of course, Vaughan was then still alive. You knew he kept late hours, probably because you'd driven past the gatehouse late at night yourself visiting patients and had seen the lights were still on in the sitting room. You drove to the cottage and Vaughan let you into the sitting room, where you knocked him unconscious. You then carried him into the garage and laid him on the floor, using his own car to run over him. We found the evidence of that this afternoon. Still using Vaughan's car, you transferred his body to the grass verge, arranging it to appear he'd been knocked down and flung sideways by the impact. Afterwards you faked the skid marks, drove back to the cottage and returned Vaughan's car to the garage, locking it up and replacing the keys where you'd found them in the kitchen. Driving your own car this time, which you'd left hidden behind the cottage, you then went back along the road to the Cross where you telephoned Neave, calling him out to the supposed accident and pretending, when he arrived and found you already examining Vaughan's body, that you'd also received a similar phone call a few minutes earlier."

All the time he was speaking, Rudd had been deliberately using his official, colourless voice that betrayed no emotion. Like Cotty, he was merely stating the facts. But his next remark was made in a more informal voice.

"For a long time, I couldn't understand why those calls were made. It seemed to me Vaughan's murderer would have been acting more intelligently if he'd left the body to be found later. Then, of course, I realised that they had to be made. They were crucial to your alibi, weren't they, Dr. Cotty? Or, at least, the one was that you made to Neave. It placed the murder at just before one-thirty when, according to the time by your own clock, you were in bed and asleep before the phone woke you up. It also gave you a reason for leaving the house. No one is going to suspect a doctor who's called out to attend an emergency at that hour in the morning. Added to which, you had every reason to be at the scene when Neave arrived. It was very clever and well-planned." He saw Cotty give a small, tight-lipped smile. "But you made a few mistakes and they were enough to rouse Neave's suspicions."

"The skid marks," Cotty said testily.

"Yes, those," Rudd agreed.

"Neave's a fool."

The comment was snapped out as if Cotty could no longer contain his impatience.

It was revealing, Rudd thought. Neave, in Cotty's eyes, was a relatively inexperienced and uneducated local bobby who wouldn't notice the significance of the skid marks on the road or, even if he did, would be too much in awe of Cotty's professional and social standing to argue against the doctor's conclusion of accidental death. Cotty would have known, of course, that Neave would have to call out the local CID but, as Rudd had also discovered when he had called in at Weldon police station that afternoon, Cotty had acted on occasions as their police surgeon in other accident cases that had occurred in the district and was highly regarded by the force as an

efficient medical man who knew what he was talking about. He must
have counted on being able to persuade them also that Vaughan had
been killed in a road accident. They had very little experience of
murder and, once Vaughan's body was removed from the scene of the
supposed accident, any of the evidence would have been lost in the
mud and rain of that roadside verge. There wouldn't have been either
any need for the cottage to be searched, or at least not so thoroughly
as Kyle and Marsh, for all their omissions, had done, and the
significance of the dressing gown and slippers, not to mention the
missing notebook, would have gone unnoticed.

All along Cotty had relied on his own experience and intelligence
being better developed than any of the officers in charge of the case, a
form of intellectual snobbery that Rudd realised he should have been
aware of when he had read Vaughan's manuscript. Even if the initials
E.C. in Kyle's notes hadn't put him onto the truth then the character
of Eliot Charteris should have pointed it out to him. But he had been
too easily taken in by the comparison with Lewis Shand and the
relationship with Hester Stewart, otherwise Hilary Shand, to realise
that the character had been based not on one individual but two, and
that although Charteris shared many of Shand's characteristics, the
pedagogic use of language, for instance, and the similar interest in
local history, there had been other qualities about him such as the
stubbornness and the abrupt manner, the elitism and the sheer lack of
imagination that were more typical of Cotty than Shand.

And it was this prosaic, unimaginative side to Cotty's nature
which had caused him to make the other mistakes which Rudd
referred to now as he made his next remark.

"It wasn't only the skid marks, Dr. Cotty, though they started off
the whole inquiry. I assume, by the way, that you were nervous about
driving Vaughan's car, which you weren't used to." It seemed the
only explanation and the abrupt jerk of his head which Cotty gave at
this point seemed to confirm it. "There were other signs that
Vaughan's death wasn't an accident. The dressing gown and slippers,
for instance, which you left in the sitting room after you'd changed
Vaughan's clothes. You'd've done better to put them in the bathroom
or bedroom. That way, it would have looked as if Vaughan had got
himself dressed before going out. Then there was the letter which you
placed in his pocket. That was a mistake, too. The bank manager let
me see it. It was only a request for a new cheque book, hardly urgent
enough to send Vaughan out in the rain to post it at half-past one in
the morning, even though I suppose that's what you wanted us to
believe. Where was it? On the desk?"

"Yes," Cotty replied. "He'd left it lying by the typewriter."

"Near his notebook?"

"Yes."

His voice was dull now, the clipped edge to it gone, as if he were too exhausted to maintain the pose. For it was a pose, Rudd realised. Underneath that curt, brusque exterior, Cotty was a shy and lonely man but too proud to admit it even to himself.

"Which you took?"

"Yes. That was the whole purpose of the visit."

"How did he find out about you and Mrs. Doulton?"

Rudd already knew the answer, but he wanted to hear it from Cotty himself. Jean Doulton had said very little when he had interviewed her and Rudd hadn't dared to question her too far. She had merely stated that she had first seen Vaughan at the bookshop and that on a couple of occasions afterwards they had met in the street when he had invited her to have coffee with him. They had talked and she had found Patrick so interesting and pleasant. It was the old story of Vaughan's charm which Rudd had already heard from Stella Maxton and Kitty Fulton, even though he doubted if Jean Doulton had been aware of what Vaughan had been doing as they chatted so agreeably over the coffee cups.

She was, he had gathered from his own conversation with her, a widow who, on her husband's death four years before, had taken a job as housekeeper and companion to an elderly lady in Haddon; a lonely woman and a bit naïve, or at least a little gullible and too easily persuaded to talk about herself. She had talked with the same readiness to Rudd with the kind of honesty which assumes that if you are asked a question about yourself it is bad manners and socially offensive not to answer fully. To Vaughan she must have been easy prey.

Rudd had found introducing the subject of Dr. Cotty into the conversation trickier, though he had got round it by remarking as casually as he could that he believed Dr. Cotty, whom he had met in connection with Mr. Vaughan's accident, attended her employer, a fact that Mrs. Cotty herself had happened to mention in passing.

Yes, Jean Doulton had replied with the same lack of guile, Dr. Cotty paid regular visits to Mrs. Grayson, who had been a private patient of his for years. He was very kind and conscientious.

There had, however, been a heightening of her colour as she spoke his name and a flustered air about her, small signs which Rudd had pretended not to notice. But Vaughan must have put two and two together, as he had done, and come up with exactly the same answer.

He might also, he added to himself, have put a few more facts together a little sooner, but it wasn't until he had received Stella Maxton's list of names and addresses that he had been able to make the final connection between the woman whom he had seen so briefly in the doorway of the bookshop and the name of the village which, as he had remarked to Jean Doulton, Mrs. Cotty had spoken of when he had called on the doctor the first time and had found that he was out making a house call on a private patient.

The link was there; all it had needed was for him to remember those two separate meetings, one with Mrs. Cotty, the other with Jean Doulton—ironically, the two women in Cotty's life whom he loved and whom he had wanted so desperately to protect that he had murdered Vaughan in order to silence him.

Cotty was answering his question in the same exhausted voice and Rudd glanced sideways at Boyce, who, standing a little behind him, was discreetly jotting down the statement in his notebook.

". . . they met at the bookshop . . . became friendly. . . . I gather Vaughan realised . . . It wasn't Jean's fault . . . no idea she was being indiscreet . . ."

It was very much what Rudd had expected. There were no surprises until Cotty was reaching the end of his account.

"Vaughan telephoned me one evening to ask me over to the cottage for a drink. I refused. I didn't like the man enough to wish to be friendly with him and I was surprised that he should get in touch with me. I had met him only once before at Mrs. Fulton's, which I believe I've already mentioned. Apart from that occasion, we'd had no conversation, even though I'd seen him from time to time round the village. When I said I had no time for social visits, his manner changed, though he still kept up the pretence of being friendly. 'By the way,' he said, 'I've been talking to a friend of yours today, Jean Doulton. I believe you know her quite well. At least, that's the impression I got from her. She was quite coy when she spoke about you.' He then went on to say that, as a writer, he'd found the encounter very interesting. 'People fascinate me,' were his exact words. 'I suppose as a doctor you must find it much the same. They tell you private things about themselves which you write down in their case histories. For my part, I find a journal very useful. It's all raw material for the next book.' " Cotty paused and added, unnecessarily from Rudd's point of view, "It was blackmail, of course."

"Of course," Rudd agreed.

"But what on earth did he hope to get out of it?" Cotty's bewilderment seemed genuine. "At no point was money mentioned.

"I think Vaughan wanted power," Rudd replied. "He enjoyed the sensation. It was a kind of voyeurism as well."

It was the same comment he had made to Boyce about Eliot Charteris, the character in Vaughan's novel, and now, for the first time, he could see how it should have been applied to Vaughan himself. Vaughan hadn't had to look far to find that particular quirk of personality. It was a piece of self-revelation, probably made subconsciously, which as an outsider, not really accepted into the village, Vaughan had used against those whom he had despised and yet whose goodwill he had paradoxically wanted to obtain. Cotty had rejected him. So, too, possibly, in her own way, had Kitty Fulton. Lewis Shand also had doubtlessly shown his dislike, and Vaughan had got his own back on all of them.

"I realised if Vaughan talked there would be a scandal in the village which my wife would suffer from most." Cotty's eyes, their expression bleak, were fixed on Rudd. "You may not know this, Inspector, but she was dying of cancer. She had another year to live, according to the specialists. I loved her and wanted to prevent her from finding out about Jean, whom I had grown fond of during the time I'd been calling at Mrs. Grayson's house. I have been married too long and too happily to wish to live alone after my wife died but, had Vaughan not found out about the relationship, Jean and I would have waited two or three years before announcing our intention of marrying. That was the understanding between us and I think it would have been accepted without any gossip."

"Was dying?" Rudd repeated, echoing the words Cotty had used earlier in his statement.

The expression in Cotty's eyes changed. It was still cold, but behind the hard centre of the pupils some other emotion showed itself that Rudd could only describe as a kind of grim humour.

"Jean telephoned me after your visit this afternoon," he continued, deliberately ignoring the inspector's question. "Not to warn me. I don't think the full implications of the interview with you had occurred to her. She imagined you were inquiring into Vaughan's death and had called to see her because she knew him. But she felt I ought to know because I, too, had met him and had been called out to the so-called accident. She had no idea, of course, that it was murder, for which I was responsible. A few moments ago you mentioned the mistakes I made when I planned Vaughan's death and I must admit that, apart from the skid marks, their significance hadn't occurred to me. But I'm not so lacking in imagination that after Jean's telephone call I wasn't aware that you knew the truth. In fact, ever since you

called on me this morning to inquire about Hilary Shand, I've realise
that if she, or anyone else, was accused of Vaughan's murder,
would have to give myself up. So I have been prepared for some tim
now. When Jean phoned, I knew I had about half an hour before yo
arrived."

"But your wife . . ." Rudd broke in sharply, trying to brin
Cotty to the point.

Cotty turned back his stiff, white shirt cuff to look at his watch

"You're too late, Inspector. By this time, my wife will alread
be dead."

As he spoke, he moved towards the inner door that led directl
into the house and stood with his back to it. Rudd, who had intende
making a dash for it, hesitated and then remained where he was.
was a hopeless situation. Unless he was prepared to struggle wit
Cotty there was no way he could get out of the surgery except throug
the waiting room and that would be pointless. The front door of th
house was almost certainly locked. Besides, what could he do whe
he reached her? He had no medical skill and, if Cotty was speakin
the truth, it was too late for anyone to revive her.

He turned to Boyce. "Get an ambulance!" he ordered, and as th
sergeant lunged towards the desk to grab the telephone receiver an
dial the emergency services, Cotty resumed his statement in the sam
unemotional voice, standing bolt upright against the door as if h
were already in the dock giving evidence.

"She suffered no pain, Inspector. I can assure you on that. As
doctor, I had both the means and the knowledge to make certain sh
died more peacefully than she had lived for the last few months of he
life."

"It was still murder," Rudd snapped.

It was the first time Cotty showed any sign of reaction. His eye
blinked rapidly and his thin lips pressed tightly together.

"I prefer to think of it as euthanasia, a possibility which Eleano
and I had discussed together when she knew the cancer was terminal
And don't try to tell me I was breaking my Hippocratic oath!" Hi
voice rose sharply as if refuting Rudd's argument, even though th
inspector had said nothing. "You can't be naïve enough to imagine i
doesn't go on—the injection that's intended to kill the pain—th
doctor or nurse who gives it knows only too well the patient will die a
a result of it. Sometimes it's done with the knowledge and agreemen
of the patient. I had promised my wife I would do the same for he
when it became necessary. And when I knew you were on your way t

rest me, it seemed the only answer. She wouldn't have wanted to
ve knowing I would be going to prison."

"You told her?" Rudd asked incredulously.

The flicker of grim humour which Rudd had seen in Cotty's eyes
uched the corners of his mouth.

"Oh, hardly, Inspector! Credit me with more imagination than
at! I killed Vaughan in order that she wouldn't discover the truth.
o, I told her that I thought the time had come; she had been in pain
l last night and this morning. She accepted my decision."

"Yes," Rudd agreed. Remembering Eleanor Cotty's face, he
uld believe it, too. She had been too worn down by suffering to put
o any objection; or perhaps Cotty had been speaking the truth and
e had welcomed it. But he still couldn't get it out of his head that,
owever much Cotty had loved her, he had regarded her in the same
ay as Neave; that they were both, in their different ways, lesser
eople and that it was his decisions alone that finally mattered.

Boyce, who had replaced the telephone receiver, came across to
e inspector and murmured that the ambulance was on its way. As he
irned his head to listen, Rudd took his eyes off the doctor briefly, and
a that split second Cotty acted.

Afterwards, Rudd came to the conclusion that it was probably
nplanned and that Cotty's decision was a spur-of-the-moment
nprovisation prompted by God knows what wild hopes of escape.
ut in the flurry of the action no such thought crossed his mind. He
as aware only that Cotty had also turned and had opened the inner
oor, which he slammed shut behind him. By the time he and Boyce
ached it, he was already at the end of the hall.

At the same time, Rudd remembered how the cars were parked:
otty's at the front of the house, their own at the side entrance and
cing away from the drive. They'd have to turn the bloody thing
und before they could follow him.

"Out the other way!" he shouted to Boyce and ran towards the
aiting room. Behind him he could hear the sergeant swear under his
reath as his feet slipped on the polished floor.

"I'll drive," he added, clambering in behind the wheel. As he did
o, he caught a glimpse of Cotty's Humber turning out of the drive
to the road and speeding away towards the outskirts of the village.
e backed and turned his own car furiously, the engine screaming and
e wheels hurling gravel against the glass door of the surgery annex.
oyce, beside him, was flung against his shoulder and swore again.

"For Christ sake, watch what you're doing!"

Rudd ignored him. The decision to drive was as impulsive as

Cotty's sudden dash for freedom; why, he wasn't sure, although t
motives behind it he was also to examine later. After all, Boyce w
much the better driver, and, under normal circumstances, Ru
preferred him to take the wheel. Perhaps it was a need to assur
responsibility for that momentary inattention which had given Co
his chance.

The Humber was well ahead of them. Whatever nervousne
Cotty might have felt when he had driven Vaughan's car and made t
mistake of braking at too slow a speed, he wasn't showing it now.
was accelerating fast, hardly slowing up to take corners, even thou
he had, of course, the advantage of knowing the road and being al
to anticipate every bend and hazard. He had, also, the incentive
desperation on his side.

They passed Vaughan's cottage, but, at that speed, Rudd hard
noticed it. It was gone before he had time to register it properly exce
for a flash of white that was the garden gate and a brief glitter
sunlight reflected back from the front windows. He was more awa
of the stretch of road beyond it, which, with its wide grass verges a
high hedges, was familiar to him. It was here that Vaughan's bo
had been discovered, lying huddled up in the rain, and it struck t
inspector as ironic that Cotty should have chosen the same route f
his attempted escape.

A crossroads came into view: a small collection of hous
grouped round a triangular piece of grass on which stood a telepho
kiosk and a pillar box—the Cross, where Cotty had put through t
call to Neave and where Vaughan was supposed to be heading to p
the letter on the night he was murdered.

The Humber was slowing down now to make the left-hand tur
and as Rudd, a few seconds behind him, braked and changed gear,
said quickly to Boyce, "There's a map under the dashboard. Try
find out where he's making for."

Boyce scrabbled to find it and opened it awkwardly as the
took the turning, rocking on its wheels.

"There's a village called Benton coming up next. After that,
could be making for the main road. He'll join it at Meacham. And
God's sake, take it easy. There's an S bend soon and then a brid
over a river."

As he spoke, they both came into sight. The ground had begun
rise behind hedges and, as they topped the hill, the view opened
Below them they could see the road bending away and the black a
white painted arrows on the roadside signboard warning of
dangerous corner. Just beyond that, on the final steep curve, the ro

narrowed into a bridge with metal railings crossing over a river that was running full and fast after the rain, its surface, broken and chopped by the wind, fracturing and throwing back the sunlight in a dazzling confusion.

It caught Rudd straight in the eyes and, momentarily blinded, he braked violently, sending the car swerving across the road. By the time he had got it under control, it was too late.

The Humber had taken the first part of the bend and was approaching the second. There were no hedges here, presumably to give drivers a clear view of the bridge and the oncoming traffic. Only a grass verge and a narrow strip of low-lying meadow separated the road from the water.

It was at this point that Cotty must have accelerated, for, as they watched, they saw the car leap the few intervening yards before plunging into the river in a great roar and crash of falling metal and flying spray.

It sank quickly, the water pouring in through the windows, which Cotty must have opened in readiness for this final act. When they scrambled out of their own car and ran towards the bank, the turbulence had already subsided and the Humber lay quietly, its black roof just protruding above the surface, the current eddying over it.

Boyce had begun to strop off his jacket, but Rudd laid a hand on his arm.

"It's all over, Tom," he told him quietly. "You'll never get him out in time."

Besides, he added to himself, what was the point? Cotty had probably died in that first impact as the car hit the water or was so terribly injured that Boyce would do no good in trying to drag him free.

There was a kind of justice about it, too, that Rudd knew Cotty would appreciate. Aware of the futility of escape, he must have decided sometime during that crazy journey to take the other way out and he had arranged his own death with the same attention to detail that he had applied to Vaughan's. Only this time he had been careful to make no mistakes.

"Do you want me to get through to headquarters?" Boyce asked. He, too, had realised the futility of a rescue attempt and had shrugged on his jacket again.

"Yes," Rudd replied. "Get the breakdown team out here and a couple of frogmen. They'll need to get the lifting gear under the chassis."

It was nearly five o'clock before they finally raised the car from the river. Rudd stood by watching. The lights that had been set up illuminated the scene in much the same way that they had lit up the verge where Vaughan's body had been found, only this time they shone onto water and the thin, bare branches of the willow trees that lined the bank.

It was the same team of men, too, that had been with him on the first occasion: Kyle and Marsh, Pardoe, McCullum and the others, waiting with him to move forward as soon as the breakdown men had finished, chafing their hands together in the cold, damp wind.

The Humber rose slowly, as if reluctant to leave the water which streamed out of it as it swung sideways onto the bank. Inside it Rudd could see a head bent forward across the wheel, the grey hair scattered and the high-nosed profile resting against the rim. But he didn't look too closely.

He supposed he'd get his promotion. Reading between the lines of what Davies had said to him when he had reported in to the superintendent, it looked likely. There'd have to be an inquiry into Cotty's death, of course, but Davies had added, "Don't worry too much about that. It'll be all right. Take my word for it."

The odd thing was it no longer seemed to matter so much, although he supposed that, in time, he'd see it in a different light. He was, after all, a professional copper and for that reason official reward and recognition were important to him.

But it would take much longer, he realised, to come to terms with that momentary error of judgement when he had taken charge of the car instead of letting Boyce drive, a lapse of self-awareness into his own limitations, as he now recognised.

Meanwhile there was this case to finish, and as Cotty's car was set down on its wheels, he moved forward briskly to take charge.

"Right! Kyle and Marsh, get those warning signs shifted so that the ambulance can move forward. McCullum, you'd better take what shots you need before Pardoe takes over. And Boyce, as soon as they've finished, I'd like you to take a look at the car itself."

ABOUT THE AUTHOR

JUNE THOMSON's previous Inspector Rudd novels include *The Habit of Loving*, *A Question of Identity*, *Death Cap*, *Case Closed*, and *The Long Revenge*. A part-time teacher and the mother of two sons, she lives in the Essex countryside.

A triumphant novel of passion, danger and
romance from bestselling novelists

PATRICIA MATTHEWS
and
CLAYTON MATTHEWS

MIDNIGHT WHISPERS

Patricia Matthews is one of America's bestselling
romantic storytellers. Now, for the first time, she
has teamed up with her husband, popular novelist Clayton Matthews, to create a stunning con-
temporary tale.

MIDNIGHT WHISPERS is the story of April
Morgan, a beautiful young heiress whose witness
of a shocking event has erased her memory. From
Cape Cod's untamed coast to the jagged cliffs of
Ireland, from the lake country of Switzerland to
fast-paced, trendy London, April searches for her
hidden past and finds romance in the arms of a
sophisticated Irish actor and a passionate young
clothes designer. But wherever she goes, she is
haunted by a mysterious voice on the phone—
"Mr. Midnight," a total stranger with the power
to manipulate April's every move—for good or
for evil.

*Read MIDNIGHT WHISPERS, available Oc-
tober 15, wherever Bantam Books are sold.*